THE Golden Empire

THE DRAGON ARTIFACTS
Book 3

MIKE SHELTON

ISBN: 978-1-7335104-2-4
Library of Congress Control Number: 2018913481
Salem, Oregon

Cover Illustration by Radovan Zivkovic and Dragana Trajkovic
https://smradagast.artstation.com/

Map by Robert Altbauer
www.fantasy-map.net

For More information about Mike Shelton and his books
www.MichaelSheltonBooks.com

Acknowledgements

I am so excited to release the last book in this series to my readers. I thank all of you for your support of my books. They are so fun to write and I have enjoyed every minute of it.

Thank you to my wife, my editors at Precision editing and my illustrators all which help to bring my stories to life. Thanks to all of them!

The Golden Empire is a work of fiction. Names, characters, places and incidents are the products of my imagination and are used fictitiously. Any resemblance to actual events, locales, or persons, living or dead, is entirely coincidental. I alone take full responsibility for any errors or omissions in this book.

-Mike-

Books by Mike Shelton

WESTERN CONTINENT BOOKS:

<u>Books of the Realm:</u>
The Cremelino Prophecy:
The Path Of Destiny
The Path Of Decisions
The Path Of Peace
The Blade and the Bow (A prequel novella to The Cremelino Prophecy)

<u>Dragon Rider Books:</u>
The Alaris Chronicles:
The Dragon Orb
The Dragon Rider
The Dragon King
Prophecy Of The Dragon (A prequel novella to The Alaris Chronicles)

The Dragon Artifacts:
The Golden Dragon
The Golden Scepter
The Golden Empire

GEMSTONES OF WAYLAND BOOKS:

The TruthSeer Archives:
TruthStone
TruthSpell
TruthSeer
The Stones of Power (A prequel novella to The TruthSeer Archives)

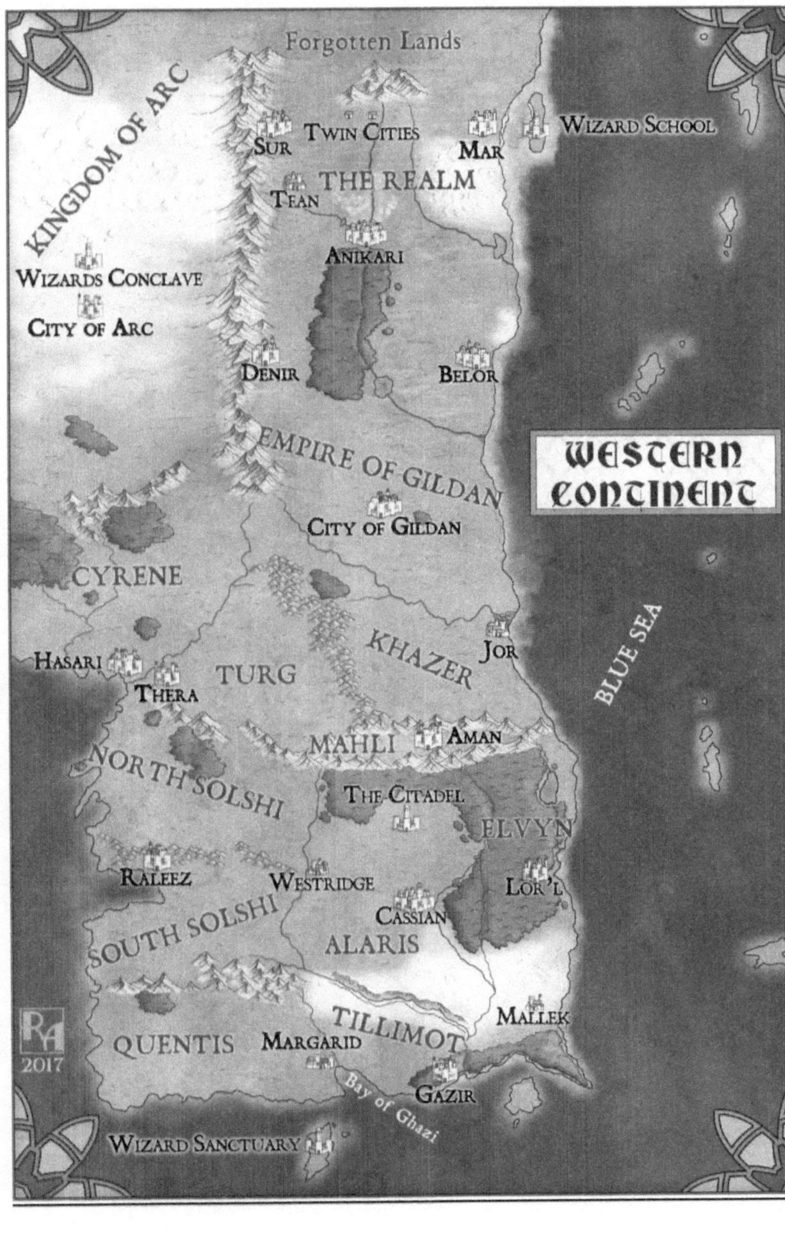

Forgotten Lands
KINGDOM OF ARC
Twin Cities
Sur
Mar
Wizard School
THE REALM
Tean
Anikari
Wizards Conclave
City of Arc
Denir
Belor
EMPIRE OF GILDAN
WESTERN CONTINENT
City of Gildan
BLUE SEA
Cyrene
Khazer
Jor
Hasari
Turg
Thera
Mahli
Aman
North Solshi
The Citadel
Elvyn
Raleez
Westridge
Lor'l
Cassian
South Solshi
Alaris
Tillimot
Mallek
Quentis
Margarid
Gazir
Bay of Ghazi
Wizard Sanctuary
2017

CHAPTER ONE

Roland Tyre paced back and forth on the wooden deck high up in the trees outside of the Elvyn council chamber in the city of Lor'l. It had been two hours since he had made his report of events, much of which the elves had met with skepticism. What was taking the council so long?

He took hold of a railing and peered out as far as he could to the east, nothing there but clear winter skies. Had he imagined it all? Had he really seen a fleet of war ships approaching the continent behind a great storm?

Unify them!

"I'm trying to!" Roland yelled out over the trees in response to the insistent pounding in his head.

"High Wizard," Gloron, one of the Elvyn guards outside the council chamber said. "Is everything all right?"

Roland turned around. "No, everything is not all right. While Lan and his councilors trudge through their debates, Delia prepares for battle and warships from the eastern kingdoms get closer and closer."

Gloron shrugged. "It is the way of our people. We don't rush into things. How old are you, sir?"

Roland shrugged. "What does that have to do with things? I am seventeen, not much younger than you, I would guess."

Gloron laughed.

Crazy elves and their sense of humor. "I don't get what's so funny."

"I am thirty-seven."

Roland brushed his palm against his forehead. He tended to forget that elves aged more slowly than humans.

"Elves live much longer than men, so we tend to be more deliberate with our decisions," Gloron said.

Roland ground his teeth. "Sometimes action is needed. You may take your time, but the rest of the world moves around you at full speed. I can't stand around here all day waiting for them to decide what to do."

Roland took a few steps toward the doorway, but Gloron and another guard moved to stand in his way.

He put his hand out in front of him to push them out of the way—he could do so with a minimal amount of power— but just before he did, the pulley behind him started creaking. He turned around.

"Protector," Gabby called out, stepping off the platform and onto the deck. At not even fifteen, the daughter of the king of Quentis—the Wolf, as he was usually called—struck Roland as remarkable. She stayed calm during difficult times and made rational decisions. Roland had recently been named by her father as the Protectorate of Quentis, one of the five kingdoms Roland had now unified under his golden empire.

"Princess Gabrielle." Roland tried to smile, despite the circumstances.

She brushed back a strand of her long, dark hair and returned the gesture. She was shorter than he but held herself regally. Her olive skin was smooth and unblemished.

"Healer Kharlia has called for you," Gabby said.

Roland turned his face back to the door of the council chambers and growled at Gloron and the other guard. Gloron only held his stance firm, but the corners of his mouth twitched.

"Looks like you are being called away just in time." Gloron's eyes twinkled.

Roland growled again. "Just call for me as soon as they are done deliberating—unless they need a nap first."

Gloron cocked his head as if not understanding Roland's insult. With a grunt, Roland turned away and met Gabby on the platform. With a signal to the operator, the pulleys began to drop them back down to the ground.

Roland watched as they moved through the massive trees. He adjusted his golden cloak around his shoulders and ran his hand through his blond hair while taking in the enormous trees around him. He marveled that, even in the winter, Elvyn stayed green and a comfortable temperature. Dropping down hundreds of feet, he spied numerous dwellings, walkways, and decks scattered through the trees. It was hard to tell for sure how big Lor'l actually was.

"How are they?" Roland asked Gabby about Bakari and Liam. The Dragon King and one of his riders had been poisoned by a spell that fought against magic, and Roland had brought Kharlia there to help them.

Gabby shrugged, but worry filled her eyes. Roland let out a deep sigh. He was angry at Bakari—well, maybe more like frustrated. They were friends, but, Roland hated to admit it, he had been jealous of the power his friend had. But now . . .

Now Roland had the Scepter of Unification, his own golden dragon, and, besides being High Wizard of the Citadel, was King of Alaris, Monarch of Tillimot, Regent of North and South Solshi, and Protectorate of Quentis. He was well on his way to becoming the most powerful wizard ever, and the people loved him. Both had been lifelong goals of his.

He reached over with a smile and patted Gabby on the back. She turned to him, and he winked.

"Don't worry, Princess," Roland said. "I'll take care of things." He always did.

After reaching the ground, Gabby directed him to a small hut, one of the few on the ground, located at the edge of Lor'l. Upon entering, he let his eyes adjust for a moment.

"Why is it so dark in here?"

"Roland!" Kharlia stood up and gave him a big hug. Her head reached his chin. Looking over her shoulder, he spied Bakari and Liam on plush pallets on the floor. Bakari's dark skin was pale, and his braided hair hung limply to the side of his head. Liam didn't look much better. Although of fair skin already, the boy was as white as a ghost.

"I've done all I can, Roland," Kharlia stood back and wrung her hands. "I think their fever is lessening. But they cannot be healed with normal magic—the poison feeds off of it. I've gone in and barricaded the poison, but I need something else besides the powers we have."

Roland shook his head. "What a mess. He should have been more careful!"

"Don't blame the Dragon King," said a voice from the corner. Roland had not realized someone was there.

Standing up and approaching Roland was Dragon Rider Jaimon. Well, Roland wasn't sure if he was still a dragon rider, since Delia had stolen their dragons. The man was two years younger than Roland. Still a few inches shorter, he had grown taller in the year since they had first met. From Quentis, like Gabby, his skin was the same color as hers. He wore a long pony tail down to the middle of his back, indicative of his being from the more rural part of his kingdom. He now glared at Roland.

"Who else is there to blame?" Roland raised his voice. "He took you, Gabby, and Alli off on a fool's quest with Delia and without your dragons."

"Don't disrespect the Dragon King." Jaimon held his ground firmly.

Roland swirled a hand around in the air. "The only person around here that has a dragon is me, Jaimon. Oh, and Delia, the one we should be out preparing to fight. But instead, the Elvyn council deems it necessary to blather on and draw out their decision."

Jaimon put a hand on the handle of his knife.

"Jaimon!" Kharlia said and put a hand on his arm. "This is enough, Roland." She glared at him, with fists on her waist. "We know how powerful and mighty you are now. So stop antagonizing others, and either help or leave. We are not forcing you to stay here."

Unify them!

Roland's right fist clenched around his scepter. "No, you are not!" It was time to force the Elvyn council to make a decision. He turned to go, when a small groan came from the floor and all four spun toward the sound.

"Bak!" Kharlia was the first at his side. His eyes didn't open, but his lips tried to move.

"What's he trying to say?" Gabby said and knelt down closer to him, next to Kharlia.

"Delia," came out a small whisper.

"What about her?" Gabby asked.

Jaimon and Roland joined the two women on the floor next to Bakari.

"Dragons . . ." Bakari croaked out another word. "Spirit."

Roland put his hand on Bakari's head and pulled upon some of his own power. Maybe he could find out what he was saying.

Bakari groaned and arched his back into the air.

"Roland, you're killing him!" Kharlia swatted his hand away from Bakari's head. "I told you the magic feeds the poison."

Roland grunted.

Gabby reached over instead and placed two hands to either side of Bakari's temples and closed her eyes.

"I thought you said no magic," Roland said.

"This is different," Gabby said with her eyes still closed. "My family has the power of *seeing*; the ability to see into someone's thoughts. It's not considered a true discipline of magic."

Roland nodded. He knew that all too well. Her brother, Kaspar, had used it on him, and her father had also tried to see into his mind.

"Must get the dragon bond back," Bakari muttered. His eyeballs moved behind his closed eyelids.

"How?" Gabby asked.

"The dragons are not our biggest worry," Roland muttered. "There's a war coming from the east."

"Shhh," Kharlia said to him.

Roland stood back up. How dare they treat him so? He was the most powerful wizard in the land. They fawned over the Dragon King like he had all the answers. It was Roland who was busy unifying the kingdoms and preparing for battle.

"I can see into his mind," said Gabby.

Roland had again turned to leave, but now he squatted back down with interest. This *seeing* ability was one he didn't have, and he didn't like that.

"The power to bind," Bakari whispered, and then his body seemed to relax, and his eyelids stopped fluttering.

"Bak!" Kharlia put a hand on his arm and rubbed it. "Bak, come back!"

"I see something there," Gabby said, and then she glowed and gasped for a moment before pulling away from him.

"Gabby," Jaimon said. "What happened? What did you see?"

Gabby shook her head for a moment, as if trying to decipher what had happened. "It was so bright, so powerful..."

Talk of power had captured Roland's attention once again.

"I think Bakari's mind is being protected while his body continues to deteriorate," Gabby continued. "But there might be a way. If we can find the thing that is protecting his mind and bring it here to where his body is . . ." Gabby talked as if she, herself, was still trying to understand what she had seen.

"What is it?" Jaimon asked.

"Where is it?" Kharlia followed with her own question.

Gabby scrunched up her brows and placed her hand once again on Bakari's head. She closed her eyes and appeared to be thinking hard. "It's south of here somewhere. I can see residuals of its power. It's similar to the Cremelinos."

"But what is it, Gabrielle?" Roland shouted. He was getting impatient. He needed to get back to the council and unify the people against the war that was coming. He had spent too long worrying about Bakari.

"It's . . . It's . . ." Gabby opened up her eyes, and a big smile spread across her face. "It's a phoenix."

CHAPTER TWO

Roland stood up with frustration. "A phoenix! You mean you saw some mythical bird in Bak's mind? That's supposed to heal him?" With a swirl of his cloak he pushed open the door. "I'm wasting my time here."

"Protector," called out Gabby.

Roland turned around at the use of his newest title and glared at the young woman in front of him. Her eyes blinked a few times, and Roland could see tears welling up in them. He let out a quick huff. "What?"

"The phoenix has been mentioned in dragon lore before. Its stories are rare, but they are there. Its power is similar to that of the dragons and the Cremelinos. Roland, we need your help to find it."

"The power to bind," said Jaimon. "The power of spirit. That's how we will save the Dragon King and Liam."

"A bird will not solve our problems." Roland shook his head. "Don't you understand we have a thousand ships coming to our shores and a mad woman to deal with first? My job is to unify the people so we can survive, not to go chasing birds."

Kharlia put her hand on Roland's arm and gazed up into his eyes. Her own held fear and hope mixed with tears. "Roland, please. This might be the only way to save Bak."

Roland hated it when women did that. It wasn't fair. He hated to see them cry.

"I know you care for him, Roland," said Kharlia. "I know you care for Bak."

"I care for all my people, Kharlia," Roland said as he hardened his resolve. She was trying to appeal to his emotions, but his plate was already full. "And that's why I can't put one person, however important he is, over the needs of everyone else."

"Unless that one person is you." Jaimon took a step forward. "You do all this for yourself, Roland Tyre. For your glory and your might. Don't talk of helping others. The only person you care for is yourself."

Roland squeezed the scepter in his hand, and light flashed out from it. It filled him and fed his craving for power. He glared at Jaimon and held his anger barely in check. The boy didn't know how close he was to having his life snubbed out. And how wrong he was.

"I do what I do to save you all." Roland slammed the scepter on the ground, and the soft dirt cracked underneath him. An echo shook the ground, and off in the distance Roland heard shouting. The power was so full in him he could hardly contain it. It was wonderful.

Unify. Unify!

"You can believe what you want of me," Roland's voice rose, "but when this is all over, I will be your deliverer. You will bow to me and sing praises to my name for what I do for you."

"Roland!" Kharlia grabbed for him again, but he moved out of her grasp. She lowered her voice. "Roland, in your quest for glory and power, please remember your friends."

Roland's hand moved off the pommel of his scepter, and he tried to remember what had been going through his head. Gabby, Jaimon, and Kharlia stood looking at him with wonder and surprise. *What? Why are they looking at me like that?*

Because of your power, the voice of the scepter spoke to him, low and husky.

Roland smiled. Of course they looked upon him for his power, wisdom, and might. He looked back into each of their eyes. Gabby's held fear, Jaimon's anger, and Kharlia's . . . what was the look on her face?

"Don't pity me, Kharlia," Roland said in a firm voice. "Pity those that stand in my way."

"Just remember, Roland; remember Bak, and Alli, and me and the dragon riders." Kharlia held his gaze. "In your quest for power, remember us." She turned and looked once again at Bakari and Liam lying on the floor.

Roland followed her gaze. When she turned back to him her eyes pleaded for help, but he just couldn't right now. Not with everything else that needed to be done.

"I'm sorry, Kharlia," Roland said and turned back toward the inner city. It was time for the council to make a decision.

As he walked back toward the great trees and the platform, Kharlia's words sank deep into his mind. Didn't she know that he did think about and care for his friends? Why couldn't they understand that he did this for them? They didn't understand him. No one did.

Arriving at the lift, he signaled the pulleys to pull him back up to the council chamber platform.

His thoughts went back to a conversation he had had with Bakari in the library in Cassian over a year ago. At the time he was only a wizard apprentice and Bakari was a level-two scholar wizard. They had spoken of the different disciplines of magic—scholar, battle, and counselor—and how Roland didn't feel like he fit in any of them. Or rather, that he was all of them together. Others talked about how they felt their magical powers, how they pulled or pushed their magic to get it to work, or how they learned over time. He was different. He always had been. He had been born to a different path.

"I am magic," Roland said out loud.

"Sir?" asked Gloron, pulling Roland out of his thoughts.

He had arrived at the top of the platform, and Gloron and the other guard met him. The doors to the council chamber were still closed. But that didn't matter anymore. He didn't need to go to them. They would come to him.

Raising his hands in the air, he pointed his scepter to the sky and called his dragon. Within a matter of moments the breathtaking golden dragon flew over the tops of the trees, the wind from its wings blowing the guards' hair around. Opening her maw, she emitted showers of golden fire, and a horrendous roar filled the city of Lor'l.

A council member strode out of the doorway to see what was going on. Seeing the dragon in the air, he stepped back inside. A few moments later the rest of the council joined Roland on the deck.

"What is the meaning of this?" said one of the women. "We are still discussing your words, and we can't hear each other over the dragon's roar."

"My good people of Elvyn," Roland began, spreading his arms out to his side. The golden scepter still sizzled with power in his right hand. "The time for discussions has ended; the time for decisions has come."

King Lanwaithian and Queen Breelyn stepped out in front of the rest of the council. They dressed in simple but fine attire; a small crown rested on the head of the king.

"The ways of elves are not always the ways of men," Lanwaithian said.

Roland nodded and smiled at the king. "As your guard, Gloron, has so well informed me."

Gloron smiled and bowed his head in respect to Roland.

Doesn't the man know I am being sarcastic? Roland shook his head in wonder and continued.

"This is how I see things," Roland pushed forward. "One, we must first stop Delia. Whether she stays ruler of Turg is neither here nor there, but she must not be allowed to usurp any other kingdoms. To that end, I will send troops from Quentis and Solshi up the coast to Turg and secure Turg and Cyrene from there."

"What about the dragons?" asked a council member. "And the Dragon King?"

Roland knew they would bring Bak up.

"I, and wizards from Quentis and Alaris, will take care of getting the dragons away from Delia," Roland said. However, he hadn't really cemented that part of the plan yet.

And get Alli back, a far corner of his mind whispered. *And get Alli back, yes.*

"Two," Roland continued, "troops from Alaris, Tillimot, and Quentis will sail here to Lor'l."

"Here?" said another council member. "Why do we need troops here?"

Roland held his anger in check. "Because, as I have told you, warships are sailing to your shores. We have a few weeks at most. With additional troops here, the power of the dragons back, and the Scepter of Unification, we can make a stand here and keep the people of the continent safe."

"We've never allowed foreign troops on our soil before," another council member said. "There has been no decision."

Unify! Unify them!

Roland raised his voice, and his dragon bellowed in response. "The decision is this: you allow foreign troops–my troops–on your soil, and hopefully we keep the invaders out of your land as well as the rest of my empire. Or you decline the help of men, and we pull back to the Dunn River and let Elvyn become the newest part of the eastern kingdoms."

The elves had never heard such an ultimatum before. They put their heads together in hushed whispers, the agitation in their voices showing how close to the edge they were. Roland heard snippets about banishing him, taking care of themselves, rejecting his proposal, and more. It went on this way for a minute. All joined in the debate—all except the king and queen. They joined their heads tightly together by themselves and more than once looked up at Roland.

Finally, Breelyn cleared her throat, and the conversation stopped. She looked directly at Roland. Those blue intelligent eyes carried power and insight that made Roland himself take a step back. After a long pause she asked a question. "And by whose authority do you do this, Roland Tyre?"

Roland took a moment to think. He tilted his head at Breelyn, and he swore he saw a barely contained grin. What was she up to? Had she set him up for failure or for a way to proceed?

Unify!

Placing his hand on the pommel of the scepter, once again he drew upon its wisdom and power. Thinking back across all he had studied and learned about leadership, power, and the elves themselves, he allowed himself more time to answer than he normally did. Something in the air—a current of magic—stood on a balancing point, and his answer would determine the fate of the western continent.

There was magic here in Elvyn. Powerful magic that was part of the trees, part of the land, part of the people, more than he had ever thought possible. They were a proud race, an independent people, a group that couldn't be pushed into a corner.

Unify them now!

But Roland and the elves needed each other at this exact moment. They needed his guidance and unification, and he needed their magic and strength. But how to do it? By what authority? He certainly didn't think it was a great idea to usurp their throne as he had done in other places. For all his frustrations at the pace of their decisions, he knew they were a peaceful and good people. A thought came to him, and he glanced at the king.

King Lanwaithian had still not said a word since exiting the council chambers. He was wiser than Roland had given him credit for. He listened first. The king, his eyes sparkling, now gave Roland a short nod.

Roland took a deep breath and prepared an answer that would satisfy all. "My friends, we need each other. I have no need to fabricate a story of approaching ships and have no desire to take over your kingdom."

There were outward sighs and a relaxing of bodies at that statement.

"There are times in history when something dark and evil threaten us all. The Dragon King and his riders have helped us in the past, but they cannot right now, so I have taken a step forward." Roland felt a stillness settle over the group, and he smiled at them. "The Scepter of Unification has been used in the past—and from what it tells me, your ancestors were involved. The people were fractured, and clans were forming across the continent. Kingdoms were crumbling, and you, the people of Elvyn, stepped forward, along with the dragon riders, to ensure the balance of things and to unify the people."

Many of the council members nodded. Roland had hoped that what he felt from the scepter was true. It was a long time ago, but they remembered.

"Once again, I call upon the Elvyn kingdom to step forward and help lead the people of this continent to peace. I now stand before you as the leader of a golden empire—one that has to stand in unity and strength to survive the coming weeks. Your king and queen have been true friends to the people of Alaris and those of the western continent, and now I bow to their wisdom."

Roland was surprised to find himself on one knee in front of King Lanwaithian. The king peered down at him with mirth-filled his eyes. Roland frowned but stayed where he was. How had this happened?

This is the only way to unify all of them, came the reply of the scepter.

"Roland Tyre," King Lanwaithian spoke loud and clear. "High Wizard of the Citadel, King of Alaris, Monarch of Tillimot, Regent of Solshi, Protector of Quentis, and holder of the Scepter of Unification . . . I, King Lanwaithian Soliel of Elvyn, by ancient authority and precedent, do now give you full authority over all our troops to oversee the battle ahead."

Roland opened his eyes wide.

"Our queen asked by what authority you spoke earlier," the king continued. "Let all in the sound of my voice hear, and all of Elvyn know, that Roland Tyre is now the Warlord of Elvyn."

CHAPTER THREE

After Roland left Jaimon, Kharlia, and Gabby, the three of them turned back inside the hut and stood in silence. The scent of sickness continued to grow, and Gabby tried not to breathe too deeply. The rise and fall of Bakari and Liam's chests were steady but small. Gabby thought about Roland's words for a few moments and was just about to say something when Jaimon spoke instead.

"It's up to me now," Jaimon said softly. "The High Wizard, or whatever he calls himself these days, has deserted us, and I am the last of the dragon riders."

"Oh, Jaimon," Gabby put her hand on his arm. She could hear the bitterness in his voice. She understood Roland to some degree. Being raised in a royal house, she was aware of the hard choices that sometimes needed to be made. "Maybe Roland is right to try and save as many people as he can," Gabby said. Maybe the life of one person wasn't worth the life of many, she wondered to herself.

"But it's the Dragon King!" Jaimon's voice broke with emotion. "By saving his life we do save many."

Gabby wondered at Jaimon's wisdom sometimes. For such a quiet man, with no magic, his thoughts were often deep and right on track. Roland had a point, but so did Jaimon. Bakari's life was worth more than others, because he could affect more lives than a normal person could. Her mind shifted, and she knew what they had to do.

"And that's why we are going to save him, Jaimon," Gabby said to his remark. "Roland will do what he has to do to bring the kingdoms together, and we will do what we have to do to ensure that his fight isn't in vain. We will save the Dragon King."

Kharlia wiped tears from her eyes. "I . . . I . . . need to stay here with . . . Bak. I'm sorry, but how are you going to save him?"

Gabby smiled and nodded. "I know, Kharlia. How are Jaimon and I, two people hardly old enough to be out in the world alone, going to save the Dragon King and restore peace to the world?"

Jaimon barked out a laugh. "You make it sound so ridiculous."

"Oh Jaimon," Gabby said. "Have some faith in us. I have magic; you have a sack of dragon artifacts. I have the power of *seeing*, and you are resourceful and wise."

"Well, when you put it like that . . . " Jaimon smiled and laughed. "How could anything go wrong?"

The three laughed, and it felt good to relieve some of the tension. After a moment, however, Kharlia returned to her original question.

"But how are you going to do it?"

"The phoenix," Gabby said, clapping her hands. "We find a phoenix and bring it back to heal Bakari and Liam. It can free the hold of the poison and bind it away, then we get the dragons back and help Roland to win the war."

"Oh, is that all?" Jaimon asked.

"When did you get so sarcastic, Dragon Rider?" Gabby punched Jaimon on the shoulder. "Don't you want your dragon back?"

Jaimon turned serious once again. "Of course I do."

"Then the first thing we do is find a ship that will take us south. That's where the phoenix will be."

* * *

Two days later, Gabby stood on the bow of a small ship heading south from Lor'l. In the past day, the lush Elvyn forest had turned into the harsh and barren desert where the southern elves lived. The sky had turned cloudy, and Gabby hoped they would be able to disembark for the evening before a storm hit.

"Ever been here?" asked Jaimon, coming up behind her.

Gabby jumped a bit but then turned and smiled. "No, but it's quite exciting, don't you think?"

Jaimon shook his head. "I just don't see why they choose to live in such a wasteland. I don't trust anyone that would choose this."

"They're elves, Jaimon," Gabby laughed. "What are you afraid of?"

"I'm not afraid," Jaimon said. His jaw tightened, and his eyes squinted. "I just want to find a phoenix and get back."

"As do I," Gabby said. "But the Lor'l elves will take us no farther. Something about honor and getting back to the warlord."

Jaimon's hands clenched tightly on the railing, and his gaze swept the docks as they approached land. "I can't believe they named him the warlord. He's already too powerful for his own good. He is arrogant, haughty, spoiled, and only thinks about himself."

"Don't worry about him," Gabby said. "He'll do what he has to do, and so will we."

Jaimon only grunted.

Soon the boat had been tied off, and the Elvyn crew escorted Gabby and Jaimon off the boat and to the dock master's office. Here they would find a new crew of southern elves that would take them around the southern peninsula and closer to their destination—a destination Gabby wasn't even sure of.

The small port and dock seemed busier than it should be. Masses of elves moved to and from ships loading cargo. Gabby noticed that the elves here were shorter, and the majority of them had red hair.

There were a dozen buildings next to the docks, but all she could see beyond that was desert.

"Where do they all live?" Jaimon asked.

"In Malek, mostly," Gabby said, pointing west. "It's about an hour's ride inland."

"Crazy," Jaimon mumbled.

They walked through the door of the dock master's office and up to a counter. "We need to charter a ship south," Gabby said.

"And who are you?" The man, with shaggy red hair down to his thin neck, glared at both her and Jaimon.

Gabby would place his age at least as old as her grandfather had been before he passed away. His pointy ears and upswept brow definitely marked him as Elvish, but his demeanor was not what they had experienced in Lor'l among the elves there.

"I am Gabrielle Von Wulf, and this is Jaimon Schaffer, Dragon Rider," Gabby said politely.

The man's eyes opened ever so slightly at their introduction, but he still said nothing. Before Gabby could say anything else a man spoke from a shadowed corner.

"Oh, such esteemed guests for our small dock," he said. He, too, had red hair and pointy ears, but was much bigger than most elves Gabby had seen. His shoulders were broader, and his neck was thick and held a strange beard coming down from his sideburns and under the chin. He appeared to be ten years her senior.

"Leave them alone, Garrick," the man at the counter said.

"Just making conversation, Wain," Garrick said. "Looks like the nice boy and girl are looking for some help."

Wain turned back to Gabby and Jaimon. "The warlord has ordered all our ships north. You'll not find anyone willing to go around the peninsula at this time of year, anyway. The pull of the tide is too strong. Many a ship has been lost making that turn around the Horn."

Gabby had heard such from her father before. The thin southern tip of Elvyn—referred to as the Horn—was indeed dangerous for ships at certain times of year.

"Oh, bah!" said Garrick. "Don't let those old stories scare you, young ones."

Gabby looked from Wain to Garrick and then back again to Wain. "Sir, we do have money. That's not a problem. But we are on an important mission for the Dragon King and . . ."

Garrick stood up from his chair and swayed closer to Gabby and Jaimon. "The Dragon King, huh?" He looked Gabby and Jaimon up and down. "Seems like the man must be desperate to send such scrawny kids to do his bidding."

Gabby almost used her powers to lash out, but if she did she would be no better than this bully was. Plus, she didn't want to tip her hand quite yet. These elves were definitely harsher than their northern cousins.

The door banged open, and three other male elves walked in. Two were older, and the third was about Garrick's age. They all had red hair and wore a type of uniform.

When they entered, Garrick slunk back to the corner. The tallest of the three stepped forward and, ignoring Gabby and Jaimon, motioned Wain over to a far corner. A whispered conversation ensued, during which, at least twice, the newcomer glanced over at Gabby and Jaimon.

The other two men circled around the youth and began asking questions.

"Why are you here?" asked one, the shorter of the three.

"Did the warlord send you?" asked the other, his voice gravelly and low.

Gabby peered around the small room. It was getting crowded and more hostile by the minute.

Jaimon took a step closer to her and put a hand on his knife.

"We are not with Roland Tyre," Jaimon answered. "We serve the Dragon King."

"And how do we know that?" said the shorter one. "You're all humans and trying to take over our land."

"Shut up, Tarryn," said the taller man off talking with Wain.

Jaimon turned back to the two men. "Your people named him the warlord, not me. King Lanwaithian rules all of Elvyn doesn't he?"

The third man took a step toward Jaimon and growled. "In title, yes, but we make our own rules here, little man. We should not let a human lead our armies."

"Paeris, Tarryn," called the other man as he walked away from Wain. "Stop blathering your tongues and get to work."

Paeris glared at Jaimon for a moment before taking a step back and joining their leader. "These people insult us by being here, Haryk. They come from Lor'l and do the bidding of the northern elves."

The door opened once again, and two other men walked in. These two were more like the elves Gabby was used to. They each had long, dark hair, slender builds, and smooth skin. Both stood taller than anyone else in the room. Their clothes were clean and pressed, and each wore an official-looking badge on his right breast.

"Haryk, what are you and your men doing here?" One of the officials took a step forward. "The warlord wants the men and your ships now."

Haryk glanced back at Wain, who all of a sudden pretended to have something else to do. When Haryk turned back to the officials he grinned a toothy smile. "Officer, we were only taking care of business." He gave a mock solute. "Wouldn't want the warlord to be unhappy now, would we?

One of our ships seems to have sprung a leak and won't be repaired until tomorrow."

The official frowned. "And the rest?"

Haryk shrugged his shoulders. "I guess we could manage without it. It's only a small ship."

Gabby jumped a bit, realizing a possible opportunity. Before she could say anything Haryk called on his two men and followed the officials out of the door.

Once they were gone, Gabby turned to Jaimon. "Did you hear that? Maybe we could use their ship once it's repaired. They could sail us south."

"Whoa, there, young humans," Garrick said, standing up again. "Don't go trusting those men. They'll just get you in trouble."

Gabby looked at the dock master, and he shrugged his shoulders. "You could ask him."

Gabby smiled back at Jaimon. "See, things are working out."

"I don't know, Gabby," Jaimon said.

"Good call, Dragon Rider," said Garrick. "I don't trust them, either. But you know who you can trust? Garrick. That's who." He poked himself in the chest. "I got a boat that can sail around the Horn . . . for a price."

"Garrick, get out of here," Wain said, pointing toward the door. "We don't need your kind snooping around our docks trying to find some coin."

Garrick grumbled and shuffled toward the door. As he put his hand on the doorknob he turned back to Gabby and Jaimon. "My offer stands."

"I don't trust him," Jaimon said after the elf left. "If he had such a good ship, what's he doing sitting in here?"

Gabby nodded, then moved closer to the counter and glanced at Wain. "But can we trust Haryk?"

The man blinked a few times and stood up straighter. "Of course, miss. Best ships in southern Elvyn."

Something sounded off in Gabby's head, but Jaimon prodded her in the ribs, and they went outside.

"I *don't* trust Haryk," Gabby said. "His men were rude to us."

Jaimon nodded. "But we need a ship. Everything else is going north."

"But the way he spoke about Roland . . ." Gabby said to herself.

"Nothing I don't think about the man," Jaimon said. "If you ask me, the more they dislike Roland Tyre, the better off I am with them."

"All right, then," Gabby smiled. "Let's find out where Haryk's ships are and if there is really one that will be left behind for repairs."

CHAPTER FOUR

Allison Stenos approached Thera, the capital city of Turg, from atop her dragon, Miriel. Looking down, she could already see signs of troops gathering and moving toward the docks. Large war ships filled the harbor flying flags of both Turg and Cyrene. However, a new flag flew above them all: the flag of the Dragon Queen. A field of red with the silhouette of a dragon stood out for everyone to know who now controlled the two kingdoms.

Delia Marinos, most recently voted in as Oracle of Turg, was their supreme leader. However, more importantly than that was what she claimed on her own. With possession of four stolen dragon bonds, she had declared herself the Dragon Queen and was now preparing to push her boundaries south.

Circling the city twice, Alli landed in a great courtyard of the castle grounds. She slid off her yellow dragon and ran her hand lovingly down its hard scales. She found that she was stalling and realized that sooner or later she would have to meet with her master.

No one stopped her at the castle doors. Although her small stature and thin frame would not automatically raise any concerns, her recent victory in the fighting games had gained her respect. Her subsequent position as one of Delia's dragon riders earned her more. Men and women saluted her as she turned down a hallway and made her way to the Oracle's office.

Her dark boots clicked loudly on the marble floor, and a cloak hung over one shoulder. A reflection in a full-length window caught her attention. She stopped and looked for a moment. Clad in red leather, sword hanging at her hip, she looked fierce enough. Moving a hand to her face, she thought she was more pale than she used to be—of course she couldn't remember much longer back than a week or so.

Shaking those thoughts from her head, she resumed her journey to the Oracle's office. Two guards saluted her at the door, and one poked his head inside to inquire about the Oracle's availability. Soon he came back out and opened the door wider, allowing Alli to go inside.

Upon entering the room, she glanced around at all the wealth. Gold and silver artifacts stood on shelves, colorful tapestries covered the walls, and a sizeable oak desk sat in front of her. Sitting in a high-backed chair behind the desk was Delia Marinos.

"Master." Alli approached and bowed her head, awaiting a response.

The response took longer than Alli was comfortable with, and she eventually raised her eyes, without raising her head. When she did Delia was staring hard at her. The woman had long, lustrous brown hair, waving down over her shoulders. Her makeup was impeccable. Sitting around her shoulders was a new fur-lined red cloak with a dragon emblazoned on it. Alli shriveled in her presence.

"Well," Delia said, "what did Queen Esmaralda have to say? And did you get to the sniveling king of South Solshi through his regent?"

Alli didn't know the best way to approach her master, so she decided to give the facts and leave any commentary out unless asked for. "The queen of North Solshi and the regent of South Solshi are both disposed. The queen is dead, the regent injured and stripped of his title. King Andre De Luz has appointed a new regent for all of a combined Solshi."

Delia slapped a hand hard on the table. "What have you done, Allison? I thought you were loyal to me!"

"I am loyal, Master," Alli said, her eyes still downcast. "*He* was there."

"Who was where?" Delia spat. "Look up at me when you speak."

"Yes, Master," Alli said. It was all she could do to obey her master. She knew she had shown a moment of weakness and failed.

"Who was there?" Delia repeated.

"Roland Tyre," Alli said.

Before Alli knew what had happened, Delia threw a porcelain mug across the room. It shattered against a back wall, and the pieces swept across the floor. One hit the side of Alli's right foot.

"What was he doing there?" Delia questioned.

"He . . ." Alli cleared her throat and tried to look directly at Delia, but it was hard. "He is now the new regent of North and South Solshi and has vowed to fight you."

Alli waited for another tirade, but only a cool glare followed. Delia walked around her desk, reached a lacquered nail up under Alli's chin, and drew her head up to look at her.

"Did he ask you to follow him?" Delia asked.

Alli's heart felt like it would beat out of her chest. "Yes." The word came out quiet and raspy.

"And he got to you, didn't he?" Delia began to pace around the room. "He's more cunning and powerful than I gave him credit for. Can I turn him?"

Alli blinked. Turn him? "Master?"

"Can we turn him to our side, Alli, or do we need to destroy him?"

Destroy him?

Alli thought about Roland's eyes; the longing and caring and compassion in them. She thought about his name and how, as the people chanted it, her mind grew more and more clear. She remembered his outstretched hand as he offered to make her his queen.

There was only one queen, and Alli stood in front of her— Delia, the Dragon Queen.

"I don't believe we can turn him, Master," Alli admitted. His blue eyes burned a memory in her mind. She also didn't know if she could destroy him or not.

"Hmmm, a pity," Delia said. "He's got that golden dragon and such grand powers. And that scepter of his . . ." Delia stopped pacing and examined Alli. Her master's eyes glazed over, and she smiled wide. "I want that scepter, Allison."

Alli's eyes went wide, and fear crept into her heart. The scepter was powerful. How could she get that from him? She shook her head slightly, but Delia caught the movement and in a swift move reached over and slapped Alli.

Tears came to Alli's eyes, but she deserved it. She had been weak. Her head lowered, and she watched as Delia retreated behind her desk once again. The Dragon Queen rummaged around in a drawer for a moment, then brought her head back up.

"Where is it?" Delia demanded.

"Where is what, Master?" Alli said. She really had no idea of what Delia was talking about.

"My artifacts," Delia said, her eyes growing dark. "The pouch with all my artifacts." Then her eyes grew wide. "Tabitha had them at the coronation. Tabitha!" she shouted. Delia threw her hands in the air, and Alli spied the bracelet with a black obsidian dragon hanging from a chain–that artifact never left her possession. Out of Delia's fingers, fire flew out at the wall in front of her, burning up an ancient tapestry. "Find Tabitha now, Dragon Rider, and bring her to me. Something is not right here."

Alli bowed in haste, then ran out of the room. She surely didn't want to get caught up in any of her master's tirades. She tried to even remember who Tabitha was. There were so many servants around the castle. She stopped to ask someone if they knew her.

"Try Delia's personal rooms," the man said. "She is one of her personal aides."

Alli climbed the stairs to the third floor and walked down the hallway. Servants jumped to get out of her way. She would find Tabitha and regain pleasure from her master. Putting a hand on the hilt of her sword, which she knew she probably wouldn't need, she carefully opened Delia's door, moved in, then closed it behind her.

The curtains in the sitting room were pulled closed, with only a slit of dull light seeping into the room. A sound in the adjacent bedroom stopped Alli, and she listened. Readying her magical powers—*oh, my sweet, magical powers*—she crept forward. The power filled her and gave her strength, sharpened her hearing, and quieted her steps.

The door to the bedroom was open only a crack. Alli peered inside and saw a young woman of her age, but taller, rummaging in a bureau drawer. She put her fingers between the door and the doorframe and moved it open.

A loud squeak ensued that alerted the woman, and she spun around, hands out in front of her. Upon seeing Alli she clenched her teeth and sent forth a sudden push of air. It caught Alli unaware, and she twisted, but it still caught her shoulder and pushed her onto the nearby bed. Within a heartbeat she stood up on top of the bed, now higher than her opponent. Tabitha peered up at her, her long brown hair swinging around in front of her tan face.

Alli faltered. Some hint of remembrance ran through the back of her mind. But it was gone before she could recognize what it was.

"Tabitha!" Alli yelled out, trying to distract the servant's attention. "Delia is looking for you—for her pouch of artifacts."

Instead of being distracted, Tabitha reached forward and pulled the top blanket of the bed out from under Alli. With embarrassment at being caught off guard, Alli fell backwards, rolled onto the floor, then came back up on the other side of the bed. Hands out in front of her, she sent a bolt of fire toward Tabitha. The woman was quick, though, and ducked, rolled a few feet herself, then came up in another part of the room.

Alli jumped back on the bed, grabbed a post at the corner with a hand, and swung around. She kicked Tabitha against the door, which closed behind her. Alli landed and walked over to where Tabitha lay.

"Give me the pouch, and I will let you live," Alli growled with a feeling of victory.

But the feeling didn't last long. As she leaned in to grab Tabitha, Tabitha stiffened, then swung her body around Alli, coming out behind her.

It was a move that reminded Alli of herself, and she groaned at the mistake she had made. This woman was no mere servant. Tabitha had power, and she been trained.

Spinning around, she caught Tabitha on the side of her head with a fist and sent her reeling once again. Tabitha might be good, but not that good.

Now Tabitha scooted up next to the bureau again and stuck her hand inside. When she pulled it out, Alli froze.

"Stay where you are, Alli," Tabitha said as she stood. In her hand she held a chain that caused such bone-chilling dread in Alli she almost lost her step backing up.

"You recognize it, don't you?" Tabitha said as she waved it in front of her.

Alli tightened her muscles, preparing to pounce, but Tabitha took a step back. How was this woman anticipating her moves?

"Alli, you don't remember me, do you?" Tabitha said.

"Remember you?" Alli asked, confused at the question.

"From the Citadel," Tabitha said.

"The Citadel?" Alli shook her head. She felt all she was doing was repeating what the servant was saying.

"You were there, Alli," Tabitha's brown eyes were focused. "We both were."

Alli shook her head. *No. No. No.* She had never been to the Citadel. She would remember that.

"It's true," Tabitha said. "You trained me."

A pounding sounded in the back of Alli's head. A brief memory of a large courtyard, of apprentices training, of a man watching from the balcony above. "Roland," she whispered.

"Yes, Alli, Roland was there too," Tabitha said, excitement filling her voice.

"No," Alli said. "I've never been there. I'm a fighter, trained by my master."

"You are the Battlemaster of the Citadel, Alli," Tabitha said, "and a dragon rider. Delia stole the bonds and did something to your memory."

"No, Roland is the enemy, and Delia will destroy the Citadel," Alli said.

"Alli!" came a voice from the hallway.

"Master?" Alli said. It was Delia. What would Delia do to her if she failed her again?

Tabitha glanced around with fear herself. "You can't let her take me, Alli." She moved toward a window that Alli knew opened up to a balcony.

Alli took a step toward Tabitha, but Tabitha flashed the chain again at Alli, and she cringed in fear.

"I can't fail her again," Alli found herself pleading. Confusing thoughts raced through her mind. "Where are the artifacts?"

"Alli, where are you? Did you find Tabitha?" Delia called from the other room. She was only a few steps away.

Tabitha's face screwed up in concentration as if deciding something. She then dug into a pocket of her dress and threw the pouch at Alli, dropped the chain back in the drawer, pushed through the curtains, and was quickly out on the balcony.

The bedroom door handle began to turn. Alli took a deep breath, held on to the pouch tightly and pulled the door open.

"Here they are!" Alli thrust the pouch into Delia's hands. "She must have put them back in your room for you."

Delia tried to push back to see what was going on in the room, but Alli moved through the door herself in such a way that Delia had to step back into the sitting room.

Delia studied the door, then back down at the pouch in her hands and smiled. Alli bowed before her, keeping her head down. "Did I please you, Master?" The pounding in her head from earlier began to recede. Tabitha had done something to her, she was sure. Why had Alli let her escape? She only knew one thing. Her master must never find out. Never.

Alli brought her head up. Delia rolled three small artifacts around in her hand, and her grin broadened.

"Yes, my dragon rider, you have pleased me," Delia said.

Alli beamed.

"And now we will go get that scepter," Delia said.

The scepter. When Alli thought about it, the blue eyes of Roland Tyre stared down at her. Memories from a balcony high above a courtyard, from across a room, from the castle grounds in Solshi. She couldn't shake them.

"Gather the other riders," Delia said. "It's time to plan our attack. Roland Tyre will be only a footnote in the histories of my empire."

CHAPTER FIVE

In the three days since meeting with the elves, Roland had been busy. Currently, he was flying from Solshi to Alaris once again. He hadn't been in Cassian, his capital there, since the beginning of all of this. He smiled and let his arms flow out to his side. Flying atop the back of a dragon was the most amazing feeling. He felt stirrings of pity for the dragon riders themselves at having lost their bonds, but he pushed the feelings away so as to not spoil his good mood. He had either met personally with or sent missives to all the leaders of his golden empire.

Unify!

Ugh. He had thought the voice would be gone by now. He had conquered, controlled, or at least directed the affairs of war in all the southern kingdoms. He tried to make himself believe that was enough to fight against the horde of ships coming closer and closer, but he didn't know if it would be. He wouldn't be able to mobilize everything in enough time.

Unify all of them!

Unfortunately, he knew what that meant. Before facing the warships of the eastern kingdoms, he had to overthrow Delia. He had to have her united territories under his banner also.

To that end, a significant contingent of troops were sailing north from Quentis and Solshi toward Turg. That was Delia's stronghold. Victory there would win him Cyrene and Khazer also. The troops would arrive in waves, and he would swoop in with his great golden dragon. If all went according to plan . . . but Roland knew by now that plans didn't last very long in the fast-changing world of politics and magic.

As if hearing his thoughts, Orelia let out a roar, and Roland felt the heat of her fires spreading to either side of him as he began his descent into Cassian.

As soon as Roland landed, hundreds of citizens came running up to see his golden dragon. Tam met him in front of his dragon. Tam was his acting battlemaster, given Alli's current condition. He was a year older than Roland, with short hair and more of a stocky build. He had been a good friend from the beginning of Roland's reign as High Wizard—one of the handful of wizards that Roland found he could trust.

"Convene the council, Tam," Roland said after their initial greeting.

Tam directed a guard to gather the ministers, then turned back to Roland. He smiled. "I'm glad you're back. The bickering of the ministers gives me headaches."

"What has been done since I've left?"

"That's just it," Tam said as they walked toward the castle. "Nothing. They can't decide on anything, so nothing gets done. The river docks are still a mess, and the people are complaining about lack of food and broken homes."

Roland ground his teeth. "Why must everything be so difficult? You would think my own kingdom would be the easiest to unify."

"Minister Patera is still posturing himself to be the leader in Mericus's absence," Tam said. "There is still no confirmation of Mericus's body being found."

Walking into the castle, Roland smiled at the guards stationed there. He stopped and talked to one he had known from his time living there.

"How is your family, Aaron?"

"Sire," the man bowed his head. "They are surviving."

Roland looked at the other guard. "And what about your family?"

The other guard blushed, not used to the attention of such high company. "I . . . my . . . well, sir," he stumbled for a bit before coming to his senses. "My home was destroyed, and we are living in the back of the church."

"Roland," Tam tried to direct him back to the council meeting, "the council will be waiting for you."

Ignoring Tam, Roland continued talking to the guard. "How many children do you have?"

"Three, My Lord," the man beamed, then his eyes turned down. "The little one has been sick, and it's a bit crowded at the church."

"What about the nobles' estates?" Roland asked. "I'm sure they have plenty of room."

The guard's eyes went round with surprise. "Sir? I'm not sure I understand."

"And, Aaron, what do you see around the town?" Roland ask the first guard. "How are the people's spirits?"

Aaron looked down for a moment, then turned his eyes back up and shrugged his shoulders. "The citizens of Alaris are a tough lot, Sire. But this battle following so closely on the civil war last year has made things difficult. It's growing colder, and many are without their homes, like Geoffrey here."

"Thank you," Roland told the guards. "It seems I have been lax in my attention here."

"Oh no, Sire," said Geoffrey. "You're a busy man. We'll survive."

"Life is not just about surviving." Roland raised his voice, and a few others in the foyer stopped and listened. "The role of a leader is to serve and make sure that the people are taken care of. On behalf of my ministers, I apologize."

Turning to Tam, Roland motioned him toward the council chambers. Roland called back over his shoulder. "This problem will be rectified soon."

"High Wizard, you can't take care of them all," Tam said.

"And why not, Tam?" Roland whipped his head around. "Why can't I take care of them all? Why should the nobles have excess when the people suffer?"

Tam shook his head. "I know you mean well, but you can't change everything overnight. The ministers, the nobles . . . that's the way it's always been."

"Well, in my empire, things will be different," Roland said. They reached the door to the council chambers. He knew he had to be tough sometimes but he really did care for his people.

Tam put his hand on Roland's arm and stopped him. "Roland, what do you mean, your empire? What have you done? Have you gone mad?"

Roland winked at his friend. "Oh, no, my friend."
Unify them!

Roland winced at the pounding in his head. Would it ever end? The guard in front of them began to open the door.

"Do you want an introduction?" Tam asked.

Roland nodded.

"And what should it be?" Tam asked. "I'm afraid rumors about you are flying."

Roland leaned in and whispered into Tam's ear as the door opened. Tam paled and took a step back. Then, clearing his throat, he called the attention of the council members.

"Please rise for Roland Tyre, High Wizard of the Citadel, King of Alaris, Monarch of Tillimot, Regent of North and South Solshi, Protector of Quentis, and Warlord of Elvyn."

Roland strode into the room, his golden cape swirling around him. He held his scepter in his hand, and the golden glow emitted an aura around him that caused everyone to stare open mouthed. A few of the ministers bobbed their heads to him, while a few others, Minister Patera included, seemed hard-pressed to remove the growing scowl from their faces.

He moved past the table to the far end, turned, and looked at each person in the room one by one. Some held his gaze; others couldn't. A few were wizards; others were long-time ministers in Alaris. They were men and women used to being coddled and in charge. With a flourish of his hand, he pointed to the chairs around the table. "Please be seated."

Everyone in the room took a seat, some more reluctantly than others. Minister Symon Patera continued to glare at Roland, and Roland found it annoying. The man was smug and rude, and Roland thought about what he could do with him.

Unify them.

Seriously? Roland spoke back in his mind. *Why is that the answer to everything? I've already unified the kingdoms.*

Unify the people.

The collective group stared expectedly at Roland, but Roland took a minute to collect his thoughts. He wanted to wave his hand and rid himself of these power-hungry leaders, but the voice in his head told him otherwise.

They are your people, too.

With those simple words, Roland experienced a sudden shift in understanding and thought. He had prided himself on looking after others less fortunate than he. He recognized the power that he had was a great gift and felt strongly about providing for the people, protecting them, and making sure they were taken care of. But he had ignored, and maybe even treated badly, those in positions of power or wealth. He had even blamed them for the condition of the people.

"Sir," Tam spoke softly from the far end of the table, trying to grab Roland's attention. "The council is assembled."

Tam's words pulled Roland from his newest thoughts. They were troubling to some degree, as he realized he may have erred in the way he had disposed of leaders and men of power. The scepter was right. They were all his people, and he needed to unify all of them.

Spreading his arms out to the side, scepter in one hand, he greeted the council before him. "My people," he began, "welcome to my golden empire."

A few of the council members cleared their throats and threw quick glances around the table. Minister Patera glared at him with arms crossed tightly. Roland waited for a moment.

His next few words could determine their reaction to him and his new empire.

"Minister Symon Patera," he called out. "Please stand."

The minister flinched. His face turned red, but he did as Roland asked. The rest of those at the table glanced from Symon to Roland and back again. He could see the worry in their eyes.

Roland bowed his head slightly to the man and spoke. "Thank you for your leadership in my absence." Those words were hard for Roland to say, but he knew the end goal to unify, so he plunged forward. "These are difficult times, and you have shown extraordinary patience and understanding."

Symon's jaw dropped, and eyes popped around the table.

"Thank you, Sire," was about all Symon could say.

"As the supreme council in my empire, each of you will play a pivotal part in unifying the people and establishing peace throughout this kingdom as we prepare for war." Roland smiled at each one of them. With mention of possibly a larger part to play, each minister now readily gave Roland undivided attention. Roland could see the gleam of power lurking in their eyes, but it was influence and control they would only get by standing in unity with Roland.

"May I ask how you have unified the kingdoms and the nature of this war?" Symon asked, still standing.

"Yes, you may, Minister," Roland said. "A great question that shows once again your ability to lead and care for our people. Please be seated."

Symon sat and looked around the table, this time with a smug smile on his face. He had received the recognition that he wanted, and now his arms sat clasped on the table in front of him. He leaned forward toward Roland, anxious to hear the answer to his question.

"The specifics of how I have unified our land will have to be discussed later, suffice it to say that the titles you have heard about are true. I am unifying the people. To what end, you may ask? Generally, to help all of our land become more prosperous and happy. Specifically, to fight against two aggressors that would usurp peace and decimate this council, among others."

The last words riveted the ministers' attention. They nodded for Roland to proceed. They surely didn't want to have any new found power or authority in Roland's new empire destroyed so quickly. They listened closely as he continued.

"Delia Marinos, the new Oracle of Turg, has stolen the dragon bonds from the Dragon King and his riders, incapacitated the riders, and is now planning to push her will on us as Dragon Queen over all the land."

The council members exploded in words of anger.

"She has no right." Minister Soren slammed down his fist.

"The wizards will not stand for this," said Jaymi, a blonde-haired lady who was an exceptional battle wizard.

"Delia has captured Allison Stenos, my battlemaster, erased her memories, and forced her to serve at her command," Roland said, his voice growing louder. "We cannot stand for this type of aggression in the southern kingdoms. Are we unified in the voice of the council that we will fight the new Oracle?"

"Yes!" came the collective voice. A few of them, possibly at odds only a few hours earlier, now turned and began discussing what could be done to stop the Oracle.

Roland smiled. He caught Symon's eye and directed the man to join him. The minister stood and walked to the end of the table, where Roland still stood.

"Minister," Roland said quietly. "What are your thoughts on this matter?"

The minister seemed surprised to be asked rather than being told what to do. Roland's training as a counselor came racing back to his mind.

"Well, I . . ." Symon stumbled for a few moments. "We have to have a united front. The people must rise up against this aggressor. Alaris will not stand for it."

"Good. Good." Roland placed a hand on the man's shoulder. "And how do we get the people behind us in this matter? They just went through a war that tore many of them from their homes. Is there something we can do to help them in their plight? Some way we might get their allegiance?"

Symon thought for a moment. "I suppose if the people are fed and housed they will more likely support us. We need more men to fight. We lost some in the last battle in Corwan, and many are still there."

"So they would be more likely to leave their families and help us fight if they knew their families were taken care of?" Roland said. "That's what you are saying, right?"

"Yes," Symon said, though he appeared surprised to say so.

"What a great idea, Minister." Roland continued to stroke the man's ego. "Where do we have the most land and food to house these people? How could you accomplish this the most quickly?"

"Me, Sir?" Symon seemed surprised.

"Well, yes, Symon." Roland pushed forward. "You could be my new minister of the people. They will love you." Roland slapped the minister on the back. "It'll be wonderful. You can use some land on your estate as a start. The other nobles will follow your example, because . . ." Roland lowered his voice and leaned in with a whisper, "because we know they all want to be like you, don't we?"

Symon looked over at Roland, and he winked back at the man. The smile on the minister's face grew broad, and his shoulders straightened.

Squeezing Symon's shoulder, Roland cleared his throat and waited until the others turned toward him. He nodded at the minister again.

"Our good man, Symon Patera, has agreed to be my first minister of the people. Let him explain to you his plans for helping our people prepare for the battle."

With that, Roland let Minister Patera have the floor. By the time he was done all the ministers were jumping to offer their lands to help the people and pledging support of other nobles they knew. They fawned over the minister's ideas and scrambled for his attention in the matter.

Roland sat back in his chair and watched the proceedings with a growing smile. Maybe unifying the people wouldn't be so hard after all. Next stop: the Wizard Citadel.

CHAPTER SIX

Gabby watched with Jaimon as ship after ship left the harbor east of Malek, in southern Elvyn. Ships from Tillimot arrived and were filled up quickly with red-haired desert elves.

"They don't look too happy." Jaimon motioned toward a group off to their right.

An argument broke out between them and the officials on the dock.

"Jaimon, something's not right," Gabby said.

"I would say everything's not right, Gabby." Jaimon stood with her on a small sand dune under a grouping of palm trees.

The two had been waiting to try and find Haryk's last ship after the others had left.

"Look, at those men." Gabby pointed to a group of thirty or so red-headed elves.

Jaimon scrunched his eyes for a moment and shook his head. "I don't know what you mean. What am I supposed to be looking at? They all look the same to me." Jaimon laughed. "I've never seen so much red hair in my life."

"No, look closer." Gabby pointed again. "Instead of marching to the ship, these are going around to the back of another building. It's the third group I have seen."

Jaimon shrugged and let out a long breath. "So they don't want to go and fight. I don't blame them."

Before Gabby could say another word she turned at a sound behind them. Paeris and Tarryn, the two elves who had been with Haryk earlier in the dock master's office stood glaring at them.

"Haryk thought you two might come snooping around," said Tarryn, the short one.

"Spies, like we thought," said Paeris.

"We are not spies," Jaimon said. "We're trying to help the Dragon King. We need a ship to go south."

"Oh, we can find a ship for you," Paeris said.

Tarryn laughed and reached toward Gabby. Jaimon jumped out in front and pulled a knife. Tarryn kicked at him with his thick sturdy boots, and in the sandy soil Jaimon couldn't move fast enough. The boot collided with Jaimon's shin, and he grunted hard, but jabbed the knife out in front of him between Gabby and the two elves.

Gabby moved around from behind Jaimon and flung her hands out in front of her, throwing a spell of wind at the two men. However, before the wind hit them, Paeris put up his own hands and blocked it deftly.

The sudden move surprised Gabby, and she missed the fist that hit her in the side of the head and knocked her over. She tried to ready another spell, but before she did she felt another power wrap around her middle and start to squeeze. Paeris glared at her and bared his teeth.

"One more move by either of you, and I'll squeeze the life out of you." His voice was low and menacing.

Jaimon threw the knife down and held up his hands. "Fine," he said. "Just don't hurt her any more."

Paeris released Gabby, and the two elves turned Jaimon and Gabby around and marched them into a back door of the warehouse. It grew darker, but not any cooler as they entered the building. Armed men and women turned in their direction, but only seeing two young people, they turned their attention back to their comrades.

The young humans were shoved into a smaller room—an office, by the look of things. A small lamp stood on the desk, behind which sat Haryk. He motioned for Paeris and Tarryn to put Jaimon and Gabby in chairs. After securing them with ropes, Paeris brought out a vial of clear liquid and forced it down Gabby's throat.

It tasted horrible, and she tried to spit it out, but her mouth was held by rough hands until she couldn't do anything but swallow. It burned down her throat and settled warmly into her stomach. Within moments a numbing spread throughout the rest of her body, from toes to fingers, leaving her unable to either move or feel her wizarding powers.

"Now, what should I do with you two?" Haryk leaned back in his chair and clasped his hands behind his head. "You've seen too much of our operation."

"We don't care about your operation," Jaimon said. "We are on an errand for the Dragon King."

"I still say they are spies," Tarryn said.

"Shut up, you two." Haryk pointed at Tarryn and Paeris. "Leave us alone."

The two glared at Gabby and Jaimon and then left the room.

"I apologize for their behavior," Haryk said. His hair was a busy mess of red, and he tried to pat it back in place. "They have no manners."

"And you do?" Jaimon spat, then turned and looked at Gabby. "Are you all right?"

Gabby's eyes were wide, her speech slurred. "I can't feel my arms or legs."

"What is Roland Tyre planning for Elvyn?" asked Haryk.

"I don't know what that man is planning," Jaimon said. "I don't even like him."

"Well, then we have something in common," Haryk said. "But tell me about him."

Jaimon looked at Gabby, and she nodded slowly.

"He is arrogant and thinks he is all powerful and makes decisions for everyone else," Jaimon began. "But he is dangerous."

"How so?" Haryk asked.

"He is very powerful and holds a scepter of . . ."

"No," Gabby pleaded, and Jaimon stopped.

"Why does it matter, Gabby?" Jaimon said. "He doesn't care about us or our dragons."

"Where does his power come from?" Haryk stood up and walked closer to the two.

Neither of them spoke. Without warning, Haryk's hand flashed out and slapped Gabby on the cheek.

"No!" Jaimon yelled out. "Don't hurt her."

"Then tell me what I want to know."

"No," pleaded Gabby. She knew that Jaimon didn't like Roland, but she believed Roland's intentions were good, and based on his title of Protector of Quentis, her father believed him also. Only a few knew that the title of Protector of Quentis was one that was rarely bestowed.

Haryk brought up another hand, and Jaimon lurched forward in his chair. "Stop!" Tears came to his eyes as he looked at her. "I'm sorry, Gabby."

Haryk took a step over in front of Jaimon. "Speak, and no further harm will come to her."

Jaimon nodded. "Roland's power comes from his scepter. It's an ancient dragon artifact that gives the holder the ability to unite people."

Jaimon's face stung with a slap from Haryk, and he peered up at the man with tears smarting in his eyes.

"I never said I wouldn't harm you," Haryk said. "Now tell me everything you know about Roland Tyre. I want to destroy him and unite the northern and southern elves under my control."

Gabby yelled out, and Haryk drew a knife out. "One more outburst from you, and I rid your mouth of your tongue." Turning to Jaimon, he thrust the knife in his face. "Now talk, and if you are lucky I might dump you in a small boat in the ocean and you can continue on your way."

* * *

"Jaimon," Gabby whispered an hour or so later.

Haryk had left the room, and Gabby could hear noises of people moving around outside. She didn't know how much longer she had before someone came back.

"I'm sorry, Gabby," Jaimon moaned. "I couldn't bear to have them hurt you more."

"That's all right," Gabby said.

Jaimon had indeed told Haryk everything he knew about Roland Tyre. She didn't blame him for doing so. He had been trying to protect her.

"It doesn't matter," Gabby said. "Roland can take care of himself. We have to figure out how to get out of here."

Jaimon seemed to focus more. "You're right."

"I never thought the kingdom of Elvyn could be so cruel," Gabby said.

"They'll kill us if we don't get away," Jaimon added.

Gabby struggled for a few minutes against her ropes. "If only I had my magic back."

"At least you have that hope," Jaimon said bitterly. "I don't have anything."

Gabby wanted to slap Jaimon upside his head. He couldn't get past the fact that he didn't have magic like the rest of the dragon riders. But she realized she could hardly commiserate with him.

"Do you still have your knife in your boot?" Gabby asked Jaimon.

Jaimon's eyes went wide. "How did you know about that?"

"Really?" Gabby rolled her eyes. "I've spent almost every waking hour with you for weeks, Jaimon. I know where you hide all your knives. You treat it like it's something special."

"It is," Jaimon said. "It has been passed from father to son in my family for generations." Jaimon's countenance turned, and he looked sad.

"What is it?" Gabby asked.

"The night my father gave it to me was the first and last time I tended sheep alone. It was during that time that I found Cholena's dragon egg, met Bakari, and became a dragon rider."

"You'll get her back, Jaimon." Gabby smiled at him. "But first we need to get out of here. What if I tip my chair and get close enough to get the knife out of your boot?"

Jaimon's eyes lifted. "That might work!"

Gabby began rocking her chair. Just when she thought it might fall, the door crashed open behind them. Paeris and Tarryn entered.

"Hey, what are you trying to do?" Tarryn yelled out and cuffed Gabby on the side of the head.

"Let's just get on with it," Paeris said as he brought a sack out in front of him.

Tarryn pulled out an identical one and walked over to Jaimon.

Paeris sneered at Gabby and pulled the sack down over Gabby's head. By the sounds of Jaimon, the same thing was being done to him.

"Hey!" Jaimon yelled out. "Haryk said he would let us go."

"But he didn't say how or where," Paeris growled.

Tarryn laughed, and Gabby felt her own sack gathered tighter around her. She felt Paeris's arms untie her from the chair and force her to her feet. The bitter taste in her mouth still made her aware that her wizarding powers were not working.

"This way," Paeris said as they moved out of the room.

Gabby heard Paeris directing Tarryn, and soon she heard a door open. The light she could see through the sack brightened. They were outdoors. She could yell out and hope someone would hear them, but this was enemy country. Unfortunately, Jaimon had no such compunctions.

"Help!" Jaimon screamed.

As suddenly as he started he stopped. Gabby heard choking and then the soft thump of a body against the ground.

"I told you not to cause any trouble," Paeris said.

Gabby stifled a cry. "Jaimon," she whispered. "Jaimon!"

"Shut up," Paeris said, "or you'll be next."

"Let's just dump them and get this over with," Tarryn said. "Hurry, before the dock officials come back from supper."

Gabby was pushed ahead harder, and she stumbled and almost fell.

"Stupid girl!" Paeris said. He picked Gabby up and threw her over his shoulder. She tried to struggle through the bag, but it was too tight around her. Her breathing came harder as the sack was now pressed against her mouth. She tried not to panic.

The air was warm against her mouth as she re-breathed in her own exhales. She could feel her breaths getting shallower and quicker. She shook her head a few times to try and clear a space around it, but she was being held too tightly.

"Please, I can't breathe," she croaked.

"Shut up!" said Tarryn, and she felt something hard hit her in the ribs.

She exhaled sharply, but when she tried to take the next breath it was harder to do so. Tears came to her eyes, and she tried to concentrate and conserve air, but she was panicking, and she knew it.

The sounds of the elves' footsteps changed, and Gabby knew they were on the docks. Then she heard the lapping of water. She squirmed again and this time couldn't help but yell out.

"Help!" Gabby yelled. "I can't breathe."

The extra exertion that it took her to yell made her head dizzy, and she began to see black spots before her eyes. Her heart hammered with fear.

Someone else nearby yelled out, and Paeris spun around.

"Trouble!" Tarryn hissed.

Gabby heard something hard hit the ground. *Jaimon!*

Tarryn screamed. "I've been hit!" he said.

Paeris moved erratically, and Gabby's ribs bounced around on his shoulder.

"Paeris, do something," Tarryn wailed.

Gabby found herself being thrown through the air. Her ribs cracked as she landed. The ground under her wobbled, and she heard the sound of waves. *I'm in a boat!*

She struggled to get out of the sack, but it was tied securely around her waist. The sounds of fighting ensued around her, and the sounds of magic being used reached her ears. Paeris was attacking someone.

Without any warning, something heavy crashed on top of her. Pain flashed through her ribs, a stinging pain every time she took a breath. She tried to squirm to get out from under the additional weight, but she was pinned down and couldn't move. The weight pressed down on her head, and she couldn't find a breath.

"Let's get out of here," Tarryn yelled out, and Gabby heard retreating footsteps on the wooden docks.

But it hardly mattered to her as she found herself slipping away into darkness. Her mind flashed with images of Bakari and Liam. No one would know where she and Jaimon were. No one was coming to help them. She shut her eyes harder and let the darkness take control. It was easier that way. The less she breathed, the less she hurt.

The boat lurched, and the weight on top of her shifted again, pushing her face harder against the ground. The last thing she heard was a grunt, then the boat grew still as she took her last breath.

CHAPTER SEVEN

Roland sat once again in his office in the Citadel. It had been a day since he had organized his council in Cassian. Soon after, he had flown with Tam back to the Citadel. The wizards there had been more than surprised to see his golden dragon drop into the courtyard there. They had scrambled around, anticipating an attack, until they realized who was riding the dragon.

Roland smiled. Though the population of the Citadel had swollen with new apprentices in the past year, there were still many older wizards who thought Roland's reign would be short. They seemed to be biding their time until he failed. But the looks on their faces when he had landed were priceless.

A knock on the door took Roland out of his musings.

"Come in," he called out.

In walked Tam, a huge smile on his face.

"What are you so happy about this morning, Tam?" Roland asked.

"A messenger from Raleez has arrived. The ships with troops from Quentis and Solshi should be leaving the bay of Raleez soon. Should give Delia quite the surprise."

"Ah, good," Roland said. "And the wizards we sent?"

"Should help to even things out," Tam said with a smile.

"And where do we stand with the rest?"

"Currently there are 240 apprentices and forty five wizards at residence in the Citadel, about fifteen more wizards spread throughout Alaris, including a few in Corwan still." Tam spouted off the numbers. "They are fairly evenly distributed between the three disciplines, but I'm worried about the battle apprentices—most of them have not been in battle before."

"I will take care of it," Roland said.

Tam looked like something was on his mind.

"Speak your mind, Tam," Roland said. "I'm not going to bite off your head."

Tam sighed. "You can't do it all, Sire."

"Please call me Roland, Tam," Roland offered. "We've been through much together. We are friends, right?"

Tam nodded. "But?"

Roland rolled his eyes. "I'm not looking for pandering, Tam. I need people who can help me fight off the aggressors and still keep the people safe."

"Very well, Roland," Tam said. "You can't do all this on your own."

Roland gave him a questioning look.

"I know all your theories about one absolute ruler being the best for the people. And under all your dramatics and thirst for power, I know you do really care for the people. I'm not questioning that. But as all powerful as you are or may become, you don't have to do everything by yourself."

Something in Roland chilled. But this was Tam. "Council me then, Battlemaster." He cracked a sarcastic smile and waved his scepter at the man.

Tam continued. "Gather the scholar wizards together and have them come up with any solutions for either beating back Delia or the horde of ships coming toward Elvyn. These wizards of the mind hold a lot of wisdom and information. Without the Dragon King's knowledge, I am afraid you will be at a disadvantage."

Roland stiffened for a moment. "You're right, Tam. The Dragon King's mind, as marvelous as it may be . . ." *Or was*, he thought to himself and he changed his train of thought. "I can't spend all the time, as you say, going through the books myself. Gather the wizards, and let them know I will meet with them in the morning to discuss solutions."

Tam nodded and began to walk away. Roland called after him. "And Tam, tell the other disciplines to do the same. The battle and counselor wizards should have an opportunity to share their thoughts. All currently in the Citadel are invited to the meeting tomorrow."

Tam raised his eyebrows. "I'm not sure that has happened in a long time. It's usually the wizard council who makes the decisions."

"You've shown me I need help," Roland continued. "Why not use all the assets at my disposal? Good ideas are not saved for the elderly or those in power only. Over a year ago I was an apprentice, and now look at me!" Roland spread his arms wide. "The mightiest wizard in the land."

Tam chuckled. "There is one power you are missing, Sire."

Roland tilted his head and gave Tam a questioning look. He couldn't imagine what Tam had in mind. He ruled a mighty empire alongside a golden dragon. What could he possibly be missing? "And that is?"

"A little humility." This time Tam did laugh out loud and turned to leave the room.

"Hey!" Roland called after him. But Roland had not taken offense. Those with power had to allow a little leeway to those below them.

As he got to the door, Tam stopped and turned his head, his eyes growing more serious.

"Yes?" Roland prompted.

"Well, Sire . . . I mean Roland," Tam stuttered, all business again. "There is one other thing. Some of the apprentice battle wizards would like to go save Alli."

Alli! Thoughts raced through Roland's mind. He had almost gotten through to her in Solshi. He needed her back.

"I'm sorry, Tam." Roland let out a long breath. "I can't afford to let them leave right now. I'm hoping to hear from Tabitha soon."

Tam's face fell. "I understand."

"But tell them she will not be left behind." Roland stood up. "Before this war is over, Delia will be destroyed, and we will have our battlemaster back. I would never leave Alli behind, Tam."

"I look forward to the day," Tam said before he turned and left. "We all miss her."

Roland fell back down into his seat. He twirled the scepter around in his hand and thought about Alli. He growled out loud thinking about what Delia had done to her. If for no other reason than that Delia deserved to be destroyed. He didn't really care about the kingdoms she had taken—that had been their choice, except he knew now that he had to unify them all somehow.

His eyes roamed over to his sizeable fireplace. A small fire had been built to take the chill off the winter morning air. But it was not the fire that took his attention; it was the décor above the mantle.

He walked over and reached his hand out to the small dragon artifact Bakari had given him. He let the carving roll around in the palm of his hand as a plan began to form in his mind. The artifact had been given to him to call the dragons in time of great need.

Well, this was a time of great need. The only question was, would the dragons come when he called? Since Delia's rise to power, Roland had taken to being a bit more careful with the use of all of the artifacts.

CHAPTER EIGHT

The next morning, Roland sat in an ornate chair—not quite a throne, but close—at the front of the large Citadel hall. Rows of benches and chairs had been set up overnight to accommodate the nearly three hundred wizards and apprentices currently at the Citadel.

Through a double side door, his dragon had entered and now sat curled around the back of his chair. Its presence appeared to intimidate the other wizards. They tried to avoid the seats closest to the front, and they eyed the beast with apprehension.

Servants stood off to the sides preparing tables of food and drink. Roland sat and watched each person walk into the room and felt a sense of satisfaction amidst the urgency that drove him forward today.

His council members sat in front of the other wizards, but still as far away from the dragon as possible. Most appeared none too pleased at being placed with the rest of the wizards and apprentices.

Unify them! Came the never-ending admonition. It was softer now, as if unifying the group before him was less important to the unification he had already accomplished. But if he couldn't unify his own people, how could he manage the entire empire?

He had thought long into the night about what Tam had said. Tam was right. Roland couldn't manage six kingdoms—and more, once Cyrene, Khazer, and Turg came into the fold—without some help.

What about Mahli? He wondered. Did he dare step there with the Dragon King unconscious? He thought about all the dragon riders. Wasn't keeping peace in the land their job? His hand tightened around the scepter once again, and he drew power from its source. It seemed the buck always stopped at him.

He stood and addressed the group. "Welcome, wizards. I convene this grand council for the benefit of your wisdom. As wizards of the Citadel, it is time for us to take our rightful place in the history of mankind. Where others have failed, we will not. Where others have run, we will fight. Where others have kept to themselves and tried to ignore the problems, we, wizards of the Citadel, will stand united. United, we will rise to the occasion and defeat the foes in front of us, and in doing so protect the people in our great empire."

Roland had them engaged. Every eye was on him. Even the council members looked at him with admiration. Gripping the Scepter of Unification, he raised his hands in the air.

"Rise," he continued. "Rise up on your feet, my fellow wizards, and pledge your loyalty to the cause of bringing the nations and her people together as one, defeating our foes, and bringing peace once again to the land." Roland paused for a moment to let the call sink in. "What say you, wizards of the Citadel? Do you stand together? Do we show the kingdoms the power of a united Citadel? What say you?"

Without pause, shouts of agreement, acceptance, and unity echoed through the halls. Three hundred wizards and apprentices stood on their feet and cheered loudly. Roland pushed his scepter to the floor, and bright lights shot out over the room, bathing the group in a golden radiance. Orelia roared for emphasis.

Roland smiled and felt more excitement than he had in a long time. There was hope for the future. A future that would include his name for centuries.

The crowd quieted down, and Roland gestured for them to take their seats. Then he opened the gathering up for discussion. The scholar wizards of the mind had indeed met and done their homework. Their greatest ideas included using some of the artifacts in the basement rooms, setting up a decoy for Delia to attack, and making sure there were enough wizards in each of the capital cities to fight against her when she attacked.

The battle wizards assured Roland that they were ready to fight and that the apprentices in training would be a valuable asset in any defense of the kingdoms.

After many other great ideas, one of Roland's council members stood. He was a counselor wizard and had served many governors in the land during the time of the Barrier. The man had never quite accepted Roland—though seeing him ride in on the dragon recently had prompted him to start treating Roland a little better.

"Yes, Councilor Hayden." Roland gave the man the floor. "Do you have a suggestion?"

Hayden walked forward, his long red robes hanging loosely on his thin frame. His blond hair was also thinning, but his blue eyes were bright and excited.

"May I suggest that you send a small contingent of wizards from our Citadel to each of the kingdoms in your . . . ah . . . empire." Hayden stumbled a bit on his words. "There are a set of artifacts in the rooms downstairs that will allow us to communicate with each other. In that way, your needs will be represented in all the kingdoms as we face our foes."

Roland's eyes went wide. He hadn't heard of these artifacts. But the man may have made the best suggestion of day. He took two steps and put his arm around Hayden.

"Councilor Hayden has given us a brilliant idea." Roland smiled, and his scepter pulsed with agreement. "You see what can be done when we are unified!"

The crowd cheered. The ideas coming from meeting all together in the grand council really were amazing. Wizard and apprentice alike had participated and found unity in their cause.

One of the doors in the back pushed open, and in stumbled a dirty young woman. Her dark hair was disheveled and fell over her light-brown face as a nearby wizard stepped forward to keep her from falling.

Each member of the grand council turned and looked back at the commotion. The young woman uprighted herself and stood for a moment, brushing the hair from her face and taking a deep breath.

"Tabitha?" Roland called out and took a few steps forward.

"High Wizard," Tabitha called out weakly. "We need to talk."

Roland understood the gravity of the situation immediately. Something had driven Tabitha to return. It had to be something important.

"Councilor Hayden, I approved of your suggestion and give to you and the rest of the council the task of creating groups of wizards and apprentices to serve as my wizard ambassadors in each kingdom. Send them on their way immediately, but leave enough here for us to defend ourselves and Alaris."

Hayden seemed surprised at the responsibility but nodded.

Roland strode toward Tabitha and gestured at her to follow him. As they moved out of the grand hall to his offices he turned to a servant and asked for food and water to be brought up immediately.

Reaching Tabitha, he regarded her with concern. "Are you all right? Can you walk upstairs?"

She gave him a weak smile, her bright white teeth contrasting with her brown skin. "I've traveled from Turg to Alaris in three days, Sire. A few more steps hardly matter."

Roland put his arm through hers. Still amazed to see her, he escorted her out of the room. On the way toward the stairs he looked down at her. She appeared exhausted and hardly able to stand. Right before the stairs he turned and walked instead to a nearby room. He flagged down a servant and told him to bring the food there instead.

Roland brought Tabitha to a chair. "What news do you bring?"

Tabitha let out a deep sigh. "Delia plans to attack you."

Roland smiled and relaxed. "I suspected that. But we have troops on the way to Turg, and we are making plans to defend all the capitals of the southern kingdoms."

"No, Sire." Tabitha shook her head. "You misunderstand. You irked her by taking Solshi away from her. She is after you now. She plans to attack you directly."

Roland nodded his head in understanding. "Well, she can try. She'll have a hard time knowing where I will be."

CHAPTER NINE

Gabby tried to rearrange herself on the small bench of the boat without her ribs hurting again. She grimaced trying to do so.

"Do you need something?" Jaimon called back to her over his shoulder.

Gabby watched as Jaimon rowed as hard as he could. They moved sideways against the current along the shore of Elvyn—but a half mile out in the sea. She glared at the other man in the boat with them until he finally turned around.

"What?" Garrik said. His red hair never appeared much different—it was always a mess. In the growing darkness, his pale skin showed white.

"Jaimon's tired," she replied. "You should row for a while."

Garrik grumbled but scooted up to Jaimon, grabbed the oars, and traded places with him. "Don't know why I helped you out anyways."

Gabby wondered the same thing. She had blacked out after being thrown into the small rowboat with the sack over her head. When she had come to, she and Jaimon were now out in the Blue Sea with Garrik paddling them farther east and then south. It seemed he had attacked Tarryn and Paeris and then jumped into the boat himself.

"What about your ship, Garrik?" Gabby asked. "Why didn't we get your ship? It had to have been bigger than this one."

Another grumble from Garrik produced no additional answers.

"Because you don't really have a boat, do you?" Jaimon asked.

"Well . . ." Garrik mumbled something unintelligible but rowed harder. The moon was now up, and a few stars made it through the wispy fog that was growing thicker over their heads.

Gabby looked to her right toward the shoreline and saw a few pinpricks of light through the trees. The trees and lights meant two things: they were further south now than the desert, and there were people. Where there were people, there was food. She was ravenous.

"Can we go to shore now?" Gabby asked. A rumbling in her stomach finalizing her plea. "We need food and supplies before going any further and we shouldn't try to go around the horn at night, if that was your plan."

"What do you know about the Horn?" Garrik asked.

"I grew up in Margarid and have been across the water to the sanctuary plenty of times."

Garrik huffed. "You two know nothing of these waters. The currents of the southern and eastern seas meet together here and cause whirlpools that have swallowed ships whole."

"And I'm sure you have survived these terrible disasters," Jaimon piped in. "You, the captain without a ship?"

Garrik stopped rowing and twisted his body to see Jaimon better. "You want to row again, young squirt?"

Jaimon stayed quiet.

"That's what I thought," Garrick concluded. He pulled a few more strokes before answering Gabby's original question. "You are right, though, we should head inland. There are more places to hide in the trees."

"Hide?" Gabby asked. "Why do we have to hide?"

"It's not us, Gabby," Jaimon said. "He's worried about someone finding him."

"Are you sure you're not a wizard, boy?" Garrick glared in Jaimon's direction.

Jaimon grunted, and Gabby laughed. "So we were saved from rebels by a wanted man."

"I'm not wanted," Garrick clarified, "just not looked at in such a good light by some."

The wind picked up, and the small boat lurched a bit sideways. Gabby grabbed hold of the edge to steady herself and winced again. She was sure she had at least a few broken ribs, and a lump on the side of her head was throbbing.

Garrick struggled with the oars to get the boat turned again toward shore. He stopped paddling a bit and wiped sweat from his forehead, even though the night was cool. He looked at Jaimon, as if wanting to ask him to take another turn at the oars. The boat had only come with one set.

"I can help," Gabby said softly.

"No, Gabby. You're hurt," Jaimon said.

"In this, I agree with your friend," Garrik said. "You can't row."

"No, but I can summon the winds," Gabby said. "I think my powers are back now. My earth powers are growing. I might be more of a battle wizard than a counselor, I've been thinking."

Garrik's eyes went wide as he glanced from Jaimon and back to Gabby.

Gabby closed her eyes to gather her concentration; it was always easier that way. When she opened them back up she lifted one hand in the air—the other holding tightly to the side of the boat—and pulled the wind from the air. As it was already windy, it was relatively easy for her to do. She just had to make it more concentrated behind their boat.

The boat lurched for a moment and tipped dangerously from side to side but then picked up speed and rode more smoothly over the waves, back toward land. Garrik used the oars to keep the boat straight, but he didn't have to turn them for power.

In no time at all, through a thin layer of coastal fog, the outline of trees rose in front of their small boat.

"Slow it down, miss," Garrick said.

Gabby lessened the wind behind them, allowing the current now to pull them to shore. Garrick jumped out in water to his knees and pulled the boat the rest of the way up onto a thin strip of sand.

Jaimon helped Gabby get out of the boat, and once they were on dry land she took a few steps to try and regain her land legs. She stumbled once and yelled out in pain, but Jaimon caught her. The three stood catching their breaths for a few moments.

On the other side of the thin beach of sand stood a small hill. Garrick motioned them up. Jaimon supported Gabby. As they walked the smaller shrubs grew more thick, until they entered a heavy forest at the top of the bank. Gabby couldn't see much farther than a half a dozen steps inside the trees. She conjured up a small light in the palm of her hand.

"What are you doing?" Garrick jumped at her and clamped down his hand over hers. "You want them to find us?"

"Who?" Jaimon said, looking around. "Who could possibly find us in the dark at the edge of the forest on the southern tip of Elvyn?"

A slight rustle of leaves was the only warning the three of them got before a dozen men and women stepped out from the darkened forest.

"Us," said a man out front.

Gabby stared hard at the man in front of her. By his pointed ears and slanted brows he was definitely an elf, but he was heavier set than those around Lor'l, and his blond hair was tied into a pony tail like Jaimon's.

Garrick took a step back, but not before the man noticed him behind Gabby and Jaimon.

"Ah," he said, "Garrickurol Aghammas; the lost child has returned."

Gabby and Jaimon gazed at Garrick, awaiting his response.

"Uh, Trae," Garrick said with a gulp. "Nice to see you again."

A woman stepped forward and glared at Garrick. "You will address a guardian by his full and proper name, Garrickurol."

Garrick's eyes went wide, and he snorted. "Very well, Merlyndra." He gave a short bow to the man standing in front of them. "Traethonylon Staizmull, first guardian of the forest elves, may I introduce you to Gabrielle Von Wulf, princess of Quentis, and Jaimon Schaeffer, Dragon Rider."

Both Merlyndra and Traethonylon's eyes went wide at the mention of who accompanied Garrick. Gabby took a step forward. "Greetings, Guardian," she said with as regal a posture as she could manage with her injured ribs. "Could we ask for a place to sleep and a warm meal?"

Traethonylon laughed out loud and slapped Garrick on the back. "Well, Garrick, you seem to be keeping high company this time around." He turned to Gabby and Jaimon and continued. "You are more than welcome in our small community. And please, call me Trae. Follow me."

Gabby and Jaimon peered at each other. Jaimon shrugged and motioned them to go along. To Gabby's surprise, the group walked through the dark forest without any lights but seemed to know where they were going.

The wind in the trees and the sound of a few stray animals made Gabby jump from time to time.

"I've never heard of elves in the southern forest," Jaimon said in a whisper. "I thought it was empty of people."

"Neither have I," Gabby agreed. She looked around with worry and wondered where they were being taken.

"You know these people, Garrik?" Gabby asked.

Before answering he glanced at Trae and then back to Gabby. "He's my brother."

"Brother?" Gabby said with a shake of her head. She was confused. By Garrik's hair he was definitely of the desert elves. "But you have different last names."

"Same father, different mothers," Trae broke into Gabby's thoughts. "He took his mother's last name. Garrick tends to live among the desert elves and has developed an affinity for the ocean, among other bad habits." He said the last with a smile that held no sting.

"I can't help it if others lose their things," Garrick said with a shrug of his shoulders.

"You're a thief, Garrick," said Merlyndra, "and that's all there is to it."

Gabby gave Jaimon a look of alarm. Who had they gotten themselves mixed up with?

A lull in the conversation ensued as they continued walking on trails that Gabby could hardly see. Trae led the way, with Merlyndra and another man behind him. Garrick was next, with Jaimon supporting Gabby. The rest of the men and women followed.

The trees grew larger, some more than ten feet across. After about twenty minutes, Gabby began to see a scattering of lights through the trees up ahead.

"Gabby!" Jaimon said as he pointed to the side.

Gabby gasped as she realized that the base of the humongous trees were small houses with windows and doors carved out of them.

"They're thicker than the trees in Lor'l," Gabby said.

The group continued past a dozen of these trees. A few people came out and waved at Trae, and he smiled back. Soon the trees thinned, and they came to a picturesque meadow. A roaring fire filled the center of it, and a hundred people seemed to be dashing about while cooking and chatting.

"Ah," Trae said. "Just in time for our midnight meal."

"*Midnight* meal?" Jaimon repeated softly.

One of the other men walked past him and slapped him on the back—making Jaimon jump. The man smiled. "Midnight is the best time for a meal."

Gabby, Jaimon, and Garrick were led forward by Trae. Garrick tried to fade to the back, but Trae grabbed his arm and pulled him forward.

"Father will be surprised to see you," Trae said to Garrick.

The man only grunted and tried to pat down his unruly red hair. "I'm not so sure about that."

"Oh," Trae laughed. "He'll forgive you for leaving, Garrick. He always does."

Gabby had traveled to many kingdoms in her young lifetime, but this group of people was stranger than anything she had encountered. Looking around the gathering, she saw older, middle-aged, and young elves moving about as if it was the middle of the day. It was all quite confusing.

Trae led them to a small gathering of people on the far side of the meadow. Bright torches surrounded a small wooden pavilion. Twisted vines with fragrant white and pink flowers wound around poles and up and over the roof. As they moved closer, the crowd parted.

Sitting on a wooden bench smoothed by years of use, sat the oldest man Gabby had ever seen. The man's pasty face had deep, chiseled wrinkles, and his blond hair, although tied back in a ponytail, hung over the back of the chair and down to the floor.

Gabby looked into the man's eyes and felt the world tilt a bit. Everything else went dark around her as his eyes leveled on hers, and she knew she was entering the magic stream.

CHAPTER TEN

In the grayness of the stream's edge, Gabby saw the glow of the forest elf in front of her. Suddenly he materialized, and his body was strong and healthy. But his eyes told her it was the same man.

"Wizard of Quentis," the man said. "I am Master Guardian Calanon Staizmull, keeper of the southern forests."

Gabby bowed in the man's overwhelming presence. "Sir, I am honored to be in your presence, but I have never heard of the southern forest elves."

Calanon laughed, and it was music to Gabby's ears. "Ah, so your father has not told you about us yet?"

"My father?" Gabby asked. "You know my father?"

Calanon smiled. "I have known your fathers for centuries. Two hundred years ago a treaty was forged between the southern forest elves and the monarchs of Tillimot and Quentis."

Gabby was still confused. She looked around her for a moment in the magic stream and off in the distance to what she thought was the south, she saw a bright light. *That's where the Phoenix is.*

"We are protectors of this forest," Calanon explained. "Among all the elves, we have always been the ones to protect the land. Over five hundred years ago, after the great eastern war, we left our homeland and sailed across the sea—tree elves, desert elves, and forest elves. There were many of us in our homeland. We each ruled a mighty kingdom. But the war split us, and our numbers dwindled. The holder of the scepter brought enough of us together, and we formed an alliance."

"The Scepter of Unification?" Gabby asked.

Calanon nodded. "Yes."

"High Wizard Roland Tyre holds it again," Gabby informed him.

Calanon's wrinkles deepened. "That is concerning. I have felt the stirrings of the power of spirit but did not know the scepter had surfaced again."

"He has united most of the land against a woman who has stolen the dragon bonds from the Dragon King," Gabby explained. "And he has said that warships are coming from the east."

Calanon wavered on his feet and Gabby reached forward to steady him. But her hand only went through him. He righted himself and pinched his lips, thinking for a moment.

"The scepter is dangerous," Calanon said. "It requires much from the user."

"How much?" Gabby asked, afraid of the answer.

"Everything."

Gabby's eyes grew wide, and she didn't know what to say.

"It has always been so. The scepter is powerful. It united the elves, but our uniter had to stay behind. I am sure it will unite man for some time, but . . ."

"The elves have joined in his empire," Gabby said. "Roland Tyre has been named Warlord of Elvyn."

Calanon's eyes went even wider. "That is surprising. I have heard that Lanwaithian has a good heart and is wise—like his father was. Maybe this man, Roland, is different. Maybe he can save us without destroying himself."

Calanon faded in and out once more.

"Sir," Gabby said. "We need to get back. You are weakening here."

Calanon laughed and nodded. "You are strong to stay here for so long yourself. But I perceive that there is a reason you have come to us. One that doesn't have to do with the Scepter of Unification."

"The Dragon King has been injured by a dangerous poison that feeds off his magic, and the dragon bond has been taken," Gabby tried to explain. "We tried to heal him, but we couldn't." She hung her head for a moment, then brought it back up and continued. "In the magic stream I saw something in the south—something of pure magic. A phoenix, I think."

Calanon smiled broadly, and excitement filled his eyes. "You saw the power of the phoenix?"

Gabby nodded.

"If you actually saw the power, then it is meant to be," Calanon said. "Very few know of their existence, and fewer still see their power."

"Do you know where it is?" Gabby asked.

"I do." The man's eyes sparkled with delight, but his voice began to fade. "It is why we are here. It is why we live deep in the forest and guard its perimeters. We are the guardians of its power. My grandfather brought five phoenixes from the east, and now there are only two left." Calanon began to fade again, and this time he didn't come back.

Gabby looked around her for a moment. Off to the south a substantial bright light reflected through the grayness of the magic stream. She took a step toward it but was transported back to the dark forest and stood once again at the edge of the pavilion.

Calanon held her eyes in his—the same blue sparkle as in the magic stream. "Welcome, Gabrielle Von Wulf and Dragon Rider Jaimon Schaefer. I am he whom you seek."

Jaimon sucked in his breath, and Gabby looked over at him. By the positioning of everyone present, her time speaking with Calanon in the magic stream had taken mere seconds.

"Who's he?" Jaimon whispered to her.

"That's Calanon," Gabby said.

"How do you know?" Jaimon furrowed his brows.

Gabby put a hand on his arm and gave him a big smile. "I just spent some time in the magic stream with him."

Jaimon shook his head, but before he could ask another question, Merlyndra stepped forward.

"Honored Keeper." She bowed to Calanon. "You do not know these people. We must be careful."

Calanon put a thin hand up in the air. "I've been careful for 200 years. Now is the time we have been protecting the phoenixes for. The Scepter of Unification is in use again."

Gasps ran through the gathering.

"They know where a phoenix is?" Jaimon asked Gabby.

"Yes, my young Dragon Rider, I do," Calanon said, "for I am the keeper of the phoenix. Just like you bond with your dragon, a phoenix waits to bond to another. As the keeper, I have been afforded some measure of communication with them, but not a full bond. Their power is strong, and they choose their bonds carefully. It must be someone that can handle the power."

"The Dragon King," Jaimon said. "He can handle the power. And he needs it to survive."

Calanon nodded his head. "Perhaps," he said with a pause, "but there may be another."

Gabby scanned the growing crowd. A bell rang, and everyone cheered and moved toward blankets on the ground. Plates of steaming meat, aromatic vegetables, and fresh-baked bread drew everyone's attention.

The group around Calanon began to move toward the food and swept up Gabby and Jaimon with them. Out of the corner of her eye, Gabby saw Calanon crook his finger at Garrik.

"Come and help me up, son," Calanon said.

Garrick looked like he had swallowed a toad, but he took the few steps toward the keeper's chair and brought his arm out for Calanon.

"Now tell me what troubles brought you to be with these two fine young people," Calanon said to his son.

Gabby couldn't hear the answer, as they were taken to a place of honor among the throngs of people. For the next thirty minutes, she and Jaimon were given as much food as they wanted. After their plates were cleared away, a tray of sweets was offered to them.

"Jaimon, don't you want some cake?" Gabby teased.

Jaimon's face paled, and he shook his head. Grabbing another pastry instead, he leaned back on his elbows and took a bite.

"Aren't you ever full?" Gabby said as she declined dessert.

Jaimon's eyes went wide as he swallowed the bite. "I don't think so."

"A boy after my own heart." Garrik had come up behind them and slapped Jaimon on the back. "You never know where your next meal will come from, so eat up." Garrick proceeded to grab a plateful of cake, pastry, and some kind of pudding Gabby didn't recognize.

Gabby glared at Garrick, but then laughed. "So you are the keeper's son? But he is so . . ."

"Old?" Garrick laughed, then lowered his voice. "Don't tell him that. But the forest elves live long and are quite prolific late in life."

Gabby felt her cheeks heat up and was going to change the conversation, but Garrik continued. "Trae's mother died giving birth to him. My father left the forest for a while and traveled throughout Elvyn. While outside of the forest, he met a young and beautiful desert Elf who fell for his charms—and ta-da." He spread his arms out wide. "Here I am."

Gabby again needed to change the subject. She was uncomfortable thinking about the aging Calanon out wooing women. So she asked about Garrik's personal life instead. "I heard mention that you were a thief? What were your intentions with us when you offered to take us around the Horn?"

"Well," he said gruffly, "I knew the desert elves were up to something, and I just didn't want to see you hurt. I felt I needed to protect you for some reason."

Jaimon huffed. "Likely story."

Garrik seemed embarrassed. "It surprised me as much as you. Helping people is not usually my forte. Not that I don't intend to, it's just that . . . it doesn't always go the way it should."

"Well, it went the right way this time," Gabby said.

Garrik jutted out his chin to Jaimon as if to say, *see?*

Jaimon licked the remaining pastry from his fingers and looked like he was thinking about something. Gabby let him collect his thoughts.

"So the forest elves are the guardians of the phoenix," Jaimon stated. "In order to protect such a special and magical creature you must have your own powerful magic here. Is that why it is always so dangerous for ships to sail around the Horn?"

Garrik choked on his last bite. After recovering, he said, "You're a smart man. We have to protect the land somehow."

Trae scooted over from where he had been sitting with Calanon. "The magic runs in our blood. It is different from that of other elves or wizards. We cannot do so many tricks with ours. Like our northern cousins, we do have a special affinity with nature, especially the trees, but for the most part we live normal lives . . ."

"Except you eat in the middle of the night." Jaimon laughed.

Trae smiled. "I forget that is strange for most people. Yes, we sleep during the day and do our work at night for the most part. While we are sleeping is when our magic is at its most potent. It is then that a phoenix needs the most protection from others finding them."

"Have you ever seen one?" Gabby asked both Trae and Garrik.

Both of their eyes went wide.

"No one ever sees a phoenix," Calanon croaked from a dozen feet away. "In two hundred years my grandfather, my father, and I have only each seen them once, and that's when the keeper's bond is passed from one generation to the next. There has not been a true bonding of a phoenix since we first arrived on the Western Continent, over five hundred years ago."

"How will we find them?" Gabby said, her face turned down. They couldn't get this far and fail.

"You will not find them," Calanon said.

"What?" Jaimon gasped. "But the Dragon King needs it to be healed."

"You will not find them," Calanon repeated, "but they will find you—if that is what's meant to be."

Gabby heard Jaimon let out a held breath, echoing her own. "Then where do we go exactly?"

"To an island just south of the peninsula, around what men call the Horn." Calanon closed his eyes for a bit. When he opened them, he nodded. "Yes, that is where you need to go."

"How will we get there?" Jaimon asked. "We will need another ship. The boat we were in isn't large enough."

"It's dangerous that's for sure," Garrick said.

Gabby frowned and glanced from Garrik to Calanon. "Is there someone who can do it? Someone who can take us around the Horn and to the island? Please, sir."

Calanon's eyes sparkled. "Oh, yes, there is one. He's a little unconventional, but he'll do."

Garrik appeared nervous and glared around the small gathering. "Oh, no. No. No. No."

Trae slapped him on the back. "But, little brother, you're always getting yourself into messes. Here's a chance for redemption."

"Father?" Garrik pleaded.

Calanon cackled. "Garrik, this must be your destiny."

"My destiny?" grumbled Garrik. "I make my own destiny."

"Well, then, my son, being the first forest elf to have been raised among the docks of the sea, you now have the opportunity to make your own destiny. Rather than going around the horn, it would be best to travel south and meet up on the southern shore. There you can find a small boat and accompany our two young friends here to the island and see if indeed a phoenix finds them. Think of it, you may be the only elf to see this magical creature in a generation."

Gabby looked at him with pleading eyes, and Jaimon rolled his.

Garrik took to his feet and stroked his red beard under his chin. "Come to think of it, there may be something on that island that makes my trip worthwhile."

"No stealing, Garrik," censured Trae with a laugh.

"It's not stealing if it doesn't belong to anybody."

Gabby laughed and clapped her hands. "When do we leave?"

"Let's get this over with. We leave at first light," Garrik said as he left the gathering.

Soon Trae had someone show Gabby and Jaimon to a place they could rest for a few hours. Before turning in, a healer came in and saw to Gabby. After a few minutes of sitting down with the healer running her hands over Gabby's injuries, she stood back up.

"Thank you," Gabby said.

The old healer bowed her head and handed her a bandage. "Keep this on while you are traveling. You will still be sore for a few days, but it will heal completely."

After the healer left and before rolling over and going to sleep, Jaimon got Gabby's attention.

"I still don't trust Garrik," he said.

"Give him a chance, Jaimon," Gabby said. "He seems to have a good heart."

Jaimon only grunted as he rolled over. Gabby smiled at their luck. Hopefully, soon they would be able to find a phoenix and return to the Dragon King.

CHAPTER ELEVEN

"Beautiful creatures, aren't they?" King Abbas of Cyrene said to Alli.

She watched their two dragons, Ryker and Miriel, red and yellow, lying in a small field just to the north of the castle in Hasari, the capital city of Cyrene. Alli agreed with the king's sentiment. They were magnificent animals.

"They look tired," Alli said.

The king stood next to her on the third floor balcony of the grand building. "They'd better get some rest, then, because Delia has it in her head to attack soon." His tone was off.

Alli turned and stared at the man. He was of the age that her father would be. The thought startled her. She couldn't remember who her father was. King Abbas had ruled Cyrene for five years. He was of medium build, had black hair down to his chin, and the bluest eyes. Quite rare for those of brown skin. He had a son that Alli had seen once; one about her age.

"You don't agree with our master?" Alli asked.

King Abbas put his hands on the railing of the balcony, and Alli could see his knuckles turn white with the exertion. He turned his head up and gazed at Alli. "She is not my master."

Alli raised an eyebrow. "She *is* our master, Abbas. She controls the bond with our dragons."

The king held his lips tight and rubbed his graying goatee with his fingers. "As the Dragon Queen, she controls the dragons, but she doesn't control me and my kingdom."

Alli chuckled. "Doesn't she?"

"I don't have to take this from you," Abbas said. "What do you know of kings and politics? You're as much a pawn in this game of hers as anyone. Why don't you stand up to her? What do you have to gain in her plans?"

Alli didn't know what the king meant. Delia was her master, and Alli did what she was told. A thought raced through her mind of letting the servant Tabitha go. It worried her. She didn't want to disappoint her master. She shoved the thoughts away and hoped Delia never found out about her momentary weakness.

When she didn't answer Abbas, he continued talking. "I don't really have a choice in the matter. If I don't follow her, I'll end up dead. If I follow her, she has promised Prince Ender and me a portion of her new kingdom, a portion of all the southern kingdoms."

"She has promised me nothing," Alli said out loud with sudden realization. All she had known was fighting, but shouldn't there be some kind of reward? Even her last master, Constantine, had rewarded her with healing and additional use of her powers.

"Then why do you stay with her?" Abbas said.

"Because she is my master," Alli said in a steady cadence.

Abbas growled and looked back down at the dragons for a few more minutes. Alli didn't know how dragons were supposed to act all the time, but something told her their lethargy was not normal. A sudden thought leaped into her head.

"Hibernation," she said out loud.

"What?" Abbas turned back to her. "What did you say?"

Alli didn't know why she had said the word she did. Where did it come from? Before she could answer, a guard came running through a nearby door and out onto the balcony. He thumped his fist to his heart and approached King Abbas.

"Sire, there is unrest again along the river," the guard said. "A ship burns."

The king ground his teeth and motioned for Alli to follow him and the guard. "This is the third ship in three days. Someone is trying to undermine us. Delia won't stand for this."

Alli found her recent melancholy lifted and a new spring in her step. She was itching for a fight. "Any idea who it is?"

The guard turned his head to them as they strode through the castle corridors. "There are rumors, Dragon Rider."

"We don't govern on rumors," King Abbas said.

"They say it is Nicholas Marinos," the guard continued.

The king stopped abruptly, and Alli ran into him.

"I thought him dead," Abbas said. "Died when the coliseum collapsed."

The guard shrugged his shoulder. "I'm sure you know best."

Alli took a step around the king and confronted the guard. "Tell us what you know—rumor or not." She looked over at Abbas. His eyes smoldered with anger at her as she took control of the situation.

The guard looked to his king for permission, and Abbas waved a hand in the air for them to proceed walking. "Tell us what you know."

"There are rumors of war coming to our shores from the south, and many don't like it," the guard mumbled. "It is said that High Minister Nicholas is building his own resurgence to fight against his daughter."

"Dangerous talk," Alli said then turned and glared at the king. "Is Cyrene loyal to the Dragon Queen?"

The king paled and turned to his guard then back to Alli.

"Of course," he said softly as he bowed to Alli in a gesture that was more than he should have. Alli would have to keep an eye on him for her master.

"In the morning I fetch Prince Ender back from Khazer," Alli said to the king. "He went to inform his father of the rise of the new Dragon Queen. Be ready when I return. Soon we will attack. Our master has a way to know where Roland Tyre will be. As dragon riders, nobody will stand against us."

King Abbas nodded in agreement. But Alli noticed doubt still lingering in his eyes.

* * *

High up in the air, Alli had just crossed over the small foothills that separated Turg and Khazer from each other. She traveled east to Jor, the capital city of Khazer, to bring back Prince Ender and his dragon. Their master, Delia, was finalizing her plans of attack. The prince, after securing his father's loyalty to Delia's cause, would travel back with Alli in preparation for the fight. Nicholas, or the ships from Solshi, could not stand the might of their dragons.

The ground beneath her was brown and flat, the air cold. Alli wrapped her cloak tightly around her, but it didn't give much protection from the fading sun behind her to the west.

Without warning, her dragon dropped a dozen feet, and Alli almost fell off. She grabbed frantically at the small rope around Miriel's neck and secured herself before her dragon fell again.

"Miriel!" she said out loud. "What's going on?"

There was no answer. There never was. It was so infuriating. She knew as a dragon rider she should feel something more than she did—and she'd had that one time. So she knew what it could be.

Why don't you speak to me, you stupid dragon.

Miriel roared and began spiraling toward the ground. Alli tried to think of what to do. She was a wizard; a powerful one, from what people told her. She should be able to do something. She closed her eyes for a moment and tried to forget that she was falling to her death.

In the far reaches of her mind she sensed Delia.

Alli! Delia spoke to her somehow through the dragon bond. *You need to take charge of your dragon.*

She's sick or tired or something, Alli yelled back in her mind. *Master, She won't respond.*

She has *to respond; you hold her dragon bond. Give her your strength, and take control.*

Alli concentrated harder. She brought up all her powers within her and felt her body sizzling as if on fire. She grew warm and opened up her eyes—lightning sparked down her arms. Looking over the side, she panicked for a moment as she saw how fast she was coming to the ground. She brought her focus back up to her dragon and thrust her hands into its yellow scales and let out an awful scream.

In the back of her mind she felt Delia share her own power with her, and she threw this into the dragon also.

"Stop!" she yelled out loud and in her mind. "I command you to fly!"

There was an instant of hesitation, then a flattening out. Alli's stomach lurched, and bright lights exploded behind her eyes. In that brief moment she saw through her dragon's eyes. As one they leveled off, barely skimming over a few lone trees, then across the brown fields they zoomed.

Now you are mine!

While still connected to the dragon, Alli dove in again with her magic and grabbed hold of the bond. She yanked it hard in her mind and tied it up with her magic.

Now you will obey me, dragon.

In the back of Alli's mind she heard Delia's laughter, and she smiled at how she had pleased her master once again.

I am tired, came the weak voice of Miriel. *I need rest. We were awakened too early.*

You almost killed me, Alli said. *The next time you disobey me you will wish you had died.*

Yes, master, came the dragon's quiet thoughts. *I will obey.*

It almost sounded to Alli as if the dragon wept. What would a dragon have to cry about? They were magnificent creatures that could fly across a kingdom in day, destroy whole towns with fire, and devour enemies with their giant maws. And she controlled this powerful creature. *She* was the master.

CHAPTER TWELVE

After a fitful sleep in a small town in Khazer, Alli took her dragon up in the air again. The farther east they flew the darker it got, and by the time she reached Jor, a downpour had descended. Miriel was finding it hard to see, hard to fly. Not wanting to walk in from outside the city, Alli brought Miriel down right in the middle of a garden that sat inside the castle walls. Miriel's long tail knocked over a statue, and her wide wings smashed into a trellis.

Despite the foul weather, a company of soldiers appeared and tried to hold Alli and her dragon in the garden until someone of more importance arrived. Soaking wet, herself, Alli was not in a mood to wait around for a greeting party. She walked toward the castle. Two men stepped in front of her, and the others surrounded her.

"Who are you?" asked one.

"I am a dragon rider in the service of your Dragon Queen," Alli said with gray eyes flashing at the men. She placed a hand on the sword that hung by her side. However, she knew that if a confrontation broke out she would end up using her magical powers—they would get the job done much quicker.

"I bow to no queen," said one of the soldiers. "Orian Asher is my king."

Alli growled at them, brought up her power and, with a flip of her head, sent the two front guards through the air and to the ground.

"Any more takers?" Alli asked. No one moved. "Where is Ender?"

The men glanced at each other and then back to Alli. One stepped forward. "Prince Ender died in an accident out at sea months ago."

"But I've just been with him," Alli said, her mind racing with the possibilities, but mental calculations were not her forte. "What about his dragon?"

The men did not look happy to continue answering her questions. They growled, and a few of them tried to convince the others to at least get under a covering. The two men she had thrown to the ground stood back up. The older of the two approached Alli again, but before he said anything another group of men walked up behind them. At its lead was a tall, elderly gentleman in dark blue robes. But it was the man behind him who caught Alli's attention. *Prince Ender.*

He smiled at her, and his eyes sparkled as if enjoying a private joke. He put a finger up to his lips to hush her questions.

"Follow me, Dragon Rider," said the older man with a crook of his finger and flourish of his robes. Alli noticed that the man somehow stayed dry in the pouring rain.

"How ? . . . " she left the rest of the question unasked.

With a wave of his hand the rain stopped, and they walked the remainder of the distance without a drop of water falling on them. Alli looked from left to right and saw that it was still raining outside of their circle. This man was powerful; she would have to watch her step.

As they entered the castle, the company of guards peeled away and moved to their prior stations. The older wizard and the man who Alli knew as Prince Ender along with two others escorted Alli through the door and into a large room.

"I'm sorry, Dragon Rider," said the older man. "We had not been informed of your pending visit. Is all well with the Dragon King?"

Alli surveyed the room. It held a few groupings of chairs and small tables. The floor was marble, and the walls rose up at least fifteen feet. A few windows dotted one side, while the other three walls held paintings and tapestries. A familiarity tickled the back of her mind. She shook her head to organize her thoughts.

"I am Counselor Ezra Karaka, Dragon Rider," the wizard said. "We met on your last visit. I'm sorry about your treatment outside. There are rumors of trouble in the land, and your sudden appearance in the courtyard gave the men a surprise."

Alli continued to gaze around the room. She ended up catching the eye of the man whom she knew as Prince Ender. Counselor Ezra must have caught her gaze.

"Forgive my manners, Dragon Rider," Ezra said while pointing. "This is the son of a visiting captain from the eastern kingdoms, Rajamani Kandori, and," he continued, "these are two counselor apprentices, Tad and Isabel. You may have met them at the Citadel."

Alli heard nothing else Ezra said. "No," she proclaimed out loud. "This is Prince Ender. He is . . ."

"Miss," Rajamani said, "I'm sorry you think I am someone else."

"Prince Ender died from an accident a short while ago, Battlemaster," Ezra said. Alli only glared at Rajamani and tried to reason out what was happening. Was this another hole in her memory?

"It appears that the dragon rider has been weakened from flying in the storm," Rajamani said with a broad smile. "Let me take her in to our rooms as our guest. My father's servants can help her bathe and change clothes."

Counselor Ezra smiled. "That is quite hospitable, Rajamani, but there are always rooms here for the dragon riders to use. I will inform the king, and we can all meet again at dinner."

Rajamani gave a small bow of deference to the counselor, but as Ezra and Alli walked past, he put a hand out on Alli's arm. She jerked back. "What game are you playing?"

"I'm sorry to startle you, but I didn't catch your name," he said. Laughter danced in his eyes.

Counselor Ezra stopped and put a hand to his gray head. "It seems I'm all out of sorts tonight. Forgive me, Rajamani, this is Allison Stenos, famed dragon rider and battlemaster for the Citadel of Alaris."

"Really?" Rajamani reacted as if he had never seen Alli before. "I'm in esteemed company." He bowed low to Alli, and when he came back up he winked at her and said, "You may call me Raj. I look forward to seeing you at dinner."

The counselor tugged Alli along once again. After Raj had winked at her, she hardly heard any other words. That wink reminded her of someone. Flashes of a large stone building raced through her mind. A courtyard, training, taking a wizard test. She shuddered at the memory, but with the memory came the face of a man slightly older than she. Blond hair to his shoulders, a contagious smile, and a wink—it was Roland Tyre.

She groaned and put a hand to her head. What was happening to her?

"Are you all right, miss?" the counselor asked.

It was all Alli could do to nod.

"I'm sure you'll feel better after a hot bath and change of clothes."

CHAPTER THIRTEEN

Two hours later, after a bath, change of clothes, and a short rest, Alli was thinking more clearly—at least she thought she was, it was hard to know these days. The farther she went from Delia, the more flashes of memory flitted across her mind.

She was led to a banquet hall, where she was offered the seat of a guest of honor, next to the head of the table. The room brought back more memories of other castles she had been in. Alaris, Quentis, and the Citadel were a few of them. She shook her head to clear away the confusion.

"Are you all right?" the king asked.

King Orian Asher, a man in his mid-forties, with light brown hair and blue eyes, smiled at Alli and then gestured his hand toward others at the table to make introductions. "This is my wife, Leeza." He pointed to a younger man across the table from his wife. "And this is Nuri, my son." Both of which had lighter hair than the king himself, though Nuri favored the coloring of his father.

Finishing the rest of the table he introduced her once again to Rajamani. Sitting next to him was his father, a man named Cherif. He bore no expression when he looked at her, but Alli could see seething frustration behind his eyes. The rest of the room contained three other tables with, what Alli surmised, were other nobles and dignitaries from the kingdom of Khazer.

Servants began bringing in enormous platters of food, and Alli found her stomach clenching with hunger. Fresh fish and rice with a yellow sauce was the main dish. Along with fresh-baked bread and some winter squash, the meal appeared delicious.

"Dragon Rider," the king said, looking in her direction. "It's nice to see you again."

Alli didn't remember seeing the man before, but she smiled and nodded just the same. "Thank you for the meal."

"Cherif and his son are traders and diplomats from the eastern kingdoms. They are here to begin trade negotiations with us." King Orian said.

After seeing how Raj handled a sword, it made better sense to Alli now knowing that he was actually the son of a trader rather than a prince of Khazer. Alli looked at Cherif, and fear as she rarely knew crept through her heart. The man's eyes held a fervor that she couldn't quite place. Her face flushed, and she suddenly had a hard time swallowing.

You will say nothing of my son or myself to the king, Allison Stenos. You now know he is indeed not Prince Ender.

The words came to her mind, and even though she had not ever heard Cherif's voice before, she knew it was he who spoke. She saw the man flex his fingers, and it felt like her heart was being squeezed.

"Dragon Rider," the king said in concern. "Are you all right?"

Alli clutched at her chest and nodded. Instantly the pain was gone.

"Yes. Yes," Alli stammered. "I'm fine."

"Flying on a dragon must be amazing," Raj said, obviously trying to unsettle Alli even more.

She glared at him for a moment and then realized that everyone was awaiting an answer. "Yes, it is," she said.

She had to regain control here. Her master expected her to bring back Prince Ender and his dragon, Cholena, to help in her fight. She had wondered why her master couldn't call him on her own, but after being in Khazer for only a short time, Alli realized that Delia's reach was not so far as she had let on.

"Sire," Alli turned to the king. "Have you seen any other dragons or their riders?" She stole a quick glance at Raj and his father. They both gave her looks that said she had better be careful.

The king shook his head. "No, it has been months since the Dragon King visited last. We hear rumors of war to the west and south. What do you know?"

Alli once again glanced at Raj and Cherif. She felt Miriel as a subdued presence in the back of her mind, and far away she knew there was still a connection to her master. A master who would be very disappointed in her right now.

"The whereabouts of the Dragon King are not known at this time, King Orian," Alli began to speak, trying to tell the truth, without giving away Raj or that she couldn't remember who she used to be. "Roland Tyre is causing problems in the south, and a new Oracle of Turg has been confirmed."

This news brought murmurs throughout the room. Khazer formed a loose association with Turg and Cyrene.

"So, Nicholas Marinos is the new Oracle?" the king asked. "This must be recent news indeed. As you know we are far away from Thera."

Alli shook her head. "The new Oracle is Delia, the daughter of Nicholas. In the Dragon King's absence she has declared herself the Dragon Queen and ruler of the united territories."

There, she had said it. She sat and waited for the reaction. She didn't have to wait long. Nobles and dignitaries at the other tables stood up and began shouting and protesting. Of course Raj and his father already knew. They sat with composure. The king looked at them, and the two smiled back at him, then turned and looked at her and nodded. Something wasn't right, here.

The king stood and raised his hands for everyone to sit down. "Friends and nobles, don't let this news upset you. Khazer will not be a part of Delia's united territories much longer." He paused a moment for a few whispers to die down. "Our friends from the eastern kingdoms have brought to us the means of finally standing on our own. The trade contracts they bring will bring us stability and power. No longer will Khazer be beholden to others. We will rise up and be the glory of the southern kingdoms."

The speech sounded familiar to Alli—it was the same thing Delia had said at her ordination.

"We will be our own sovereign kingdom," the king continued. "We will be independent of any other association here in the west. Indeed, we will be part of a new empire." He then turned and waved at Cherif to stand.

Cherif stood and waved at the others. His simple attire made him seem actually more powerful to Alli. He rubbed a hand down one side of his clean-shaven face and over his chin as he peered around the room with a smile.

Alli's hand went to the dagger in her belt.

Stand down, Dragon Rider. The voice echoed in her head once again, and Alli's hand froze at her waist.

"On behalf of the empress of the eastern kingdoms, I welcome Khazer as the first kingdom of the west to join with us." Cherif walked around the room, touching the shoulders of many and giving smiles to those in the room as he spoke. Alli was sure he was somehow manipulating their minds with his invasive magic. "You will experience highly favored trade terms with exotic products from the east. Your boys and girls will be afforded the opportunity of our great centers of enlightenment. When they return to you they will have knowledge far surpassing those in your neighboring kingdoms. Khazer will be a beacon of light throughout the western continent. Gold and silver will flow freely throughout your land, and the city of Jor will become the center of all activities on the continent. Be assured, each of you will have an honored place in this mighty empire."

Danger rang through Alli's mind. This had the sound of something planned for years. She needed to get back and warn Delia. Roland Tyre and his Citadel were not the most dangerous foe they had to beat.

"In celebration of tonight, I bring to you a special dessert of the east prepared by my servants," Cherif said. His speech and his touch had won the nobles over, and they clapped for him.

Cherif waved his hand, and in walked three ladies. Two had beautiful brown skin with high cheekbones and long flowing hair; one had blonde hair that fell just past her shoulders. Her walk mesmerized all the men in the room.

The platters they carried held small bowls of something that resembled pudding with a dollop of cream on top. They began placing a bowl down in front of each person in the room.

Alli couldn't let things go on like this. She was a dragon rider, and her master expected her to secure the kingdom. The dessert began to be passed around, Cherif moved back toward his chair, but before he got there Alli pulled him aside and spoke in a low voice.

"What about the other kingdoms, Cherif Kandori?" Alli asked. "They won't all fall to your charm. As far as I see, there are only two of you here with a few servants."

Cherif glared at her. "You have no idea who we are, Allison Stenos. But I know each of you. I know your greed, your thirst for power, your never-ending bickering."

Her mind went to Roland again—his own thirst for power had already afforded him the rule of numerous kingdoms in the south.

"I think you may find things more difficult than you imagine," Alli said. "Khazer is the weakest of all the kingdoms on the continent." She stopped for a moment as she realized the king and others at the table were watching her. She wondered how loud she had spoken. It was true, and she surmised that's why they had jumped on board for a chance to be more than they were.

Both Alli and Cherif moved to the table and took their seats once again.

I told you not to interfere.

Pain erupted in her head this time. She glared at Cherif as he walked back to his seat. After sitting down he took up a fork and twisted it into the table. As he did so, the pain in her head increased. She leaned forward and tried to keep from passing out. She pushed all her magic back at him and felt a weakening.

Cherif smiled to the room, as if nothing was happening. "Please eat. It has been prepared specially for each one of you. You will never taste anything better the rest of your life."

Flooding her mind with power, Alli gave one last internal and powerful push against Cherif. He dropped his fork and beads of sweat stood out on his forehead.

"Are you all right, Father?" Raj leaned over to his father, then turned and gave Alli a warning look.

She just shrugged her shoulders. They shouldn't have pushed her.

The rest of the room hardly noticed; they were too busy devouring the creamy dessert. She wasn't hungry anymore and pushed hers out of the way. It was then that she looked two chairs down, past the counselor, and caught the eyes of Nuri, the king's son. His face blushed at her attention, but his eyes were grave and concerned. He gave her a slight nod.

Alli stood. "I ask for your leave. I'm not feeling very well."

The king stood to bid his goodbyes. Ezra, standing a few tables back with a group of nobles, looked her direction and offered to escort her, but Nuri jumped up between them.

"Father, I will escort the dragon rider to her room."

The king smiled. "That is kind of you, Nuri, but Counselor Ezra can get one of his apprentices or a servant to take her. Stay and enjoy the dessert."

"I have lost my appetite," Nuri said. "You know I can't eat desserts with milk anyway."

His father smiled with a nod of understanding. Out of the corner of her eye, Alli saw Cherif and Raj give a start. Their eyes went wide as they turned and eyed each other.

"I'm on my way to my chambers anyway," Nuri said as he moved over next to Alli.

The king nodded. "Very well, then."

Alli fell in step with Nuri. As she walked away from the table, she caught a murderous glare from both Cherif and Raj.

They walked silently out of the room until the sounds of the banquet were gone. Alli breathed deeply and rubbed her temples with her fingers. The headache caused by Cherif was still lingering.

Nuri motioned her down a corridor and put his finger to his lips.

When they were a few corners down the hallway, he stopped her.

"You must help us, Dragon Rider." His light eyes pleaded with her. "I saw what Cherif was doing to you and the others. This treaty, this deal my father is making with them, is not right. My father is not in his right mind. You must find the Dragon King and get help."

Alli's mind flashed again at mention of the Dragon King. She pictured the man named Bakari at the Coliseum. His eyes were intense and full of caring for her. She shook her head to clear away the thoughts. "I'm not sure what I can do," she said more abruptly than she meant.

Nuri took a step back, but then his eyes grew hard. "I met you before, Dragon Rider, and you are not the same. What's happened?" He stood a few inches taller than she and glared down at her.

Alli put her hands to the side of her head and growled. "That man in there—Raj, was pretending to be Prince Ender. He has a dragon from Delia and I'm not sure of what he and his father plan."

Nuri's eyes went wide at that. "But can you help us? You are a dragon rider."

"I don't know what is wrong with me, Nuri," she said, her shoulders slumping down. "I can't remember who I am."

"But you must. You must remember. We need your help."

Alli was about to open her mouth when a yell came from the banquet hall.

Nuri gave her a questioning look, and they ran in that direction. Sprinting by the kitchen first, they almost ran into one of the cooks. Seeing Nuri there, her eyes opened wide and she grabbed his hand and pulled him back away from the banquet room.

Nuri tried to pull away, but the woman was strong.

"Nuri," she said, "stop!"

Nuri looked furious, but he stopped and gave his attention to the woman. "Your father and mother have been murdered—poisoned."

Nuri's face turned ashen, and his knees gave out.

Alli glared at the cook as she caught Nuri mid-fall. "What are you saying?"

"They've all fallen down, Dragon Rider. Everyone in the room, but the two visitors." Her eyes were red, and she wiped the tears from them. "You must get Nuri to safety."

Alli immediately understood the implications. Cherif and Raj would make for Nuri's chambers immediately. Without any thought, she grabbed Nuri's hand and ran toward the nearest door.

Miriel, she called in her mind. *Miriel, please hear me. I need your help!*

CHAPTER FOURTEEN

Roland had to be careful. Delia was close by. He knew he could beat her, but he was still worried about the other dragons she controlled—and Alli. He gritted his teeth wondering if she thought about him at all.

"Always having to fix everything," he mumbled to no one in particular.

However, Tabitha sat behind him on his golden dragon, and she nudged him in the ribs.

"Did you say something, Sire?"

He had taken Tabitha up on Orelia and asked her to direct him to the cave where Orelia had come to life. Currently they flew low over the coastal range so as to not attract Delia's attention; Turg was just a few miles north.

"Nothing," he said.

"There!" Tabitha pointed down and to their right. "I think that's the place. It's hard to tell after all the destruction."

That is the place, his dragon spoke to him.

And why didn't you tell me before where all these powerful artifacts were?

You never asked.

Growling to himself, he took the dragon down to a spot just to the left of most of the destruction. He wasn't in a good mood today. He did not like the thought of Delia's plan to attack him personally. He needed to get Tabitha back into

Delia's household and get more information. She had risked much by coming to him and had been gone from Delia for five days now.

Roland's golden dragon landed on the ground; shale and rock broke beneath Orelia's weight. Roland dismounted and helped Tabitha off. He stood and looked in front of him at a pile of broken rocks.

"Are you sure this is where it was?" Roland asked. There really was no cave anymore.

Tabitha nodded her head. "I'm sure. When the dragon walked out, the cave began to collapse. The rest caved in when Delia and Korax blasted the side of the mountain to keep the Dragon King from following."

A cool winter wind blew at their backs, causing Tabitha to wrap a thick cloak around her body. Roland could have warmed himself with his magic but he didn't know how much of his powers he would need to get through to the remaining artifacts.

Roland went back to the first part of Tabitha's sentence. "And how, exactly, did the dragon change?" Through the magic stream he had seen portions of what happened, but really only small glimpses.

The two of them walked over to the pile of rocks while the dragon stayed sitting at the edge of the small flat platform of rock they had landed on.

"When we first found the cave, the dragon was not alive," Tabitha explained. "Dragon artifacts were scattered on the ground around it. Its eyes blazed and came alive when Delia and Korax started to pick up some of the artifacts. When the

Dragon King and Rider Jaimon and the girl with them—Gabby, I think her name is— showed up, Delia had found the artifact that would control the dragon bond. She used it to steal the bond from the dragon riders. By now, Rider Liam had also shown up from the Realm."

"I felt something here, when I used the scepter in Cassian," Roland said. "I saw the dragon in my mind and knew I was meant to have it."

You do not have me, wizard! The voice in his mind shook the ground.

"Roland!" screamed Tabitha as a boulder rolled down and smashed between them.

Roland turned to his dragon in a fury. "What was that for?" he said out loud.

You did not take me, Orelia said. *I gave myself to you.*

Roland repeated the words to Tabitha.

"Then how can Delia have the dragons bonds?" Tabitha asked, looking at both Roland and Orelia.

Roland thought for a moment. Suddenly it dawned on him. "She doesn't have the bonds," he said with excitement in his voice. "She only thinks she does. The artifact creates a false bond!"

"Then there is a way to break it?" Tabitha said. "You can get the dragons back to the Dragon King and his riders."

Roland ground his teeth in frustration. He found himself holding his scepter.

Unify them all.

"Why should I give them back their dragons?" Roland said. "They are the ones that caused this problem in the first place. Maybe I'll take them all."

Tabitha backed up a step and had to put her hand out on a rock to keep from falling. "High Wizard, that would be a lot of power."

Roland waved his hand in the air, dismissing her concern. "Nothing I can't handle, I'm sure. If I am the ruler of my golden empire, why shouldn't I have everyone united under me—man, elf, and beast alike?"

Tabitha bowed to him. "As you wish, my Lord. I'm sure you know best."

Roland tossed his head to the side and lifted his scepter up in the air. Why did everyone question his judgement? "You do not agree with me, Wizard Tabitha? You are only weeks out from being an apprentice, and you know more than me?"

"Of course not, Sire." Tabitha pointed to the cave-in. "What do we do about this?"

Roland collapsed the scepter and placed it back in his pouch. He chuckled at her change of topic. He had been too hard on her. She had performed a great service to him, being his eyes and ears in Delia's court.

"Stand back," he ordered Tabitha. Then he himself moved back a few steps.

Waving his hands, he drew in a large amount of magic from deep inside. He let the power fill him, then directed his hands and thoughts toward the pile of rocks in front of them. At first one rock lifted, and moved to the side, then another, then a larger one. Soon a dozen rocks moved at once, and a small hole appeared in front of them.

"The cave!" Tabitha said.

Roland smiled and took another minute to move enough rocks for the two of them to walk into the cave. He created a flame in his upturned hand and moved into the darkness.

He stood at the entrance for a moment, letting his eyes adjust. The cave opened up at least thirty feet in all directions. He lowered his hand toward the floor and saw a littering of artifacts at his feet.

"What do you think they all do?" Roland asked.

"I'm not sure, my Lord," Tabitha said. "Delia knew about many of them and took a few, but there were more than this when we left."

Roland stood back up and gazed around the room. "Who could have been in here?"

"The dragon riders were still here when we left them," Tabitha said. "Maybe they took some."

"And didn't tell me?" Roland raised his voice. "Sounds about right. I never did get a straight answer on how they got to Lor'l so fast." He reached down and scooped up a handful of the smaller artifacts and studied them in his hand.

Most were miniature replicas of dragons or parts of dragons, made from all sorts of materials. He turned over a wooden one and rubbed his finger on it, trying to figure out what it was.

"How do I work them?"

Tabitha shook her head. "I don't know. Some can only be used by the dragon riders, but I've seen Delia use one, and also Gabby."

Roland sighed. "I'm sorry about my words earlier, Tabitha. I was too harsh. I forget sometimes that not everyone has lived with magic as I have."

Tabitha smiled. "It must be wonderful. I've only felt it for less than two years, and only been training for less than half of that time."

"I've had some kind of ability ever since I can remember," Roland said as he gathered up a few more items. He could see the scattering of gold stone from where his dragon had been encased and began to walk around the area. "All wizards have some abilities, but, Tabitha, I *am* magic. Not everyone believes me. They don't understand that the source of my powers are different from everyone else." He leaned down and picked up one more item and stuffed it in a small sack. "Do you believe me?"

"I wouldn't be here if I didn't believe in your cause," Tabitha said. "From the first time I met you, I knew you were something special; someone greater than us all."

Roland laughed. "Do you really want to help me unite everyone, Tabitha? Do you understand what that really means?" Roland took a step closer to the young wizard.

Tabitha smoothed back a strand of brown hair behind her ear, and excitement glowed in her eyes. "Yes, my Lord."

Roland found that his hand once again held the Scepter of Unification. It was a glorious artifact. Whether originally intended for a dragon rider or not, it was his now, and he would wield it to unify them all.

Yes! The deep voice spoke to his mind. *Yes, Roland Tyre. You are the unifier. Only you can turn back the tide of evil and power that is heading to our shores.*

Roland raised the scepter up in the air and glanced out of the cave. His beautiful dragon stood waiting for his return.

Roland slammed his scepter to the ground, and a blast of light filled the cave. He was transported into the magic stream once again.

CHAPTER FIFTEEN

Grayness swirled around Roland, and he lost all sense of direction. He stumbled on a ground that didn't actually look to even be there. There was no distance or objects to focus his eyesight on. Dizziness overwhelmed him for a few moments before he could take a deep breath and steady himself.

That had never happened before.

He wondered if it could be the artifacts he had been holding in his hand. Maybe they had interfered somehow. Pushing the problem to the back of his mind, he began walking. Each time he had come to the magic stream of late, there had been a purpose, something for him to see or do. As he concentrated more, he saw the familiar pinpricks of light around him—each one signifying a wizard or other powerful creature or artifact.

Roland reached his hand toward a random spark and could feel the presence of a relatively weak wizard. He moved on. This time he saw two bright specs racing east—at least, that is what he thought the direction was.

Ah, the Cremelinos. He didn't understand them yet, but they were magnificent.

Looking around again, he spied other bright lights. Two were close by, and two were farther away. Of the four new dragon riders, Roland wondered which one was which.

The scene shifted around him, and he saw Delia standing outside next to Abylar. The wizard, Korax, stood next to her with a scowl on his face.

"King Abbas is ready to go," Korax said, "but says his dragon is acting strangely, tiring easily."

Delia stroked Abylar's scales, and Roland felt dissatisfaction from the dragon.

"It's only an excuse," Delia says. "The man has no spine."

"What about the other riders?"

Delia's face grew dark, and she walked away from the dragon. As she did so, the dragon turned and seemed to look right at Roland. Shock ran through his mind.

Save us! came a weak pleading.

Roland had never heard the voice of any of the other dragons before. He tried to communicate back, but Abylar's head only dropped and turned away from him.

Unify them. The thumping began again.

Roland rubbed his head with his hand. *Unify the dragons too?*

How many things did he have to unify? He stepped away from the scene, and Delia and Korax faded back into the mist.

A new scene opened in front of him.

Alli!

He watched as Alli walked out of a cave with a light-haired young man about her own age. Back in the cave, Roland saw a pair of eyes staring out at him. The eyes came closer, and Roland saw Alli's yellow dragon, Miriel.

Where are you? Roland yelled out. *Alli!*

Alli turned and glanced around the cave, then shrugged her shoulders and walked to the edge of it. White crested waves splashed against the shore in the background.

"Nuri," Alli said as she pushed the young man back inside the cave. "Get back inside."

Alli herself followed. In Roland's vision came another dragon—the red one, flying low over the waves and heading south.

"Where is he going?" Nuri said.

Alli squeezed her eyes shut for a moment and then re-opened them. "He pretended to be your brother, Ender, and got the Dragon Queen to give him a dragon bond."

"But where is he taking the dragon?" Nuri asked.

Alli shook her head. "I don't know."

"You must help me, Dragon Rider," Nuri said. "I'm all that is left of Khazer's royal line."

"I'm not here to help you or your family," Alli shouted and rubbed her hands around her temples. "I was supposed to bring Prince Ender and the dragon back to the Dragon Queen."

Tears filled Nuri's eyes and he yelled back. "You're right, I don't understand. You're supposed to be a dragon rider and famed battlemaster. You're supposed to help us. That's what the Dragon King and his riders do."

"No!" Alli screamed and walked back farther toward her dragon. "I am not a battlemaster. I am not doing this for the Dragon King. I'm a bad person, Nuri. I don't even know why I helped you."

Nuri took a few steps toward the cave opening.

Roland's heart thumped with pain for Alli. He couldn't bear to see her so torn up inside. He knew she was good. What could he do?

Unite them!

No! It was Roland's time to yell. *What do you want from me? I can't do it all!*

You wanted all power, High Wizard, came the scepter's voice. *You wanted to be the most powerful wizard in the land. You told others that one all-powerful person would be better than all these other kings, wizards, and dragon riders. If you want all that—if you really want to be the most powerful wizard—you need to unify them all. They are all your responsibility now.*

You never told me that, Roland said and slammed his scepter to the ground.

Once again the scene changed around him, but Roland tried to pull back to Alli. He couldn't leave her like that. The power of the scepter pulled harder against him and he saw the sea—and dark clouds. In the midst of the dark clouds, a hole opened up, and he once again saw the fleet of warships he had seen earlier.

Roland's cry caught in his throat. There were so many of them. *They will destroy us all,* he whispered.

Not if you unify them all—men, elves, and creatures. Bind them together. Only then can you save them all. Only then will you be truly worthy of the Scepter of Unification and receive the glory you desire.

"Sire!" called Tabitha from outside of the magic stream.

Her voice brought him back to his senses, and he looked around the grayness once more. Breathing hard, he thought about Tabitha and the cave they were in. Finally, he broke out of the magic stream and fell to the cave floor in exhaustion.

Tabitha knelt next to him. "High Wizard, are you all right?" Her eyes furrowed with concern. "You were just standing there bathed in golden light, and I couldn't get you to respond."

Roland didn't trust his voice yet and only nodded. He opened his hands and found that the artifacts he had been holding were now only dust in his hand. Tabitha studied the remnants, then turned back to Roland's face.

"What happened?" Tabitha asked.

Roland shook his head. "What if I can't do it?" he asked with a shudder. He had never felt this way before. "What if I can't save us all?"

Tabitha helped him to his feet, and they left the mouth of the cave. He looked out at his dragon and tried to think.

"Why isn't my dragon affected by what Delia did to the dragon bond?" he asked out loud.

After a moment of silence, Tabitha caught his attention. "High Wizard, you are the most powerful wizard in the land. You have united Alaris, North and South Solshi, Tillimot, Quentis, and even Elvyn. You have a golden dragon and the golden scepter. Isn't that enough?"

"Apparently not!" Roland snapped. "I must unite the rest of the southern kingdoms. Turg, Cyrene, and Khazer must come into the fold, it seems. As well, the dragons, Cremelinos, and any other creature of power."

Tabitha opened her eyes wide.

Roland nodded his head and began to steel his resolve.

"I believe in you," Tabitha said. "If not you, then who else can save us?" Her voice pleaded with Roland. "Sire, you must save us."

And things clicked into place for Roland once again. He took a deep breath, let it out, and smiled. "You are right. If not me, then who? Certainly not Delia. We only have a short time until the war ships approach our land. We need to take care of her now."

"But how?" Tabitha asked.

Roland walked to his dragon and opened a large travel bag attached to one side of the small saddle. He opened it up and pulled out a small but beautiful silver canister. The scroll work on it was indicative of a master's work. He handed it to Tabitha.

She raised questioning eyes at Roland.

"Go back to Delia," Roland said. "Tell her that I tried to get information from you about her plans. Tell her we are weak at the Citadel and she should attack there. We will be ready for her."

"What is it?" Tabitha said referring to the canister she now held in her hands.

"Just find any of Delia's artifacts that you think would be helpful to us and put it in here."

"And then what?" Tabitha asked.

Roland shook his head. "I can't tell you. If Delia finds it, then she can't get the information from you."

"Sounds intriguing," Tabitha said, her eyes going wide. "This is actually quite fun."

Roland grunted. "Just be careful. She is a dangerous woman."

Tabitha grew serious. "I know that. I've traveled with her and seen what she can do."

"I'll drop you off a little closer to the city," Roland said. "Then I need to get to Solshi before returning to the Citadel to prepare for Delia's attack."

They both mounted Orelia. With a few flaps of her giant wings and a short run, she lifted up high in the air. Roland put a hand on the golden scales in front of him. He still didn't understand the nature of his relationship between the dragon and himself.

He directed Orelia closer to the city, but not close enough that they would see them. They landed behind a small forested hill. Tabitha jumped off and gave a quick, informal salute to Roland.

"Take care, Sire," Tabitha said.

"Tell Delia that I seem afraid of her attacking me," Roland said. "Tell her that the Citadel is weak right now and I don't have many wizards there with me."

"You don't," Tabitha said. "I'm not sure you can withstand a direct attack by her four dragons."

"I don't think she'll have four anymore." Roland smiled, remembering his time in the magic stream. The yellow dragon was with Alli in Khazer, and the red dragon seemed to have flown east. Though Roland did frown at that. There was nothing east, but the warships. "Tell her I am running around trying to hold things together and that it would be a good time to attack."

Tabitha frowned. "She's building a transport that will hold dozens of wizards and soldiers."

"I'm counting on it!" Roland said. "Let her feel overconfident. The Citadel will be ready for her attack."

Roland watched as Tabitha ran out of sight. Then he lifted back up on his dragon. He took a deep breath and directed Orelia to fly south down the coast. So many moving pieces to direct. But as he drew upon the power of the scepter once again, plans began to form in his mind. Plans that made him feel better.

Two nagging thoughts seem to always churn in the back of his mind. The first was the enigma of his own dragon. Was it real? Why hadn't Delia stolen its bond at the same time—it was in the cave with her. The second was the worry for Alli. He didn't know who the young man was that she was with, but she appeared to be in trouble. He needed to get her back before Delia dug her claws into her once again.

His two visions of the warships scared the daylights out of him. The constant pounding in his head to unify things put him on the edge of driving him crazy. But the scepter seemed to think he could handle it. And perhaps he was a little crazy—but maybe that's what happened when you became the most powerful wizard in the world.

CHAPTER SIXTEEN

Gabby, Jaimon, and Garrik stood on a thin beach on the southern coast of Elvyn and looked out over the water. It had taken two days to hike through the thick southern forest. Garrik grumbled most of the time, but Gabby ignored it and figured he was one to complain about anything.

"I can't see anything through this fog," Garrik complained—once again.

"Garrik." Gabby smiled and followed his gaze. "If it was clear and you could see for miles you would gripe about it being too bright."

Jaimon snickered, but Garrik only grunted.

"It's cold out here too," Garrik said and wrapped a warm cloak around him.

Gabby agreed. The temperature had dropped drastically once they had left the trees, only a few dozen feet away. The wind blew, and both Gabby and Jaimon had a hard time keeping their ponytails from blowing around their faces. Garrik didn't seem to care about his hair—it looked about the same no matter what kind of weather he was in.

"How do we get through that?" Jaimon asked, pointing to the rough water directly between them and the nearby fog.

"My thoughts exactly," Garrik said. "You're the ones wanting to go there. I'd rather stay off that cursed island."

"Cursed?" Jaimon's face grew worried.

"Well, full of magic, at least."

"Figures," Jaimon mumbled.

"Now, you two." Gabby pointed her finger at each one of them. "Quit complaining. We are going to the island, and there's no turning back."

"Yes, Princess," Garrik gave a mock bow.

Gabby glared at him for a moment and turned and peered up and down the coast. "Where's the boat?"

"Boat?" Garrik raised his hands up in the air. "You mean we forgot the boat?"

Jaimon grew worried again. "You mean . . ."

Garrik slapped the boy on the back. "You're too serious, Dragon Rider. Lighten up a little."

Jaimon blushed, and Gabby stepped in.

"Cut it out, Garrik," she said, but smiled to let him know she wasn't all that mad at him. "I assume you do have a boat hidden somewhere here."

Garrik pointed west—but of course they couldn't see far in the fog. "A half a day's walk will bring us to a small village of forest elves. There will be a boat there for us to use. But for now we make camp for the night."

Gabby sighed, but she knew it was for the best. It grew dark early this time of year.

Soon they had two tents set up—one for the men and one for Gabby. Jaimon had built a small fire, and Garrik pulled out a small pack of dried meat and a loaf of bread.

Using her powers, Gabby rolled a few larger rocks over for them to sit on.

"That could come in handy at times," Garrik said.

"As an elf, don't you have magic?" Gabby asked as she sat down with a small groan. Her ribs still hurt.

Garrik grunted. "The northern elves inherited most of it. A few men and women of great power—wizards, you would call them—arise from the desert elves every once in a while, but the only magic most have is the ability to control the land and water in some minor way."

"But what about the forest elves that protect the phoenix?" Gabby asked.

Garrik let out a long sigh. "My ancient father has abilities, and my brother, Trae, has some also, but besides being in tune with the trees around us, we don't have much. Me being a half-breed, now that's a different matter altogether. Besides an affinity for getting out of unlucky situations, I'm not sure I possess much magic."

"Well, magic isn't everything," Gabby said.

"Says one with powers of her own," Jaimon mumbled between bites of bread.

"Jaimon Schaefer!" Gabby swatted at him. "Stop being sorry for yourself. You have a dragon! That's much rarer than having magic."

"*Had* a dragon, Gabby," Jaimon said. "I *had* one."

With abnormal caring in his voice, Garrik turned to Jaimon. "Tell me about your life, Jaimon Schafer. What did you do before keeping company with princesses and dragons?"

That got a slight smile from Jaimon. "My family raised sheep in the foothills in northern Quentis. My best friend was Bug."

"Bug?" Garrick laughed. "What kind of a name is that?"

Jaimon smiled wider. "We grew up in the same small village. Ever since I can remember he liked bugs. As a little kid he would walk around with them on his hands showing everyone."

Garrik nodded and tore off a piece of meat and stuck it in his mouth. "Sounds like a nice life."

Jaimon nodded. "Yes."

"But then you found a dragon," Garrik continued.

"The first time Bug and I went out to tend sheep alone we got stuck in a storm up in the mountains and found the dragon egg." Jaimon's eyes brightened with the memory.

"And you bonded to it then?" Garrik asked, eating the last of his food.

"The moment she hatched from the egg, I felt the bond," Jaimon said. "It's like having another mind with yours. No," he paused a moment, "it's like they complete who you are. Cholena brought me comfort, knowledge, and power."

"Ah, so you do have powers, young Dragon Rider," Garrik said with a grin.

"Yeah." Jaimon smiled back. "I guess I do . . . when I have my dragon."

"Then you are luckier than most," Garrik said.

He winked at Gabby, who was surprised by his caring. He had cheered up Jaimon.

The three sat in silence for a few moments until Garrik excused himself to his tent. After putting out the fire, the other two followed suit.

Gabby lay with a blanket pulled up over her and thought about how close she was to home now. Just along the coast, west a few days, was the Bay of Ghazi and her home. It had been a few weeks since she had left there with Jaimon to answer the Dragon King's call.

Her life was quite incredible. She had been to Mahli, Turg, and Elvyn since she had left. She thought about her family. She had learned from Roland that her father, the king, had seemed more aware of events transpiring than he had let on. That sounded like her father. Secretive, powerful, and the head of not just Quentis, but of the Followers of the Dragon in the southern kingdoms.

She wondered about her classmates at the Wizard Sanctuary. As princess, there had been times when she had left for state events, but she had never been gone from the sanctuary so long as this. As sleep began to overtake her, she thought about Guardian Calanon and his directions. Suddenly, in that space between waking and sleep, he appeared to her once more.

Be careful, wizard, he issued her a warning. *There is a disturbance of magic on the island. Something else is there besides the phoenix.*

What is it? Gabby asked.

But the guardian faded away with only an echo. *Be careful.*

* * *

Around noon the next day, three men jumped out of a tree in front of Garrik. Gabby and Jaimon jumped in surprise. Jaimon had a dagger pulled instantly and moved around next to Garrik.

"Now that's a fine way to greet an old friend," Garrik said to the group in front of them.

"Garrik, you old scoundrel. What are you doing here?" said the apparent leader.

All three men had shoulder-length brown hair, pointy ears, and upswept brows. All three carried bows on their shoulders and wore brown and green garb that blended well with the forest. In fact, they looked so much alike that Gabby wondered if they were triplets.

Garrik pointed his head at Gabby and Jaimon. "Escorting these two to the island."

The three looked at Gabby and Jaimon, and their right eyebrows lifted at the same time. They turned back to Garrik.

Jaimon still held his knife out in front of him. Garrik reached an arm out to him.

"Put the knife down, Dragon Rider," Garrik said. "They are friends."

The title of dragon rider seemed to make an impression on the three, and they looked at Jaimon with newfound respect.

"We need a boat," Garrick said, "and then we'll be on our way."

The three nodded, but one spoke up. "In this fog?"

Garrik nodded toward Gabby. "I don't think the princess wants to wait any longer."

Once again the three appeared impressed. Gabby only smiled at them.

"Of course," said the third. "Of course."

As they followed the three men, the first asked a question. "Is the guardian well?"

Garrik shrugged. "As well as he'll let on. There is trouble afoot, and he wants to see it through, I surmise."

"We've heard about trouble in Tillimot. Seems like Queen Ameena Shabon attacked Alaris and barely kept her life. Minister Daymian Khouri from Alaris holds the kingdom for Roland Tyre, the High Wizard of the Citadel. Something about uniting the lands."

"He has also been named the Warlord of Elvyn," Gabby said.

The three stopped and stared at Gabby, then turned to Garrik for confirmation. He nodded. "He has asked for the desert elves and men from Tillimot to come to his aid in Lor'l."

"But the desert elves are deserting him," Gabby said.

"Grave news," said one of the three, and the rest shook their heads at the information.

"And where is the Dragon King in all of this?" the first one asked Jaimon.

Jaimon seemed surprised by the question and blushed at being caught off guard.

"That is why we are here," Gabby said. "The Dragon King is ill and needs a phoenix to heal him."

All three of their escorts sucked in their breaths.

"What?" Gabby said looking from them, to Garrik, and then back again. "What's wrong?"

"Not wrong, but . . ." said the first.

"Different," said the second.

"Strange," said the third.

"Maybe wrong," amended the first. "Something else has gone to the island; something of power. You must be careful."

Gabby recalled the guardian's warning.

At that point they stopped at a boat. It had a broad, single sail and sat on the shore. It was about twenty feet long, painted white, and Gabby could see three sets of oars sitting on hooks just inside of it. There were three benches spaced evenly with a small wooden locker at the back.

"With such low visibility I wouldn't use the sail, Garrik, unless you get in trouble and have to move fast," said the first elf.

The second elf walked away for a moment to a small hut that stood nearby. He came out carrying two bags with straps.

"Food and water for three days," he said. "And I see you have your own gear."

"Only three days?" Jaimon asked. "What if we need more time than that?"

The three elves glared at Garrik. "You didn't tell them?" said the first.

"Apparently," Garrik said to Jaimon and Gabby, "one only stays three days on the island. The power of a phoenix is too strong. If you haven't found what you are looking for by then, you never will, or at least you never return."

Gabby put her hands on her hips. "And you never mentioned this?"

"Would it have mattered if I did?" Garrik said gruffly.

Gabby paused, then shook her head. "No it wouldn't. But are you sure?"

Garrik laughed out loud. "Look here, both of you, I've never actually been to the island before."

"What?" Jaimon said. "Why did your father send you, and not another guide?"

The three other elves moved the boat to the edge of the water, took a few steps back, and motioned Gabby, Jaimon, and Garrick into the boat.

The three climbed in and were busy for a few minutes getting seated and arranging their packs. But Gabby wasn't going to let Jaimon's question go unanswered. Once they pushed off, the three began to paddle forward.

"Garrik?" Gabby said.

"Thought you'd forget," he mumbled.

"Why not another guide, someone who's been there before?" Gabby prodded.

Garrik sighed, and for a half a minute the only sound they could hear was that of the oars pulling through the water. "My brother has been to the island, but left after only one day inland. He's never spoken about what he saw there to anyone but my father. My father won't take a chance with Trae going there again; he is the designated heir. No one else has ever returned from the island."

CHAPTER SEVENTEEN

The three rowed in silence for quite some time. The cool fog matted down Gabby's hair, and she continually had to wipe water from her face. She had a warm cloak, but the cold began to seep through her body, making her miserable. Besides the sound of the paddles in the water, the world became eerily quiet and small.

"How do we know if we are going in the right direction?" Gabby whispered, breaking the silence.

"Ah," Garrik said. "I was born with a perfect sense of direction."

"Finally, something of use," Jaimon mumbled.

Garrik sucked in a breath but had the good graces to not rise to Jaimon's provocation.

"So how do we find a phoenix once we get to the island?" Gabby asked.

She saw Garrik shrug his shoulders. "That seems to be for you wizards and dragon riders to figure out. My job is to get you there."

Gabby let out a deep breath and watched as the eerie fog swirled around their boat. She knew with surety that she had seen the phoenix in the magic stream as a means to help heal Bakari, but now she doubted other things.

"What if we can't find it?" Jaimon echoed Gabby's own concerns.

There was no answer to the question, and all three only continued to row. Soon, however, the water became rough and they had a hard time keeping the boat straight.

"The Straits of Gazir," Garrik said to no one in particular. "This is why ships going around the Horn to and from Tillimot and Quentis go farther out and around the island and into the ocean before heading north."

After another hour, Gabby's arms were burning, and she had to rest. The three decided that from that time forward only two would row at a time. Water splashed up the side of the boat onto Gabby's legs, and she pushed the packs farther under the seat and hoped that they were as waterproof as they were supposed to be.

"Are you sure we're still going straight?" yelled out Jaimon to Garrik.

"We'll hit the island, don't you worry," Garrik said, then mumbled under his breath, "I just don't know where and how hard we'll hit it."

A half hour later Gabby took up her oars again. She could feel the blisters forming on her fingers.

"Wizard, can't you do something about this?" Garrik called back.

Gabby was reluctant to use up too much power, not knowing what she would need on the island. She was still young and became tired soon after exerting herself. But she had an idea. "Put the paddles up for a moment," she called out.

Closing her eyes, she tried to concentrate. Having grown up on the coast, she was familiar with the water and its waves and currents. She thought about the wind, the water, and the earth underneath the water and pulled up her power. It slipped for a moment, and she wondered what was happening. Finally, with determination, she grabbed a hold of her reservoir. With a few flourishes of her hands she gathered the wind around them, focused it behind them, and pushed them forward.

The boat lurched ahead a little too fast, and both Garrik and Jaimon fell to the side. Garrik almost tumbled out of the boat.

"Hey, steady," Garrik called out over his shoulder after righting himself.

Gabby grabbed ahold of the bench to either side of her and tried to steady the wind behind them. The current underneath was unpredictable, and it was hard to keep the boat steady. They traveled this way for a short time, when all of a sudden, a large shadow flew over them in the fog.

"What in the guardian's name was that?" Garrik cried out.

The fog still hung thick around them, but there had definitely been a large shadow.

Gabby held her hand up in the air and flashed a bright light over them to see if she could see anything. However, the thick fog just reflected it back.

The shadow came over them again, followed by a loud roar receding in the distance.

"Cholena!" croaked Jaimon. "It's my dragon! Go faster, Gabby."

"Stop your magic," Garrik ordered Gabby.

Jaimon turned his neck around toward her. "No, Gabby. We have to find her. She's in trouble. I have to get her away from that man."

"It's following your magic," Garrik said. "Stop."

Gabby felt for Jaimon, but Garrik might be right. The last they saw of Cholena, Prince Ender of Khazer had been riding her with Delia. She released her power and left the boat to the waves.

Jaimon looked like he might jump out of the boat as it lurched back into the currents, but after shifting around a bit he stayed quiet with the rest of them.

"What is he doing here?" Gabby whispered.

"I don't know," Jaimon said. "But it can't be a coincidence."

Gabby agreed with that. "Delia is after the power of the phoenix, too, it seems."

"This Delia," said Garrik from the front, "is the new Oracle of Turg? The one that is trying to destroy the Dragon King?"

"And everything else she can get her hands on," Gabby said.

"Two powerful wizards trying to run things is not something I want to get in the middle of," Garrik said. "Maybe we should turn back and wait until the fog clears. Then we can see what we are getting ourselves into."

"No," said both Gabby and Jaimon at the same time. Jaimon's was more forceful.

"We keep rowing to the island," Gabby said. "You're already in the middle of this Garrickurol Aghammas."

"Now you sound like Merlyndra," Garrik moaned. "Too many bossy women in my life."

Jaimon blurted out a laugh, and Gabby splashed him.

"Hey!" Jaimon said.

"Who is Merlyndra to you, Garrik?" Gabby asked.

"My wife," he said.

"Your wife?" Now Gabby laughed.

"Well, we've been betrothed to be married since we were young—you know, trying to keep things among the forest elves close in," Garrik said. "I've just not been able to stay in the forest long enough for it to actually happen."

"You're afraid?" Gabby gasped out loud. "The brave ruffian outcast is afraid of getting married."

"Now, that doesn't sound very nice," Garrik said, but there wasn't much spite in his words.

"But you are afraid?" Gabby clarified.

Gabby saw Garrik's head bob up and down. "I'm caught between two worlds. I don't belong in either, and I . . ."

Gabby felt bad for the man. She had pushed too far. "I'm sorry, Garrik," she said. "I shouldn't have pried. But look on the bright side. Once you help us find a phoenix, you'll be famous, and Merlyndra will be begging to marry you."

Jaimon laughed, and Garrik only grunted and pulled the oars harder.

The day wore on with no further sign of the dragon, or anything else, for that matter. Soon the air around them grew darker, and they knew that night was approaching.

"Are you sure we're not out in the middle of the ocean?" Jaimon asked. "How long will this take us?"

"We're headed in the right direction," Garrik said. "You would know if you were out in the ocean past the island. This little boat wouldn't stand a chance. Why don't you two take a break, and I'll keep us on course for a while."

Gabby surely wasn't going to question Garrik's suggestion. She put the oars down and rubbed both of her upper arms. She heard a moan from Jaimon up ahead of her and smiled grimly. Her muscles burned, and she wondered if she could actually row any more at all. Sitting her hands in her lap, she tried to relax her muscles. She closed her eyes and breathed deeply, willing the pain in her arms to lessen.

Listening to the quiet but sure rhythm of Garrik's oars slipping through the water, she began to feel the tension leave her body. A few faint splashes to her left signified fish jumping out of the water, and a gull's cry overhead through the fog made it seem as if they were at least in sight of land—that is, if they could see anything. The moist air was cool on Gabby's face, but it mixed with sweat from the effort of rowing. Her body shivered a few times before she was lulled into a light slumber.

* * *

Without any warning, Gabby began to fall backward. She flailed her arms to the side and caught hold of the sides of the boat. Her heart beat wildly as she gasped for breath. Her eyes darted around, trying to figure out what had happened.

Up in front of her, Jaimon fell sideways. Halfway to the boat's edge, he jerked himself up, but Gabby was already behind him and put an arm out to the side, stopping him from falling any farther.

"Thanks," he said weakly. "What happened?"

"We fell asleep," Gabby said.

"Wake up, sugarplums," Garrik laughed. "We are close to the beach. The tide on the island is pulling us in."

Another wave ran under the boat, and the boat turned sideways, almost capsizing. A small wave splashed over the side of the boat next to Gabby, and she scrambled to move out of the way. But in doing so she fell to one side of the boat.

Without thinking, Jaimon moved over to help her.

"Stop!" Garrik called out.

But it was too late. With the weight of both Gabby and Jaimon on the same side, the mast swung their way also—all combining to bring too much weight to the port side of the small boat.

"Move over, Jaimon!" Garrik yelled, trying to counter-balance the weight.

But it was all too much at once, and the boat tipped over. Gabby went flying out first, followed by Jaimon. Garrik tried to stay in while pulling himself and the mast to the other side, but to no avail, and he flew out into the water also.

Having grown up near the ocean, Gabby was an excellent swimmer, though her thick cloak, now wet, began pulling her under. She went with it and took herself down, then while underneath slid out of it and kicked her legs to bring herself back up on top.

Jaimon was not so lucky. He floundered in the water, arms flailing to either side.

"Help!" Jaimon yelled out.

Garrik tried to get to him, but the current had turned the boat between him and Jaimon. Gabby kicked her feet and tried to reach him too, but the cold water was already seeping into her bones, and she felt herself starting to get hypothermia.

Jaimon went under the water once.

"Jaimon!" Gabby screamed. "Grab the boat."

But she knew he couldn't hear her under the water. She tried to swim over where she had seen him last, but the current seemed to be pulling in different ways at the same time, and she couldn't get there quick enough.

The fog settled in thicker around them, and the light continued to fade, making it even harder to get to each other.

Garrik threw a paddle in Gabby's direction, and she grabbed one end of it and pushed it toward where Jaimon was. His head popped up out of the water again, and he sputtered and spit up. His eyes were wild and unfocused, and he kicked without going anywhere.

"Grab the paddle, Jaimon!" Gabby said. "The paddle!"

Jaimon coughed again and yelled, waving his arms around in a panic. The paddle was only a few feet away, but it could have been twenty.

Gabby pulled her arms hard, trying to swim over to him, but they were so weak with the recent rowing. Her right arm started to cramp in the cold water. She couldn't let Jaimon drown. She pulled upon her magic—which came slowly in her exhausted state.

Calling upon the powers to manipulate the water, Gabby tried to change the direction of the floating boat and move it toward Jaimon. It barely moved. Then she realized it would be better to try and push Jaimon himself toward the overturned boat.

With a burst of energy she yelled out and pushed Jaimon forward, away from her, but closer to the boat. "Grab the boat, Jaimon!"

But the sudden push, instead of helping him, scared him, and he yelled out for help once again before going under.

"Garrik!" Gabby cried out.

She watched as Garrick used his powerful arms to push against the boat from the other side, trying to get it closer to Jaimon.

Breathing hard, Gabby looked around for what else she could do. Her body was shivering, and her lungs were on fire. Her weakened arms could hardly keep her above water.

A loud roar sounded overhead, and Gabby turned her head up into the darkening fog. Breaking through the fog was a flame of yellow and red burning down toward the water. Following the flame was Cholena, Jaimon's mighty green dragon. Prince Ender sat atop her. He seemed to be fighting with the beast to turn back—but to no avail.

The dragon screeched as if in pain but dove down to the water, its claws reaching underneath—a dozen feet from Gabby. When Cholena lifted out of the water again, she clutched Jaimon in her claws. He lay limp and wasn't moving.

"Get him to safety!" Gabby yelled, not knowing if the dragon understood her or not. She looked up at Ender. "What are you doing here?"

"Same as you, wizard, I surmise," he shouted.

The dragon roared again—a painful wail—and flew off into the night before Gabby could ask any more questions.

CHAPTER EIGHTEEN

Alli stood at the edge of the cave once again and glared out at the churning sea just east of the city of Jor. A raging storm sat off in the distance, and the gray waves crashed on the rocks down beneath her. Nuri stood beside her, silent and brooding.

"What is wrong with me?" she whispered out loud and brushed a few stray tears away from her eyes.

A low moan came from behind her. Her dragon, Miriel, sat in the back of the cave, barely moving. Alli turned and walked back, leaving Nuri. She put her hand on her dragon, feeling the familiar rough scales. Miriel had barely made it away from the city and into the cave before collapsing.

"Something is happening to the dragons," Alli said as she ran her hand lovingly over Miriel's yellow hide.

We need to rest, came a faint reply deep in the recesses of her mind. Just hearing the voice thrilled her. For the last week she had craved to hear her dragon's voice. *Again?* The thought came to her mind.

Yes, again.

She knew that somehow she used to hear Miriel's voice all the time. But that had all changed.

Alli growled and stomped her foot hard on the ground. "It's infuriating not remembering."

"What *do* you remember?" Nuri said, coming up behind her.

She jumped a moment at his approach, berating herself for not paying more attention.

"I remember fighting in the arena," she snapped at him.

"What arena?"

"In Thera. My master, Constantine, trained me, taught me, and helped me to be a great fighter." She remembered loathing and loving the man at the same time.

"Ahh," said Nuri. "I've heard of the underground of Turg. A dangerous place. But you survived."

Alli nodded and slid down to the ground, resting her back against the side of her dragon. She could feel Miriel's heartbeat vibrating into her back. It was a comforting feeling, and she closed her own eyes for a moment.

"Yes, I survived," Alli said. "And I was given to a new master." Delia terrified her, and she blanched at talking about her so openly.

"But what about before then?" Nuri prodded before sitting down next to her on the ground.

Alli swung her head from side to side and squeezed her eyes tighter. "Only glimpses. I remember the Citadel, portions of a few battles, and Roland . . ." After they had arrived in the cave, she had sworn she had heard his voice.

"The High Wizard?"

"Yes," Alli said. "But he has now declared himself as the leader of some golden empire. His quest for power has him trying to unite all the southern kingdoms under his rule." She slammed a fist down against her leg. "Arrogant man!"

Flashes of his warm smile and sparkling blue eyes came unbidden to her mind, and she pushed them away. "He is the enemy," she said.

"The only enemy I see is those two men who killed my family." Nuri stood again.

Alli opened her eyes and watched the young prince—now the next king of Turg—pace around the small enclosure.

"Who are they?"

Alli shook her head. "I don't know for sure. Raj pretended to be your dead brother to get a dragon and his father has the ability to speak to people's minds. If they are really just a vanguard from the eastern kingdoms, then more may be coming."

"I have to go back to the castle," Nuri said. "I have to check on my people."

"But they will kill you, Nuri," Alli said.

"Maybe someone survived," Nuri said. "We saw Raj leave. Surely you could take care of his father. You are a mighty warrior and dragon rider."

Alli smiled grimly at his assessment of her and laughed. "I'm not truly sure what I can or can't do any more."

"But we have to do something," Nuri said. "If you won't, then I will."

"And get yourself killed doing it." Alli stood.

"What do you care?" Nuri yelled at her and turned away.

Alli stumbled a bit, but recovered quickly and stood and glared at Nuri.

Alli, Miriel's voice came quietly to her mind. The more she was away from Delia, the more often her voice came now. She turned her head back toward her dragon, who still appeared to be sleeping.

Remember who you are, Miriel spoke softly.

Alli scowled at Nuri. "Fine. I'll help you."

Nuri smiled and bowed his head to her. "Thank you, Dragon Rider."

"Don't push it," Alli growled. "I don't know why I'm doing this."

"Because you are a good person," Nuri said. "I'm not sure what happened, but the dragon riders always come in times of danger to establish peace in the land."

Alli grunted, not knowing what to believe at the moment. Roland and Delia both thought they could rule everyone. Her heart seemed to pull toward one, while her mind pulled toward the other. But it was time she started making her own decisions—an ability that seemed easier the farther she was from either one of the great wizards.

"Miriel!" she called out to her dragon. "We need to get back to Jor."

Her dragon stirred a bit but said nothing. A growing irritation rose within Alli again, and she remembered the words of her master. She needed to be more firm with her dragon.

"Miriel!" she said out loud and in her mind as she smacked the dragon on the side. "I command you as your rider."

Before Alli could even think, her dragon snapped its head around and let out a loud roar. Fire flew from her maw as Alli grabbed Nuri and dived out of the way. The wall of the cave behind them glowed and sizzled with the heat.

When Alli turned back, Miriel's emerald eyes pierced her own. The power and intensity in them caused Alli to fall to her knees. Tears sprang to her eyes at the passion in her dragon's eyes.

I chose you, Dragon Rider, came the familiar voice—soft but firm. *After Breelyn lost the bond, I felt your heart and told the Dragon King that I chose you. I carry you and bond with you willingly, but never under command. Delia used an abominable artifact to steal our bond. But it is not hers to give.*

Nuri stirred at Alli's side and stood back up, but Alli stayed where she was. She felt hot shame at what she had done. Her master had told her to be firm, but . . .

She is not your master, Allison Stenos, Miriel said with a low growl. *And she is not mine. The only one that can command us is the Dragon King.*

All of a sudden, Alli's vision went dark and gray and she found herself in a void of nothingness. A vision opened up in her mind. Bakari, the Dragon King, lay still on the ground. A soft blanket sat under him, and a white pillow cradled his head. His long, dark braids were scraggly and dirty, and his face was more gray than brown. Remorse welled up inside Alli, and she swallowed hard.

As she reached her hand forward to touch the frail body, the scene rippled in front of her and disappeared. She opened her eyes to find that Miriel had laid her head back down on the ground, her beautiful eyes barely open to a slit.

Alli, still on her knees, leaned forward and put her forehead against the orange-tipped scales of her dragon. Her breath shuddered. "Miriel," she said out loud as well as in her mind. "Please forgive me. I don't know who I am. Tell me what to do. Please help me."

Tears ran down her face as she waited for an answer. She could feel Nuri pacing behind her. He was anxious to get back to his people. Her heart went out to him. Losing his entire family at once had to be hard. Why hadn't she been able to stop that? But that wasn't what she had been sent to do. Delia had sent her to retrieve the other dragon and Prince Ender—whom she knew now was Raj.

As if thoughts of Delia made her more aware of her master, Alli felt the Dragon Queen's voice in the back of her mind. *Dragon Rider, where are you? Return to me at once.*

Alli stiffened at the command. It was the first time she had heard Delia since arriving in Khazer. She was trained to obey her master and moved her knees, preparing to stand back up. But before she could, Miriel stirred just a fraction, and Alli's attention went back to her dragon.

Dragon Rider, Miriel said, her voice a distant echo in Alli's mind. *Resist her. She does not command you or me. Rise up and be who you are meant to be!*

But I don't know if I can. Alli didn't remember feeling more hopeless and lost in her entire life—well, at least as much of her life as she could remember. *I don't know who I am*, she wailed in her mind. *Tell me who I am!*

You are the battlemaster. Miriel's voice grew stronger and louder in her mind. *You are a dragon rider!*

A small crack appeared in Alli's mind, and flashes of memories began to come through. The first time she had ridden Miriel—with Roland—following Bakari into the mountains of Mahli on the way to Turg. Seeing Jaimon fall to the ground helpless as she had been captured by Constantine. The memories came forth slowly, one by one, and with each came shooting pains. A flash of a man—Doctor Abaddon—laying his hands against her head to heal her.

Alli roared with pain and fell back on the ground. "Stop! Stop!" she pleaded with her own mind.

"Alli!" Nuri came to her side and tried to help her to sit back up. "What's wrong?"

"The doctor did something to me. My head . . . the memories." She gasped for air. "It hurts too much."

"Don't think about it right now," he tried to console her. "Think about the cave here, the ocean outside, your dragon."

Alli did as he suggested. She listened to the waves of the ocean crashing against the rocks below them. She felt Miriel in the back of her mind and leaned on her for more comfort. Finally, the pain subsided, but so did the memories, and she was left once again with gaping holes in her mind.

Find Roland. Only he can save us now. Miriel's last words came before the dragon closed her eyes completely and the bond receded, leaving only a small spark of life in the back of Alli's mind. *I need to sleep.*

Nuri helped Alli to her feet. She put a hand against the rough cave wall to get her balance.

"Are you all right?" Nuri asked with compassion in his eyes.

Alli turned to him and nodded. "Yes, I'm fine. Better than I've been for a while, though I am still afraid Delia's voice will come back."

"What happened?"

Alli shook her head. "I saw things—the Dragon King, glimpses of my past—and heard the voice of my master." She paused a moment and stood up straighter. "No, not my master." Her voice grew stronger. "I am my own master. I am the battlemaster and a dragon rider."

A smile grew wide on Nuri's face. "You remember?"

"Only small pieces," Alli said. "Many of the memories are too painful right now. I can't bear to remember more."

"And your dragon?"

Alli's gaze took in her sleeping dragon. "She needs to rest awhile. I guess we are on our own for now." She clapped Nuri on the back. "Let's go and get your city back, then I need to find Roland Tyre ."

Upon saying his name, a memory tried to surface. They both stood in the doorway of a grand building holding hands, and then Alli let go and walked down a hallway. She tried to remember more, but as she did so her head pounded again, and she had to turn her attention away.

"Memories again?" Nuri asked.

"Yes," Alli said, trying not to wince. "Memories of a friend. Roland Tyre may be the only person who can save us from whatever is going to happen."

CHAPTER NINETEEN

Gabby opened her eyes and found herself on her side. In front of her was a narrow, sandy beach. Farther inland grew tall palms, ferns, and other plants that seemed to hint at a warmer climate than she would have thought existed here in the wintertime. She assumed she was on the island they had been rowing toward.

Hearing a groan behind her, she sat up and turned over. Garrik, too, was slowly sitting up. He turned and spit, then rubbed his hands over his face.

"What happened?" Gabby said as she ran her hands over her body to make sure nothing was broken.

Garrik grunted. "After the dragon took Jaimon, the wind picked up and pushed the boat to me. I was able to get to you and hold on until the current took us to shore."

They both turned and looked a dozen feet away at their boat, which now sat on its side, the mast broken off. But besides that it appeared intact.

"Are you all right?" Gabby asked.

Garrik took a few moments to stand up and then nodded. "A little sore, but nothing broken."

Gabby stood up also and smiled back. "Me neither, though I don't know if I'll ever be able to use my arms again. I can hardly lift them."

Garrik laughed. "Rowing will put some muscles on you, that's for sure."

"Not sure I'm looking for that." Gabby raised her dark eyebrows at Garrik. She turned around for a bit. The fog stopped twenty feet out from shore, and the island itself was bathed in beautiful morning sunlight. "Now, we need to find Jaimon and a phoenix."

"We?" Garrik turned serious and shook his head. "It was my job to bring you here, not to go looking for some crazy bird."

Gabby put her hands on her hips and scowled at Garrik. "You afraid?"

Garrik shook his head, but before he said anything they heard the distant roar of a dragon, followed by a loud screech. They looked at each other.

"Well, maybe a little," Garrik admitted. "No one has ever come back from this island, Gabby. I don't care if you're a wizard, a princess, or just a smart girl—I have no intention of traipsing through this jungle. That's your quest, not mine." He stooped down and began gathering firewood. "I'll be right here next to a warm fire, getting the boat ready. After you find a phoenix, come back here, and I'll be ready to take you back to the mainland."

"Aren't you worried about Jaimon?" Gabby asked. She couldn't believe what Garrik was saying.

Garrik let out a deep breath and looked up from gathering wood. "Of course I'm worried about him. But what can I do against a dragon? He's the one who's a dragon rider. If I stay here, I will give him a place to come back to."

Another screech, this time louder, came once again. Gabby glanced up the small bank of sand to where the trees began. "That must be a phoenix." She turned her eyes back to Garrik, but he just resumed gathering wood. So she started walking slightly uphill and away from the shore.

Their packs of food and extra clothes were lost somewhere under the sea. Luckily her shoes had stayed on. She hoped she could find a phoenix—and Jaimon—quickly and return before she got too hungry.

She hoped Cholena hadn't hurt Jaimon. But she didn't trust the man riding Cholena. Grabbing a short vine, Gabby pulled herself up the rest of the small hill, took a few steps, and stopped.

With mouth open, she turned slowly around. It was the most beautiful place she had ever been. Tall palms swayed in a warm breeze overhead. Broad ferns and other wide-leaf plants grew all around her. The leaves were almost as tall as she. Bright yellow and pink flowers dotted the landscape—some growing up from the ground, others hanging down on vines from the wide-trunk trees that filled in around the giant palms. A few birds flitted in the air around her, and a butterfly landed on her shoulder.

Studying the area more closely, she realized also that the sun was warm, unlike the weather on the mainland or the water just a dozen yards away.

"Garrik!" she cried out. "Garrik, come quick."

In a matter of moments, Garrik's head appeared over the embankment, and then he pulled himself up the rest of the way. He glared at her when he saw her standing there.

"I thought you were hurt," he said.

"So you do care," Gabby said with a broad smile. "I'm fine."

"Then why all the yelling?" Garrik said.

"Look." Gabby spread her hands around and took a deep breath. The scent of the flowers was sweet to her nose, and the air itself smelled clean and fresh.

Garrik took a few steps and turned his head around, seeing his surroundings for the first time. His jaw dropped as he ran a hand over one of the green large-leaf plants. A small animal scurried out from underneath, and he jumped back.

Gabby laughed, and Garrik glared at her again.

"Afraid of a little squirrel?" Gabby laughed again, her eyes sparkling in delight.

"What if you had really been hurt?" Garrik said.

"Then you would have come and saved me," Gabby said. "It's a paradise. Have you ever seen anything so beautiful in your life?"

Garrik let out a long breath and stared up into the sky. "No. No, I haven't."

"The magic of the phoenix must keep it like this," Gabby said.

"Powerful magic, indeed," said Garrik. "No wonder no one ever came back from here."

Gabby walked over closer to Garrik and put a hand on his arm. "I need you, Garrik. Come with me. We'll find a phoenix faster together."

"My father said you don't find a phoenix; it finds you—if it wants to."

"Well, then walk with me, and we'll let a phoenix find us," Gabby said. "I need to see if Jaimon is here, too. That man riding Jaimon's dragon seemed to have plans of his own."

"Plans that might include killing us," Garrik said.

Gabby nodded. "Yes, so we'd better hurry." She grabbed Garrik's hand and pulled him forward. There appeared to be a small trail leading inland.

* * *

Three hours later they had found no sign of a phoenix. The sun now beat down from overhead, and Gabby was beginning to feel hungry. By Garrik's growing sour mood, she suspected that he was also.

Before she could see, Gabby heard a flapping of great wings overhead. She pulled Garrik over under a broad tree and knelt on the ground. Through the leaves and vines she followed the dragon with her eyes as it circled around.

"It's searching for us," Gabby concluded. "But I don't see Jaimon on it anymore."

"Who is that man?" Garrik whispered.

Gabby shook her head. "Prince Ender from Khazer, but now that I think of it, he doesn't have the look of one from Khazer."

"Hmpff," Garrik said. "How does such a young girl get herself mixed up with warring wizards, dragons, and evil strangers?"

"And a southern elf," Gabby added to the list.

The dragon flew farther away, and the two of them began to emerge from under the tree, when all of a sudden Garrik cried out. When Gabby turned around, hands out and ready to strike at whatever was attacking Garrik, she stopped and gave Garrik a puzzled look. He just stood rubbing his head.

Looking up into the tree, Gabby saw round yellow fruit hanging down. One such fruit lay by Garrik's foot.

"Mango!" Gabby exclaimed and moved forward.

"It fell on my head," Garrik explained his outburst.

Gabby covered her mouth to stifle a laugh.

"Fine," Garrik said. "Go ahead and laugh."

She did.

And he joined in.

After a few moments of mirth, Gabby picked up the fruit, produced a knife, peeled off the outside, and bit into the fruit.

"This is the best mango I've ever tasted," she said, wiping a bit of juice off her chin.

"We don't get many mangos in the desert," Garrik said. "Those down in Quentis, where they grow, seem a little stingy with their price." He said the last with a laugh and twinkle in his eye, while pulling another one off the tree. It was mostly red, with only a bit of yellow and green on one end. He, too, had a knife and peeled the mango, and the two of them stood in silence for a few minutes enjoying the fresh fruit.

After tossing the pit aside, Gabby motioned for them to continue forward. "Where do the phoenix live? The guardian said there may still be a few left. What kind of area would they be in?"

"They are said to build nests in the tops of the highest trees or on cliffs that overlook everything else. They stay as close to the sun as they can."

Gabby went over to a tall tree and peered up through its branches.

"What are you doing?" Garrik asked.

"I'm going to climb up as high as I can to see where the tallest point on the island would be."

Garrik huffed but moved over next to her and started climbing himself. "Not a bad idea."

Gabby smiled and watched the elf scurry up the branches and through the thick vines of the tree. He was nimble.

"I'm part forest elf," he yelled down at her, as if reading her thoughts.

While he climbed, Gabby looked around and marveled once again at how beautiful it was there. It would be a nice place to stay. She looked up through the branches and tried to follow him with her eyes, but she lost sight of him in the thick branches. Finally, he shouted down at her.

"There's a mountain in the center of the island, with a waterfall and steep cliffs," Garrik said. "And wait. . . Uh oh."

"What?" Gabby yelled up the tree.

Garrik didn't answer, and all she heard was him scoring down the branches at what sounded like a breakneck speed.

"Garrik, what's wrong?" Gabby yelled out again. She spotted him about thirty feet up.

"Smoke . . . and people," Garrik said between puffs of breath. "Hurry, hide!"

Gabby turned around, but before she could go on, three men and a lady came up in front of her. One of the men was old, but the other two appeared to be only a decade older than Garrik. All three were elves by birth, so age was hard to tell.

They wore bright red and orange feathers in their hair—from a phoenix, she guessed—and had a bright red mark painted on their foreheads.

She heard Garrik drop to the ground behind her but kept her focus on the elves in front of her. The older one took a step forward, and Gabby brought out her hands in front of her in preparation to defend herself with a spell.

"No need for that, young one," said the man. His accent was thick, but Gabby caught the words, nonetheless. "Your magic will not work here."

Gabby moved her hands away from the people and pushed out what should have been fire from her fingertips, but nothing happened. She tried wind next, still nothing. Looking inside herself, she concentrated harder, trying to bring her magic up to do her bidding. But there was nothing there, not even a spark.

"What is this place?" Gabby said with a whisper.

"Come," said the older man with a pleasant smile on his face. "There is no need for magic here. There is nothing to be afraid of."

The other two motioned Gabby and Garrik forward as well.

"Come to our village," said the woman.

Gabby and Garrik turned to each other, and he indicated with a shrug that it was her decision to make. The people didn't seem harmful, and maybe they could help her find the phoenix. She took a step forward, and Garrik walked up beside her.

"That's my oldest cousin," said Garrik softly in her ear. "He doesn't seem to recognize me. He left many years ago when I was younger. My brother went after him, but was very tight-lipped about things when he returned, only saying that my cousin would be fine. We must be careful here."

Gabby's heart raced as they followed the strangers down another small trail.

CHAPTER TWENTY

Roland felt like he spent all his time flying from one kingdom to another. He guessed that was the price he paid to be a great wizard and leader. He knew time was growing short, but the list of things to do didn't seem to be getting any shorter. At least from his short vision in the artifacts cave, he knew that Delia's powers over her riders and dragons seemed to be weakening, and currently she only had King Abbas siding with her.

He had spent the last day in Tillimot. While there he had met with Daymian Khouri, who seemed to have things well in hand. The queen had been banished to a countryside home, and her son, the previous heir, was being watched carefully. So far he hadn't done anything against Roland's wishes.

Roland continued to arrange for men to sail around the Horn and up to Elvyn. It was there they would have to make their stand against the invading eastern warships. There were rumors of people from Tillimot seeing a green dragon flying to the southeast over an unpopulated island off of the Elvyn coast. Roland didn't have time to look into it. If the dragon was away from Delia, that was all that mattered to him.

Now in Quentis, he was about to meet with the Wolf and his son, Kaspar. They appeared to be strong allies, but they had many secrets Roland knew they weren't sharing with him. Leaving his golden dragon in the beautiful gardened courtyard,

Roland strode through the front doors of the domed palace. Guards stood at attention and saluted him.

"Protector Roland," came Kaspar's voice from Roland's left.

"Kas." Roland nodded at the man only a year or so older than he. The women who walked down the hallway, whether servants or nobles, stopped and ogled—that's the only word Roland could think of—at their prince.

"You always have the attention of the lovely ladies." Roland chuckled and ran a hand down his own smooth blond hair. It was hard competing with the man.

Kaspar smiled and lifted his dark eyebrows. "If I remember right, you have become quite close to your own beautiful woman."

Roland felt his cheeks redden and leaned over to adjust his scabbard, drawing attention away from his face. He remembered Alli blushing as well with every mention of Kaspar, but in the end she had chosen to stay with Roland in the Citadel. The thought lifted his spirits. "I guess you can't have everyone, Kas."

Kas didn't take offence and just laughed as he led Roland down the wide hallway to the Wolf's private office.

As they entered the room, the man looked up from his desk and stared into Roland's eyes for a moment. Roland felt the familiar push against his thoughts and, with a smile and nod, pushed back.

The Wolf chuckled. "You're getting stronger."

"I have gathered more artifacts and am learning at a faster pace," Roland admitted. He held his golden scepter in his right hand—a fact he hadn't noticed until just now. The artifact seemed as much a part of him as his own appendages.

"How is the Dragon King?" The Wolf asked. "Did you get the healer there in time?"

Roland shook his head. "He is no better, from what I know. Kharlia couldn't help him. She is there with him and Liam, watching over them while Gabby and Jaimon search for a phoenix."

The Wolf jerked up from his desk, and before Roland knew it, the man stood a foot in front of him. His eyes smoldered, and his visage was dark.

"You let those two go and find a phoenix by themselves?" the Wolf roared.

Roland wasn't afraid of too many men, but he took a step back now. His hand tightened around the scepter.

Roland waved a hand in the air and tried to regain control. "My business is to unify the kingdoms. I don't have time to traipse around the continent in search of some mythical creature that probably doesn't even exist."

The Wolf glared at him. "That is my daughter—my barely fifteen year-old daughter—you sent off with the youngest dragon rider," the Wolf said. "Surely you could have provided them with an escort."

Roland cringed inside. Maybe he should have. But outwardly he wasn't going to take this from the man he had let retain his kingdom. Pounding the scepter against the marble floor, Roland took a step forward and stopped mere inches from the man's face. The Wolf was slightly taller than Roland

and quite a bit more broad. But Roland had the scepter and the dragon.

"I am the Protector of Quentis, sir, and also recently named the Warlord of Elvyn," Roland began, raising his voice. "I am certainly not your daughter's babysitter."

Before Roland knew it, the Wolf reached out and slapped Roland in the side of his face. "Impudent boy!"

Roland brought his hands out in front of him and pushed out against the leader of Quentis. The man went flying across the room and crashed into the front of his desk. Kaspar ran to his side.

A knock sounded on the door. "Is everything all right in there, sir?" came the voice of one of the guards.

Roland looked from the door, to Kaspar, and then back at the Wolf.

"Everything is fine," Kaspar called out. He turned toward Roland with a murderous look on his face before helping his father up.

Roland sucked in a deep breath and let it out slowly. He shouldn't have done that. All three stood and glared at each other for a few moments, then the Wolf went back to his chair and motioned for Kaspar and Roland to sit.

"I'm sorry, sir," Roland said softly.

"What was that, Protector?" the Wolf asked with just a hint of a smile on his lips. "I didn't quite hear you."

Roland ground his teeth for a moment then barked out a loud laugh. "I'm sorry to have let my temper get the best of me. I know you care for your daughter, and I shouldn't have provoked you. But I will let you know that she is one of the most capable young women I have ever met."

"Of course she is," the Wolf said. "She is my daughter."

The three relaxed and without any more words on what had happened the Wolf explained more to Roland.

"The phoenix are real, Roland Tyre," the Wolf said, "and the most dangerous of all magical creatures. They have been guarded and protected by the forest elves for hundreds of years. They live on a small island to the south of the southern Elvyn forest."

Roland nodded. "Your daughter should be successful finding it and bringing it back to the Dragon King. She said he needed their power to be healed."

"It's not that easy," the Wolf said, his face lined and worried. "From what I know, no one has ever returned from that island."

Roland let out a sigh. "There are also rumors of one of the dragons—the green one—flying around the island."

"Delia couldn't know about the phoenix," the Wolf said. "Only the royal families of Quentis, Tillimot, and Elvyn have ever been told."

Roland shrugged. "Delia appears to have lost some control over the dragons and their riders."

"Alli?" Kaspar asked, leaning up in his chair.

"Last I saw her—in the magic stream—she was in a cave in Jor with her dragon and another man about her age. She called him Nuri."

"The prince of Khazer," said the Wolf. "What are you doing about Delia?"

"I came to tell you Delia isn't our biggest problem—though hopefully I have put events in motion to stop her soon at the Citadel. She will find quite a few wizards and artifacts defending it when she attacks," Roland said. "The bigger problem is a thousand warships from the east that will be at our shores soon; a week, perhaps a few days more by this time, is all the time we have to unify and fight them off."

The Wolf leaned back in his chair, the blood draining from his face. "Are you sure? How do you know?"

"I do. Let that suffice." He didn't have time to explain everything. "What I need from you is all the wizards you can spare up to Lor'l as fast as you can, then soldiers and sailors to follow."

"It is dangerous this time of year to go around the Horn," Kaspar said. "We will have to go out farther before we turn north."

"Then you had better hurry," Roland said. "Tillimot is already on its way."

"And what about the Dragon King and my daughter?" the Wolf asked, anger clearly still smoldering inside of him.

"They will have to take care of themselves, Sir," Roland said with a sigh. "If they are able to help us in the end, fine. I will take all the help I can get. But if not, I cannot spare worry about a few people, no matter how much I would like to, when the fate of the entire southern kingdoms hang in the balance. I hope you can understand."

The Wolf opened his mouth to say something, but appeared to think better of it and closed it again. He didn't look happy, but as a king himself he understood that hard choices had to be made sometimes.

"I will use all the power at my disposal," Roland continued, "but only if I unify everyone will we win. That is the truth of it. And that's where I have to spend my energy right now."

After a brief silence, Kaspar spoke up. "I will go help her. I will find Gabby."

Roland beheld Kaspar with respect. "That would be fine," he said.

The Wolf growled but kept his voice low. "That is not a decision you make for us, Protector. Whether my son goes to help my daughter is my decision alone."

Roland nodded. "And it is my decision alone how I determine to protect my people, King of Quentis."

The Wolf nodded and stood. "You are a dangerous man, Roland Tyre. The decisions you have to make and the power you play with may yet destroy you."

"They may indeed," Roland admitted. "But not until I unify the land and beat the enemy from our shores."

"Then good luck to you." The Wolf seemed to consider for a moment, then put out his hand and shook Roland's.

Kaspar turned to Roland. "I will find my sister; you just make sure that Alli is all right in all of this."

Roland held his lips tight as he nodded. So many people and priorities to deal with.

He called to his dragon in his mind as he escorted himself out to the courtyard.

As he flew off, he called down to those watching from the ground, including the king and his son. "For those who fight in Elvyn, double the pay!"

The small crowd cheered as Orelia flew higher up in the sky.

Nice touch, the dragon said.

Roland laughed. *Well, If I'm going to save the people, I do want them to love me for it.*

Orelia roared, and a golden stream of fire flew from her mouth. Roland drew upon a defensive spell to keep from being singed.

Hey, a little more warning next time, oh mighty dragon!

The dragon roared again, this time without any fire.

Roland turned around and watched the sea fade away behind them. It really was great to be so powerful.

He needed to return to the Citadel and ready his forces for Delia's attack, but first he had one more stop to make.

CHAPTER TWENTY-ONE

Atop Orelia, Roland circled the city of Raleez, now the combined capital of both North and South Solshi. Down below people stopped what they were doing and pointed up into the gray sky. The golden dragon flying down toward them was a joyous reminder of how Roland had liberated them from a tyrant queen.

Cheers floated up to Roland as he took the dragon down toward the castle courtyard.

I really like this place, Roland said to himself and to his dragon.

And from the looks of it, they like you, wizard. The dragon's voice was almost a purr.

Roland smiled and waved at his constituents as he landed softly on the ground. A group of royal guards greeted him, with King Andre De Luz coming up front. The young man, a few years younger than Roland had to wait until his sixteenth birthday to become king by right in his kingdom. In the meantime, he had named Roland as regent; a role that Roland hoped was good enough to unify the lands.

"Regent Roland!" Andre bobbed his head toward Roland. When he brought it back up, his eyes sparkled with delight. "So good to see you again. Our troops are traveling north to Turg and Cyrene in Guildmaster Ferdinand's ships. He has been very accommodating."

"I'm sure he has," Roland chuckled. "I'm paying him enough."

Roland put his arm around Andre as they walked together back inside the castle. "Are the people well, Andre?"

Andre smiled. "Oh, yes. The textile guilds are now selling to Alaris and other neighboring kingdoms. With fewer taxes, the fishermen are more energetic and determined and are actually bringing in more than before. The people are happy."

They entered the castle, and Roland glanced around him in awe once again. The ancient building was a wonder to behold. Tall columns led down the long hallway; tapestries and paintings dotted the walls between. Dull light streamed through high windows. While pushing down the people, the previous queen had amassed a good portion of wealth.

After a brief lunch with the king and a few of his advisors, Roland was ushered down a long hallway of the castle. His black boots echoed off the tiled floor while Andre led him down a long corridor and around a corner. Roland could hear sounds of people behind the thick walls and wondered what was going on. Andre brought Roland up a half a dozen steps to a landing in which a large double door stood in the center. A newly carved dragon was inlaid with gold around the doorframe. Roland raised his eyebrows in question to Andre.

"The people have a surprise for you, Sire," Andre said, with almost a giggle in his high voice.

"A surprise?" Roland was intrigued. It had been some time since anyone surprised him.

Andre motioned for two guards next to the door to open them, then he motioned for Roland to follow. Roland took a few steps inside, then put a hand against a marble column as *déjà vu* raced through his mind. It was almost identical to the vision he had had when he had first found the scepter.

Roland took a few steps and was ushered up on a circular raised dais and looked down at an immense hall. Throngs of people stood shoulder to shoulder, many of them still entering in a hurry through various side doors. Both sides of the hall had tall windows—one side looking out at the churning waters of the bay of Raleez. Evenly spaced in the hall were wide, alabaster columns. Looking up, Roland saw that the ceiling was gold and carved in beautifully intricate patterns.

Bringing his gaze back down to the people, he studied the crowd carefully. Nobles stood with other citizens of varying degrees of wealth. Most had the brown hair and tan skin indicative of this part of the continent, but he saw a few blond heads mixed in as well as a few darker-skinned people from Mahli. Some of the people wore their finest; for others their finest was barely more than rags. He was touched deeply and didn't know what to say.

Without any words, a drum beat started slow and deep, then increased in speed until each beat ran into the other. Then it stopped, and trumpets blew a fanfare. The people as one dropped to their knees, their right fists going to their hearts. A cry caught in Roland's throat. He fought back the tears by taking a deep breath.

As one the people peered up at him from their knees and shouted, "Hail Roland Tyre! Hail the Golden Wizard!"

Roland couldn't hold back the tears any longer. It was the most beautiful thing he had ever seen. But then to his surprise, huge thirty-foot doors opened in the back of the room, and a dozen honor guards escorted his golden dragon into the room. The people parted, and the dragon walked with his head high toward Roland.

"She's so beautiful," he whispered to no one in particular.

A pleasing sound echoed in his mind. *I am what you made me to be.*

Roland wasn't sure what that meant, but for now he didn't worry about it. Bringing his scepter out in front of him, he held it high in the air and spoke out loud for the first time since entering the room.

"Rise, my people," he said, his voice growing louder and clearer as he spoke. "Rise and be one. Rise up and be unified as part of my golden empire."

The people rose and cheered; then Andre stepped forward. He directed Roland toward a chair that sat on the dais. A gold-gilded back and arms surrounded a red velvet seat.

"Today you will sit on my throne." Andre directed him to sit down.

Roland removed his golden cloak, handed it to a servant, and lowered himself onto the seat. It felt right. Four men came forward, each holding a velvet pillow. They knelt in front of Roland, and Andre took an item from each pillow and handed it to Roland. Two silver rings and two golden bracelets. The bracelets had dragons scrolled around them.

"Where did you get these?" Roland asked. "They are exquisite."

"Deep in the cellars," Andre said. "They are artifacts."

Roland turned them around on his arm, amazed at the

workmanship. Something familiar about them tickled the back of Roland's mind, but once again he shoved the thought away. He wasn't going to let anything hamper this moment.

"Roland Tyre," Andre said, "you are our deliverer, our regent, and will always be known as the Golden Wizard. These gifts are only a token to show our appreciation to you. You will always be welcomed in Solshi and will have permanent rooms in the castle."

Roland brushed a few stray tears from his eyes as he looked out over the people. They were waiting for him to say something. But what could he say? He almost laughed with giddiness.

He took a deep breath and tried to relax and enjoy the moment. "You sure know how to put on a show," Roland said with a wide grin and a wink. "I'll have to have you teach the other kingdoms." His thoughts went to Quentis and Elvyn. Two proud kingdoms that had in word become part of his golden empire, but he was sure that behind his back they disparaged him.

But *these* people understood him. These people knew how powerful he was and how much he truly cared for the welfare of his people, and for that he would take care of them.

Unify them. The voice came to his mind again. It had been awhile since he had heard the directive. The words brought his thoughts back down to earth. He had a war to win and needed to focus on that. He shook his head a few times to clear away the grand thoughts he had been having. But when he looked back out over the people, he could feel their love.

His mind went back again to when he had first found the

scepter, and he felt a sudden fear dig deep inside of him. That vision hadn't ended well. His visage darkened as he thought about the dragon crumbling before him and the people rotting away. What had the woman in the vision said to him? *Choose.* She had said he had to choose his heart or his mind; he couldn't have the people love him and be all powerful.

Roland laughed. Well, she was wrong. It was only a silly vision, anyway.

"Are you all right, Sire?" Andre leaned over to him. "Do you need something?"

"No, no, Andre." Roland smiled. "I am perfectly fine."

Before Roland could even finish his sentence, a loud crash sounded on the roof, and pieces of ceiling began to fall. The people screamed and tried to get out of the doors, but there wasn't enough room. Many fell to the floor and were trampled upon by others.

Roland stood and tried to understand what was happening. Another loud boom echoed through the room, and two windows burst open, glass flying everywhere. Chaos overtook in the hall. Guards came up around Andre to keep him safe.

"My Lord," said one. "We must get you to safety."

"No," Andre said. "Save the regent first."

Roland heard the words and was momentarily washed over once again with the love these people held for him. But the horror of his vision was coming to pass in front of his eyes. He slammed his scepter on the ground, and golden shots of fire wound their way through the room, over the heads of the people, and out through the broken windows, searching for the problem.

Then he heard the sound. The roar of a dragon was unmistakable. The blue and red dragons appeared outside the open windows. Delia sat on one. She was using her powers to burst holes into the castle.

"I thought she was going to attack the Citadel!" Roland roared. "Tabitha told me Delia was going to attack me, and I thought that meant the Citadel." Was it all a ploy? Had Tabitha turned on him? He couldn't believe it. But he knew he had to do something. Solshi's main army and navy had traveled north and should be attacking Turg at this very moment. There weren't many left to defend the land against Delia.

"Orelia!" Roland called out to his dragon. He jumped off the dais and high into the air. The dragon came up underneath him, and together they flew through a broken window to confront Delia and her dragons.

She will not have my people!

CHAPTER TWENTY-TWO

Roland rose above the castle on his dragon and scanned the area. Chaos met his eyes. Citizens of Solshi were fleeing from the castle and through the city. Two dragons swooped overhead; one with King Abbas and Wizard Korax on top, flinging down powerful bursts at the castle itself. The other dragon, Abylar, held Delia and was now heading east to the city walls. The dragon carried a transport of some sort underneath him and seemed to be straining to stay up in the air.

Glancing down at the ground, Roland's attention somehow was drawn to two small children separated from their parents by a tide of running people.

They were going to get killed!

He brought the dragon down lower, and the distraction moved people to the side enough for the parents to come running back to find their son and daughter.

"Thank you, Sire!" yelled the woman up to him as she clutched her daughter in her arms.

Roland growled inside. Moments before things had been so perfect.

"Well, I still am the most powerful wizard," he said to himself.

He hated to leave the people in Korax's line of fire, but Roland needed to stop Delia. His dragon raced toward her just as she let down the transport. Twenty men and women disembarked.

The men and women raced toward the city walls. Many of them wore armor and colors of both Cyrene and Turg. All had knives or swords hanging at their waists. But what worried Roland the most were the bolts of lightning and fire they used to blast the city walls apart.

Wizards!

"Delia!" he yelled over at her. "Stop this madness. These are my people, and you cannot have them!"

Delia laughed. "This is what happens to those that defy me, Roland Tyre. Soon your mighty empire will be in ashes."

Delia pushed out a gust of wind at Roland, and his dragon was swept sideways. Roland grabbed the reins with one hand while holding on to the scepter with the other.

"And your people will be mine," Roland called out.

Delia gave a puzzled look and came at him again. He rose to meet her. She must have come straight south from Thera and hadn't noticed the ships coming in from the sea.

"Where do you think all the ships and soldiers are?" Roland asked as he drew the power of the scepter into him.

Delia shot out a bolt of fire, and Roland raised the scepter and blocked it; showers of sparks burst through the air. Orelia growled and rose straight in the air to get the higher ground.

A loud boom caught Roland's attention, and he turned toward the city and saw some of Solshi's own wizards clashing with the ones Delia had brought. Turning back to Delia, who was now directly below him, he directed Orelia down hard and fast. They landed on the back of Abylar, sending the blue dragon into a somersault.

Delia hung on with both hands. "Kill them, you stupid dragon!" she cursed Abylar. "Spit fire on them, or whatever you do!"

But nothing came out. So Delia brought up both hands in the air and fired ten shots of fire in a row at Roland. Swinging the scepter from side to side, he hit away every bolt of lightning in quick succession.

Unify them!

Not now! Roland couldn't believe the one-track mind of his scepter. Delia was his enemy. His dragon swerved, and he dodged another blast of fire.

Without warning, Abylar dropped and went down underneath them.

Follow him! Roland commanded and Orelia obeyed. *But don't kill him.* He didn't want to destroy the dragons. He needed to unify them.

"Where are the other two dragons, Delia?" Roland called after her, as she continued to drop. "Already left your mighty empire?"

Roland raced toward Abylar, getting ready to attack if needed. What trick was Delia pulling? Delia screamed, and Abylar leveled out a bit, but not before crashing into the ground, taking a few small trees with him as his gigantic bulk rolled over. Delia went flying through the air.

Orelia took Roland closer to the ground, and he jumped off. Using his powers he floated down to a brown field, golden cloak flying out at his side, and golden scepter held firmly in his hand. He was about fifty feet from Delia when she finished rolling on the ground and came back up in a fighting posture.

She squinted her eyes at Roland and laughed. "What are those dragon manacles you have there, Roland?"

"Manacles?" Roland glanced down at his wrist. He had forgotten the thick golden bracelets Andre had gifted him. He skidded to a stop twenty feet in front of Delia. Something didn't feel right.

Delia reached into a pouch at her side and brought out a small dragon artifact. Roland could see it was a band of sorts itself, of similar size to Roland's own—but black as night. Delia slid it on her wrist and with a flick of her hand sent a jolting pain into Roland.

He threw his head back and roared.

"I've spent my entire life studying the dragon artifacts, Roland." Delia stopped and smiled. Her dragon lay on its side, panting. "Those golden bands capture people like Alli for me."

"What did you do to her?" Roland yelled out.

"I made her my slave," Delia said, a sneer on her face. "Just like I will do to the mighty Roland Tyre. Bow to me, mighty wizard!"

Another jolt of pain brought Roland to his knees. He bellowed. He tried to claw the bands off his wrists, but every time he tried Delia shot more pain into him.

Orelia came and landed between Roland and Delia.

What are you doing? he asked his dragon.

The bag of artifacts, his dragon spoke to him. *Use them.*

Roland stumbled to his feet, opened his saddlebag, and pulled out a handful of artifacts. He hardly knew what they did, but now was as good a time as ever to find out.

He pulled out a small jade dragon head and grasped it in

his fingers and poured his power into it. Suddenly his dragon shrunk down to no more than the size of a horse.

Delia laughed and tapped her wrist again. Once more Roland fell writhing to the ground. He concentrated as hard as he could, and Orelia grew back to full size—with a roar that shook the ground.

Alli had always warned him about using unknown artifacts. He crawled back behind his dragon. He didn't dare use another artifact without knowing what it was. As his dragon roared at Delia, Roland tried to take the manacles off, but he couldn't seem to find the release on them. He caught a glance of something shiny in his pack and dug it out. It was the silver canister, the twin to the one he had given Tabitha. He opened it up and smiled.

She hadn't turned on him. Inside sat an artifact. But once again he didn't know what to do with it. But he knew how to find out. It was dangerous at the moment, but he didn't have any choice.

Keep her busy, Orelia, Roland directed his dragon. *I need a few moments.*

Ignoring the pain, he pulled upon the power of the scepter, closed his eyes and entered into the magic stream. He had to move quickly as he didn't know how long his body could withstand more attacks from Delia. He was used to how the magic stream worked now, and even though it was gray and directionless, he thought about Tabitha, and a small spark came within his reach. He put out his arms—which he realized didn't have the manacles on them in the magic stream.

He grabbed ahold of Tabitha's light and was pulled into

another place. He surmised he was in the castle in Turg. A woman sat in a chair in a small room, back facing him. Her hands cradled her face, and she was crying.

"Tabitha?" he whispered.

She jumped and turned around. "Roland . . . I mean High Wizard . . . Sire . . ."

Roland smiled. "It's fine, Tabitha. Are you all right? Why are you crying?"

"I let you down," Tabitha sobbed. "She didn't trust me, and when I tried to coax her toward the Citadel, she hid her real plans from me. I didn't know until just after she left that she met to attack Solshi."

"And the ships?" Roland asked. "Are they here yet?"

Roland heard a loud boom outside and raced to a small window. He got his answer. "Find General Ferdinand," Roland directed. "He should be here with the ships. He will keep you safe."

Tabitha nodded. "But what are you doing here?"

Roland felt weak; he was finding it hard to stand straight. Delia must have done something to him again.

"The canister, what did you put in the canister?" Roland asked.

Tabitha perked up at that and rubbed the tears from her eyes. "I took it from her room after she left. It's what they used to capture Alli and other magic users for the games. When the other person uses their magic you flip the chain out at them. It will wrap around their magic and bring them to their knees. If you can get close enough to Delia you can capture her."

"She's right in front of me." Roland smiled. This could be

fun. But before he could say more, he felt his body pulling his spirit back out of the stream. He wished he had more time to see what else was happening at Turg, but he didn't.

The room and Tabitha began to collapse on themselves and back to a pinprick of light. But before they were totally gone Roland heard Tabitha call out.

"You must put the other band on your own wrist first!" she said in a voice that Roland barely heard.

For a brief moment he was in the grayness of the magic stream again and then, without warning, thrown back to reality. He was on the ground, shuddering with pain. The box lay next to him, and he pried it open and grabbed the chain. From around the side of Orelia, he heard Delia coming closer.

"Your dragon can't stop me, Roland," she said in a loud but calm voice. "You will be mine."

Roland jumped up and moved around his dragon. Pain began to rack his body, and in desperation he flicked out the chain. It pulled Delia's magic to it but then conducted it into Roland's arm and into his body.

Falling to the ground, he blacked out for a moment. His body felt like it was on fire. His scepter lay on the ground next to him, and even his dragon stumbled and appeared weakened.

What's wrong? he moaned inside his head.

I am only as strong as you are, wizard.

Roland scrambled back and peered inside the box again. Tabitha had said something about another band.

Delia laughed. "Are you looking for this?" She held up another black manacle. "You didn't think I trusted that spy of yours, did you? I knew about her all along, High Wizard. I used her to get you exactly where I wanted you. You are pathetic. You think you can beat me? I am the Oracle of Turg! I am the Dragon Queen!" She screamed into the wind and once more sent fire into Roland. It was almost more than he could handle—almost.

Roland growled. This wasn't how it was going to end. He had to unify everyone and save them. That was his destiny. She might have the dragon artifacts, but he had something, too.

She blasted him again, both through the manacle and physically with a ball of fire. He swatted the fire away as a gnat and, grabbing his scepter, slowly stood back up. With each painful step, he walked closer and closer to Delia. For the first time, fear spread across her face as she saw the power radiating from him.

"I am the King of Alaris," he began, "the Regent of North and South Solshi, the Protector of Quentis . . ." With each step his strength and power grew. "I am the Monarch of Tillimot, the Warlord of Elvyn, and right about now the Conqueror of Turg and Cyrene." This he said with a smile on his face.

Delia's face fell and she took a step back and looked toward her dragon. "Get up, you stupid beast. Get me out of here." She turned back to Roland and sent another bout of pain into his wrist.

Roland bent over and roared in anguish, but then stood back up and continued walking. Twenty feet, ten feet, five feet. And Delia backed up as far as she could before she hit the great blue dragon.

"I am the High Wizard of the Citadel." The titles continued to roll from Roland's tongue. "I am the rider of the golden dragon. I am the holder of the Scepter of Unification." He raised the golden scepter high in the air and brought one end down hard on the ground between him and Delia. He stood and raised his head high, golden cloak billowing around his sore and tired body and roared out into the air. "I. Am. Magic!"

As the scepter hit the ground, a large crack opened in the earth below Delia's feet. Abylar stirred as the crack widened, traveling in his direction.

"Move, Abylar," Roland yelled at the weak dragon, but he stayed still.

As the fissure opened in the ground, Delia floundered to get away. She tried to use her powers against Roland, but they were nothing to him now. Her face darkened into anger, then worry, then fear as she tried to run away. But the crack in the ground followed her, opened wide and finally devoured her whole.

"I am the Dragon Queen!" Her last words echoed down into the deepening fissure as she fell.

"Not anymore, you aren't," Roland whispered and collapsed onto the ground barely able to stay conscious with the amount of power he had held.

But the fissure next to him continued to grow, and now Abylar was indeed in trouble. Roland tried to stand up but was too weak.

"Orelia, help me," Roland croaked out loud.

Before his dragon could do anything, a hefty dark red shape flew down over them. Liam's dragon, Ryker, ran into Abylar from the side, his rider, King Abbas falling off onto the ground.

"What are you doing?" Roland called out to the dragon.

The giant red dragon roared and pushed at Abylar again, this time rolling him over and away from the fissure. The ground shook with the movement, and King Abbas lost his footing and fell, barely avoiding the fissure himself.

Ryker took a giant step and brought his long neck down low and stared into Roland's eyes.

Thank you, mighty wizard. Delia's power of the bond is broken. Ryker's voice was deep and tired.

The ground stopped shaking, and Roland went up on his knees, grabbing the scepter with both hands to pull himself up. *I will need your help, all of you, to defeat the eastern war ships.*

A long sigh followed. *We are tired, High Wizard, but we owe you a debt. We will be there when you need us.*

How will I call you? Roland asked, but then remembered the artifact that sat on his mantle in the Citadel and knew what he would have to do.

The dragon's tail swished around and knocked King Abbas to the ground.

"Please don't let him kill me," the king pleaded with Roland.

"Tell me why you deserve my mercy?" Roland asked.

"I was deceived," King Abbas said. "My people need me. My son is still too young to rule in my place."

Roland thought for a moment. Delia had indeed deceived many people. "You will remain as a prisoner until this is all taken care of. In the meantime, know that your kingdom now has been conquered by my men."

The king's face paled as he stared up at Roland.

Roland glanced back at the city of Raleez. Crowds stood on the walls and cheered. Delia's wizards stood out in front of them, bound and gagged. Lying on the ground at the foot of the wall was the dead body of Korax Arvanitis.

"Hail, Roland Tyre!" the people called out. "Hail the Golden Wizard!"

Roland smiled. He motioned for a group of guards to come and take King Abbas away. Then he jumped on the back of his own dragon. He wondered briefly why all the other dragons still seemed weak, while his didn't, but didn't linger on the thought too long. It was probably because he, himself, was so powerful.

Now to take care of those eastern warships, Roland thought as he soared out over the bay of Raleez and then turned around and headed back east. King Luz waved up at him with a smile and Roland returned the gesture. He would have liked to help in the aftermath of the attack, but other duties called him east. He needed to check on the progress in Elvyn.

CHAPTER TWENTY-THREE

Alli stood next to Nuri in a dimly lit room of a rarely used older house. It sat on the back of the castle property in Jor. She sneezed at all the dust in the room. It had been a well-kept home at one point, with quality furniture, glass windows, and crown molding. Now the floor slanted slightly, the drapes on the windows were faded, and the furniture's coverings had holes in them. Nuri had used it in the past as a place to get away from the bustle of the castle and to have some time by himself.

"I used to come here with my brother," Nuri said to Alli.

"Ender?" Alli asked, knowing the answer. *The real Prince Ender, not the pretend Rajamani Kandori.*

Nuri nodded, and they both turned their attention back to those who were slowly gathering into the room.

After leaving the cave, the two had snuck back into the city. There were not many people out, and those they had seen were only scurrying to whatever place they had to be. Cherif held the city along with about twenty of his own men, who had come on the ship with him. Nuri was resourceful in getting around the city unnoticed. Alli surmised that the quiet prince must have done his fair share of escaping crowds in the past.

In the last two days they had found out that somehow Counselor Ezra Karaka had survived the poisoning, along with a handful of nobles—some of which had been together in the back of the room talking. Before they had returned to the tables to touch their desserts the others had begun to get sick. In the chaos, Ezra had snuck away through castle passageways Cherif didn't know about.

Now, the counselor, along with three other wizards, two nobles, and two city leaders, had gathered with Alli and Nuri to discuss how to get their city back.

Before the meeting started, Ezra stood in front of Nuri and spoke solemnly. "Nuri Asher, as the last remaining member of the royal household, you are now king by right and would normally assume full entitlements of that position on your sixteen birthday. However, these dangerous times necessitate pushing up that schedule. There is a provision in our law for times just as these." He knelt in front of Nuri.

Nuri glanced over at Alli and the others and then looked back down at the counselor.

"As the last remaining member of the royal court," Ezra began, "I, Wizard Ezra Karaka, do recognize you, Nuri Asher, as full king of Khazer, with all rights, privileges, and honors. I pledge my loyalty to you and do so in the presence of those gathered with me as witnesses according to our law."

With a grieving seriousness Alli hadn't truly seen in Nuri before, he brought his hand out and touched the top of Ezra's head. "I accept this responsibility and promise to protect our people to the best of my ability. Arise."

Ezra arose and took a step back. Nuri's eyes gazed at the others, and Alli swore that she saw a mantle of authority settle upon his young shoulders. He stood taller, and his eyes flashed brighter for a moment.

"Do you all so agree to this action?" he asked the others.

"Aye," they all said. Then they all knelt on the dusty floor and bowed their heads.

Nuri touched each on the head, in what, Alli assumed, was a type of ceremonial gesture. After doing so, they all arose and waited for their new king to direct the meeting.

"What is the situation, Counselor?" Nuri asked.

Before answering, Ezra glanced over at Alli. His gray hair hung to his thin shoulders, identifying his age, but his blue eyes were piercing and held Alli in his gaze.

"Sire," Ezra turned back to Nuri. "Begging your pardon, but may I ask the dragon rider where her loyalties lie in this? These are troubling times, and she has not bowed to you."

Alli clenched her fist and took a step forward. She bowed to no one . . . well, except her master. A master that, Alli realized, hadn't called out to her in a while. Thinking of Delia brought her thoughts back to her dragon. Miriel had stayed behind in the cave when they left, citing a need to rest. But the bond burned brighter than ever before—at least as far back as she could remember, which still wasn't very far.

"Dragon Rider Allison saved my life," Nuri said as he looked in her direction. "I trust her."

Alli raised her brows. She wasn't sure she even trusted herself.

"And whom do you serve?" Ezra asked Alli.

That was a great question. Whom did she serve? Who was her master now? It was all so confusing. She put a hand to her head to think better, but her memories were still all a jumbled mess.

"Are you all right?" Nuri asked, taking a step toward her.

Alli took her hand down from her head and nodded. "Just trying to remember." Turning to the counselor, she decided to be honest with him. "Counselor, you know me as the Battlemaster of the Citadel and a dragon rider, but I barely remember those things. Something has been done to me in Thera. My mast . . ." she broke off her sentence and changed what she had been about to say. "Delia has used me, and I'm not sure when she will try to do so again. I helped Nuri escape because I wanted to do the right thing, and I will see that through. I will see the usurpers gone and Nuri on the throne of Khazer, but beyond that, I can give no promises."

Ezra regarded her for a few more moments and then nodded. "Seems as if you are being honest with us, Dragon Rider. So I will take your words at face value."

Alli nodded her thanks.

Turning his attention back to Nuri, Ezra spoke, "Sire, Cherif holds the castle, but not much else. The people are afraid, but the undercurrent in the city is hopeful. They put their hope in you."

Nuri took a deep breath and let it out in a long sigh. "What can we do?" He took all of those in the room into his gaze. "Give me some ideas."

"We could destroy his ship," said one of the city leaders.

"But that wouldn't get him out of the castle," said another.

"But it would keep him from escaping, once we did get him out," said the first.

"Does he have wizards with him?" Alli asked.

Counselor Ezra nodded. "At least three, maybe more of his men are wizards–of what strength, I do not know."

"And Cherif can speak to others' minds," said one of the wizards.

Alli nodded. "Yes, I heard him. He is powerful. So he must be the center of our plans. The other wizards are not worth worrying about."

"But—" started one of the nobles.

Alli cut him off with a growl. "I can take care of them."

Many in the room raised their eyebrows at her bravado, but Nuri stepped into the conversation and steered any arguments away from her.

"Alli is right. Cherif and his son are the key. Do we know where Raj went?"

Alli shook her head.

"We need to find a way to lure Cherif out of the castle," said one of the wizards. Alli assumed he was a battle wizard by the weapons he carried. "If we can do that, the guards and wizards can retake the castle."

"I agree," Nuri said. "But how do we get him out of the castle and keep him out of our heads at the same time?"

Without any warning, Alli cried out and clutched her head. Bright lights exploded behind her eyes, and she fell to the ground. *What's happening to me?* She couldn't think or breathe. The room was spinning around her, and she felt like she was going to vomit from the pain. Torturous stabbings dug deep into her head, and she wrapped her arms around it to try and keep them out. Voices filled her mind all at once. She heard

Roland, Gabby, Delia, and the dragons. It was going to burst her ear drums.

I am the Dragon Queen! Delia's voice boomed and echoed through Alli's head. The statement was full of terror and alarm, and then ended.

As soon as Delia's voice stopped, the pain in Alli's mind ended. And in its placed rushed the most joyful feeling she had ever had. Gladness, delight, pleasure filled her soul to bursting.

Alli, came the soft but real voice of Miriel.

The bond! It's back! Alli yelled out loud.. "Oh Miriel!"

Miriel's presence filled Alli's mind and soul. She was whole again.

She found herself in a gray nothingness. She hadn't been there before, but she had heard about it—the magic stream.

Alli took a deep breath, and a flood of memories poured back inside her. Training at the Citadel, her mentor, the Dragon King, flying on Miriel, Roland—*Oh, Roland, I'm so sorry!*

She took a deep breath and let out a sob. She couldn't handle it all at once. She tried to push them back. Too many memories; a lifetime, jumbled up in no particular order. Using the power to run fast when she was younger, growing up in the eastern forest of Alaris, being captured by Constantine. She couldn't bear that one and tried to push it away.

"Alli! Alli!" Nuri called out from far away. "What's happening?"

Alli tried to call out to him, but couldn't. She used all her might to push the memories back to a safe place. Opening her eyes, she looked around her in the grayness and noticed dots of light. A bright one was close by, and she reached to touch it.

In an instant, she was transported to a different place. She now stood in the corner of a room, but no one seemed to notice her. In front of her sat Cherif, in a chair behind a table. A map was spread out in front of him, and others were there looking at it. Alli walked over carefully and peered down to see what they saw. It was a crude map of the Western Continent.

Cherif pointed to a spot out in the sea. "Four or five days—a week at the most—and they will be here. We must bring enlightenment to this people and help them see the way."

"What about your son? Where is he?" a man asked.

"He will be back with a prize that will ensure our triumph. We will give the empire the way to victory. The empress will Reward me—all of us—and let us rule here."

One of the men turned around just then and stared directly at where Alli stood. "Someone is here, my lord, a spirit."

The other men turned and scanned the room. Alli stood very still. She wasn't sure how the magic stream worked, but she knew she couldn't afford to get caught. The information she had learned needed to get to Roland and Bakari.

"A spirit walks with us here," said the same man as before. "I can feel her. A stranger."

"It's a sign, my Lord," said one of the other men. "We shouldn't have come early. The empress will be angry with us."

"Nonsense," said Cherif. "If we would have waited for the warships to conquer, who do you think would have ruled the land? Them, that's who—the generals. We would have come later and been relegated to our normal trade compensation. No, this is our chance. I'll not have you messing it up with talks of spirits and such."

The others murmured their agreement to Cherif's warning and then turned back to the map.

"My son will return with a great power of the spirit, and we will greet the empress and give her our gift. The dragon will ensure he returns in time."

"What if he doesn't?" asked another man.

"Silence, doubters," said Cherif. He turned and looked each of them in the eye. Their bodies relaxed, and they nodded and smiled.

"Now go and prepare for the funeral tonight." Cherif waved his hand, dismissing those in the room. "We want the people to see we are benevolent rulers." He bowed his head as if in sorrow. "It's hard to imagine that the dragon rider killed their king and his family."

"What?" words burst from Alli's mouth.

This time, Cherif did lift his head and look in her direction. She shuffled backward to the corner of the room and hoped he really couldn't tell if she was there or not.

She considered the others standing there, all nodding at what Cherif had just told them.

He just did something to their minds, Alli thought. She had to be careful. The only one that didn't seem affected was the man who had sensed her. He still peered around the room with a frown on his face.

Alli thought back to the magic stream and was soon back in the grayness. She saw other lights around and touched a few of them briefly. Other wizards in the castle, a few throughout the city, but nothing of importance. She remembered how

Bakari and Roland had traveled in the magic stream and thought about going to them herself, but a voice called to her.

"Dragon Rider!" It was one of the wizards in the room with Nuri. She felt the magic stream begin to dissipate around her and finally disappear altogether. She blinked her eyes a few times and saw the wizard bending over her in concentration, his hand on her head.

"Alli, are you all right?" Nuri leaned down, his eyes filled with worry.

Alli tried to remember what had happened in the magic stream. But it was hard to concentrate. She remembered the conversation, but not much before that. She recalled having memories of the past flash through her mind. But now she couldn't quite grasp them. Only fragments remained—as if waking from a dream.

"My dragon!" she suddenly remembered and sat up quickly. Her head swam for a moment, but then she recovered enough to talk. "My dragon bond is back, Delia is dead, and we may have a much bigger problem than Cherif."

All in the room stared down at her with confusion.

"Cherif and his men are only a vanguard of what seems to be an attack by the eastern kingdoms upon our continent." Alli broke the news to the stunned group.

Before anyone else could start talking, Alli pushed forward with a plan. "There is a funeral tonight, and I have an idea." Alli stood and folded her arms across her chest.

CHAPTER TWENTY-FOUR

Gabby couldn't remember long they had been on the island. Had it been hours? Days? Weeks? But did it really matter? The people here were so kind, the food delicious, and the scenery gorgeous.

"Gabrielle," Garrik's cousin, Calen, said to her, "are you enjoying your meal?"

"Very much so," Gabby said. "Thank you." She bit into another juicy bit of roasted pineapple. It was the most delicious thing she had tasted in a long time.

Calen had been very helpful in showing them around the small village—about thirty huts and fifty or so people interspersed through tall palm trees. The houses were made of mud and bark, the roofs from palm fronds and large leaves. A few children ran laughing by Gabby now, and she smiled at their joy.

It seemed so long ago that she had been a child and running carefree. Of course, growing up in the household of the heir to the throne made for a more formal upbringing. Two of the children came back and grabbed her hands and lifted her up from her seat. Gabby turned and looked at Garrik. He shrugged his shoulders and waved her along.

The two children, five or six years younger than she, wound their way, laughing all the while, through the jungle until stopping at a pool of water. Gabby took in a quick breath. It was breathtaking. The deep aqua-colored water sparkled with the setting sun. A small stream ran both into and out of the pool. Stepping closer and looking upstream she noticed a small waterfall about a hundred feet away. The children beckoned her there.

Gabby thought she had something else she should be doing and tried to remember what it was. A nagging thought that she was trying to find something haunted the back of her mind.

"Come on, Gabrielle," the girl called out. "Come and see the gemstones!"

Gabby couldn't help but laugh at their excitement. Whatever she needed to be doing could wait. As she followed them, a sweet fragrance drifted up to her from the side of the path. Large, palm-sized pink, white, and yellow flowers seemed to follow the children's course.

Coming closer to the falls, Gabby giggled at the rainbow that fronted them.

"Look," the young boy drew Gabby's attention from the rainbow to the pool that sat below them. Gabby opened her eyes wider at the color spots shining through the clear water.

"What are they?"

"Gemstones," the girl said.

"Cylindra, they're not just gemstones," said the boy. "They're stones of power."

"Stones of power?" Gabby asked. She hadn't ever heard of stones having power. "What do they do?"

The boy opened his mouth, but Cylindra jumped in.

"Danlon, you know we are not supposed to speak about them," Cylindra said. She glanced around nervously. "We shouldn't have even brought her here."

"but we never get visitors," pleaded Danlon.

Gabby knelt down to be more at their height. "I won't tell anyone," she said. "I've studied magic my whole life. Have you heard about dragon artifacts?"

They both shook their heads.

"What if you tell me about the stones, and I'll tell you about the dragon artifacts?"

Danlon's eyes lit up. He turned a pleading looking to Cylindra, whose frown turned to a smile, and she sat down between Gabby and the pool.

Gabby looked back at the pool and closed her eyes for a moment. She drew upon her wizarding powers and tried to see if she could feel anything. At first there was nothing, but then. . .

"I can feel them," Gabby said with excitement. A different kind of power seemed to call out to her.

"What are you doing?" Cylindra asked, breaking Gabby's concentration.

"I feel something," Gabby said. "What do they do?"

"No, you mustn't do that," Cylindra said. "The Keepers will be angry at us."

"Keepers?" Gabby asked.

"They are the only ones to touch the stones," Danlon said. "A long time ago, elves were sent here to watch over the stones to make sure that no one takes them. They are called Keepers."

"But they never use the magic?" Gabby asked. "I can feel something strong in the stones."

Cylindra and Danlon looked at each other, and their eyes went wide. A few moments of quiet followed.

Cylindra stood up and brushed her long, red hair behind her pointed ears. "We should be going."

Danlon followed her suggestion, and they started walking back down the river. Gabby followed but was perplexed by their reaction. Through a small break in the trees, she stopped and stared up at a large stone cliff off in the center of the island. When she didn't follow, the two children turned around and beckoned her on.

"Gabrielle, we must get back." Cylindra's face grew worried. "We shouldn't have brought you here."

Danlon took a few steps back in Gabby's direction. His thin face and long red hair appeared almost identical to Cylindra's, but he stood an inch or two shorter.

"What is up there?" Gabby pointed to the cliff rising up above the tree line. She could feel something drawing her there but didn't know why. She realized she was feeling light-headed, and she leaned a hand against a rough palm tree for support. Something wasn't right here.

"Nothing for you to worry about, Gabrielle," Danlon said more forcefully than he had sounded before.

"But . . ." Something tugged at the back of Gabby's mind. Something important. "Why am I here?" she said more to herself than the others.

Danlon grabbed her hand and pulled her along. "You're here because the island wants you here," he said. "Don't you like it here?"

Gabby looked around and took a deep breath. Holding onto Danlon's hand made her forget what all the urgency about the cliff was about. She could always look into it later. "Of course I love it here. It's the most beautiful place in the world."

Cylindra let out a sigh of relief at Gabby's words, and Gabby smiled at the girl. Soon they were skipping back through the jungle and found themselves back in the small village.

An older man came up to them with an angry face. His hair was a mix of gray and red and hung halfway down his back. His face was wrinkled and thin, his cheeks and mouth sunken in. A loose, colorful robe hung over his thin body.

"Where have you two been with our guest?" he said.

Cylindra looked down, and Danlon followed her lead.

"Well?"

"They took me to the waterfalls, sir," Gabby said.

"Keeper, we are sorry," Cylindra said, her slanted eyes filling with water. "We didn't mean any harm. We were just trying to be friendly. If they are going to be with us now, we wanted to be friends. We didn't know she could feel them."

"Feel them?" the keeper said. "Feel what?"

"The stones," Danlon said.

The keeper turned his attention back to Gabby. Wonder, fear, and distrust filled his eyes.

He opened his mouth to speak, but before he could, a loud roar sounded overhead. The man grabbed both Danlon and Cylindra's hands and pulled them toward a hut, while beckoning Gabby. Others who were outside ran inside other shelters.

"A dragon!" Gabby said, and a memory of what had brought her there surfaced. "I'm here to save the Dragon King."

"Shush, child," the keeper said.

The four of them, with three other villagers, stood huddled together in the hut.

"Close your minds," the keeper ordered, as he himself closed his eyes. "The stones will protect us."

The others followed his orders.

Gabby glanced around and wondered what was going on. She took a few timid steps toward a small window, pulled back its thin cloth covering an inch or so and peeked outside.

There was no one left in the village commons. Within moments they had all run indoors. She wondered where Garrik had gone. Then movement up in the sky drew her attention. Flying in circles above them was Cholena, Jaimon's large green dragon. Gabby could see the spikes coming out of the top of her head and streaming backwards. The dragon's generous body was filled with thick scales, and spikes pointing upward jutted up from her backside. Her long tail swished through the air as her wings flapped slowly. Cholena dropped lower, and Gabby thought her flying appeared more labored than it should.

With an otherworldly shriek, the dragon spit out a long stream of fire and dropped hundreds of feet. Now barely over the trees, she wailed again and bucked off the man riding her.

The man fell through a tree and landed on a grouping of large plants.

Without thinking, Gabby ran and opened the door.

"Get back inside!" the keeper shouted.

Gabby paid no attention. She had to find out what Prince Ender—or whoever he was, was doing here. That dragon belonged to Jaimon and had been stolen by Delia. The dragon herself skimmed over the bushes, barely getting back into the air and soared off toward the middle of the island, wings tipping dangerously from side to side.

Gabby reached the man's side, as Garrik and a few others joined her.

"Get back," the keeper said. "He's dangerous."

"How do you know?" Gabby said.

"Because anyone who comes uninvited to the island is dangerous," he said.

Gabby let it go, wondering what that meant about her and Garrik.

Gabby walked up, with the keeper at her side. The keeper kicked Ender in the side with his foot, and he stirred, slowly opening his dark brown eyes. His skin was dark, not as dark as Bakari's, but now that she paid attention, his features appeared different from anything she had seen in her life—though admittedly she hadn't been everywhere in the western continent.

With great speed, the man snaked his hand out and grabbed the keeper's ankle and pulled him to the ground. Gabby reflexively jumped toward him, bringing a knife out from her side, she quickly had it at the man's throat. She blinked a moment in surprise at her own actions.

"What are you doing here?" Gabby asked. "Where is Delia?"

The man turned his head and spat. "Delia is dead."

Gabby jerked in surprise.

The man moved to sit up, and Gabby moved her knife closer to his throat. Garrik and a few others encircled him. He made to move and apparently tried to draw on a spell of power. He raised his hands in the air, but nothing happened.

"Your magic is no good here," the keeper said. "This island is protected."

Gabby still felt a faint echo of residual power from the stones she had seen in the pool. She wondered if she could harness their powers. Could anyone else feel them?

"Who are you?" the keeper asked. "I will know if you lie or not."

The man, five years or so older than Gabby, nodded. "I am Rajamani Kandori, son of Cherif, the mightiest trader in the eastern kingdoms."

The reminder of the warships Roland had seen jogged through Gabby's mind once again. *Why is it so hard to think around here?*

"What do you mean, Delia is dead?" Gabby asked him. "And I thought you were Prince Ender."

"I heard it in my mind," Rajamani said. "Delia screamed and fell to her death, and I lost the bond with my dragon—the one she gave me. That's why the dragon threw me off of her."

The dragons? "That's why I'm here," Gabby said out loud.

"What are you mumbling about, Gabby?" Garrik asked.

"That's why we are here, Garrik. I remember why we are here."

"Remember what?" Garrik said. "I thought we were staying here. It seems like a nice place."

The keeper gave a grave look to Gabby and then sighed. "This island is protected. Those who come here cannot use their normal wizard powers, and their memories are altered. In time they cannot remember not being here."

"That's not right," Gabby frowned.

The keeper spread his arms out to his side. "Is it so bad to live in paradise?"

"It is when I need to help save the Dragon King and stop eastern warships from destroying our continent."

Rajamani frowned. "How did you know?"

Gabby didn't have time for this. She didn't know how much time had already been wasted in lying around enjoying paradise. "We do have powerful wizards here, too, Rajamani."

Rajamani's eyes opened wider, then he recovered himself and scowled. "You will bow before our might. My empress will destroy you all!" He pulled on the men that were holding him, but to no avail.

Gabby turned to the keeper. "We are here to find a phoenix. Where are they?"

The village crowd, which had grown to full size during this exchange, sucked in a collective breath.

"You don't find a phoenix," the keeper said. "It finds you!"

"So I have been told," Gabby said. She grabbed Garrik's hand and began to pull him away from the group. "Let's go get found."

"Where are we going?" Garrik asked.

"To the cliffs," Gabby said as she pointed with her other hand toward the middle of the island.

"But I liked it here," Garrik grumbled.

"So did I. So did I."

CHAPTER TWENTY-FIVE

Gabby and Garrik made their way through the jungle foliage alongside Calen, Garrik's long-lost cousin. Sometimes they used a path; at other times they had to hack their way through with the help of Calen's long, curved knife.

"Is it always warm here?" Gabby asked.

"Yes," Calen said. "It rains a bit at night, and it is clear and sunny during the day. Fruit grows on the trees year round, and small game is plentiful. It's a very giving land."

"And you never thought of coming back?" Garrik asked.

Calen shook his head as he whacked off a low-growing palm frond and cleared a space for them to continue walking. "It's paradise. Would you?"

Garrik grunted and pushed forward through the trees.

"There is a magic here that keeps them here," Gabby said. "We don't even know how long we've been here."

Garrik grunted again. "I knew I should have stayed on the shore."

They had been walking for half a day now, and Gabby thought she would be tired. But instead she felt invigorated. Although she couldn't use her own wizard powers, there was another power that permeated the island. She could feel it humming in and around her. It was powerful and comforting.

At a small clearing, Calen motioned for them to stop, and he removed a sack from his shoulder and brought out some food. Mangos, pineapple, bread, and some kind of roasted meat. After a few large bites, Garrik wiped some juice from his chin and sat back on a small patch of grass.

"Calen is right," Garrik said. "Why would anyone want to leave this place? I've lived my whole life caught between the desert and forest elves. But here . . ." His eyes wandered around the small clearing. A colorful bird flew down from one of the vine-covered trees and landed mere feet from him.

Garrik reached out a piece of bread, and the bird came tentatively toward him. With a quick peck, it picked up the bread from Garrik's hand and flew off.

"See what I mean?" he said with a sigh and lay all the way back with his hands behind his head.

Calen copied him, and they both lay in silence for a few minutes. Gabby began to agree with them and ran her hand over the soft grass as she took the last few bits of her food and tossed it out for another patient bird that had hopped toward them.

Gabrielle Von Wulf, wizard of Alaris, spoke a voice deep in the back of her mind. It was Guardian Calanon Staizmull, keeper of the forest elves.

Calanon must be powerful indeed to reach her across such a distance. *Yes, sir?*

Do not get lulled by the island's magic.

Gabby sat up straighter. What had she been doing? She looked over at Garrik and Calen, both resting peacefully on the grass, their eyelids barely open. She had almost fallen into the same trap.

Thank you, Guardian Calanon, Gabby said.

She thought she heard a deep chuckle. *Young wizard, you are stronger than you think. I can feel power in you. Have you found what you seek?*

No, she said in her mind.

A phoenix finds you, Calanon reminded her. *Don't look with your eyes. Look with the power you have inside you. Then it will find you.*

But I can't use my power here.

There are more powers in the world than those of the four wizard disciplines, wizard of Quentis. Look at the island. Look deep inside yourself.

Gabby sighed. He sounded like one of her teachers at the Wizard Sanctuary. Her mind wandered there for a moment, and she almost wished she was back in school. Life would be so much simpler. All the dragon riders she had set out with almost six weeks ago had left her side, and it was just her now, a newly trained young wizard, trying to save the Dragon King.

Go, child, came Calanon's voice again, this time more urgent. *Go quickly. The time of reckoning is coming soon. She is coming.*

Who's coming? Gabby left her own musings behind and concentrated once again on the task at hand.

The empress. She will stop at nothing. Go, now!

She jumped. Her bones shook with those last words.

"Garrik, Calen, get up," she ordered.

The two forest elves jolted awake and jerked to their feet.

"What?" Garrik asked, wide eyes darting around the clearing.

"This island has magic to lull us to security. It keeps people from leaving and talking about what's here," Gabby said. "But you must resist it. Both of you."

Calen's slanted eyes opened wider.

"Garrik, how long has Calen been gone from the forest?" Gabby asked.

Garrik thought a moment before responding. "Maybe fifteen or twenty years."

Calen's mouth dropped. "It can't be!"

"Calen, you have children here now," Garrik pointed out to try and make his point. "How old are they? Nine or ten?"

Calen nodded slowly.

Gabby pulled them both with her. "To protect the stones of power and the power of the phoenix, the island keeps you here, just like it has already tried to keep Garrik and I, but we can't do that. I need to find a phoenix. I need to save the Dragon King."

The empress is coming, Calanon's voice echoed in her mind. Gabby didn't understand all of what that meant, but there had always been rumors of the eastern kingdoms attacking them someday. The histories said the people in this land had escaped the wizard wars over 400 years ago; maybe the elves had come even before that. That was a long time for the eastern kingdoms to hold a grudge. But as Calanon had said, the day of reckoning was approaching.

"Lead the way to the cliffs, Calen." Gabby pointed forward.

Only a short distance farther, she could see a mountain with sheer cliffs sticking up in the middle of the island. "That is where we will be found."

Calen walked forward. "Found?" he asked.

"Guardian Calanon told me the phoenix finds us," Gabby said.

"You spoke to the Guardian?" Mist formed over Calen's bright green eyes. "I had forgotten him. I hadn't realized it had been so long. Is he angry at me for being gone so long?"

"No," Gabby guessed. "He knows what this island is and what it does to you."

"He is well?" Calen asked.

"He is getting old," Gabby said, "and I'm afraid is weakening."

The three moved forward in silence after that, with only the sound of birds overhead and a few ground animals scampering out of their way as the three continued to hack through the vines—vines that seemed to grow thicker the closer they got.

Another hour of hacking through the jungle brought Gabby and her group to a clearing. Looking straight up from where she stood, she saw a sheer cliff hundreds of feet tall. A twenty-foot-wide waterfall cascaded down its face, plunging with roaring force into a large pool of water before snaking away in a stream that she assumed led to the ocean.

"Wow!" Garrik said. "I've never seen its like before."

Gabby nodded. Behind the cliffs rose higher mountain peaks. Despite the mild temperatures down below, a sparkling patch of snow still sat on the flat top of the mountain.

"I never knew . . ." Calen gasped.

"You mean you've never been here?" Gabby asked their guide.

"No," Calen said. "We've been content to stay where we were. Maybe the keeper has been here."

While speaking, Calen began walking closer to the pool of water at the waterfall's base. To get there they had to climb up and over large, rough, volcanic rocks. A few stray plants grew in the cracks of the rock, watered from the spray of the waterfall, but besides that nothing grew up against the edge of the mighty cliffs.

From there they climbed upwards on a windy and barely used animal trail for an hour or so before reaching a flat-rock area that was about half way between the top of the falls and the bottom of the pool. The three moved simultaneously to the edge of the cliff. Gabby first peered up at the top of the waterfall, hundreds of feet above them, and then down anther hundred feet to the pool.

As she did so, she felt a strange power well up inside of her.

"Gabby!" Garrik yelled out and grabbed her hand.

She opened her eyes, which she hadn't realized she had closed.

"What are you doing?" he asked. "You almost walked over the edge."

Gabby peered down and gulped. What had she been doing?

"I felt the power," she whispered. "Down there. Don't you feel it?"

Garrik and Calen looked down, following her gaze. Amidst the churning water were reflections of light—red, blue, orange, pink, and green.

"Stones of power," Calen whispered almost in reverence.

Garrik glanced back over at his cousin with a questioning look. It was hard to hear each other over the fall's roar. He motioned all three of them back away from the waterfall.

Gabby wiped the mist from her face as the rumble of the falls receded behind them. Back thirty paces or so, Calen turned to them and tried to explain.

"The keeper says the stones of power were brought to the island hundreds of years ago by our ancestors from the eastern kingdoms," Calen began. "They provide the life and light of this small island. Their powerful magic feeds the magical creatures of our continent and keeps things in balance. Each stone has its own magical powers, but no one in recollection has been able to use them or to take them away from here. They stay hidden and protected."

"But what does that mean that Gabby can feel them?" Garrik asked, looking from Calen to Gabby and back again.

Calen shook his head. "I am not the keeper, so I don't know."

Gabby paced around on the rocks while Calen and Garrik continued to stare in amazement at the mighty waterfall.

She was close; she knew it. She could feel power all around her. She tried to pinpoint where it was coming from. When she had been in the magic stream it had been so bright and powerful that even from Elvyn, and not being a dragon rider, she had sensed it.

"They're connected somehow to the power of the phoenix," Gabby said. "I can feel something here" she pointed to the stones on the pool, "but there is also a great power up there." She pointed up to the top of the cliff.

Garrik's eyes went wide. "You're not getting me up there."

"And you call yourself a forest elf?" Gabby laughed. "You should be used to heights. I've seen trees in Lor'l that are hundreds of feet tall."

"Not in the southern forest," Garrik mumbled. "And what makes you think there is a way up there? That cliff is straight up and unless you can fly. . ."

However, an idea came to Gabby, and she clapped her hands together with glee. "That's it! You're right, Garrik. We fly up there."

"So now you think you can sprout wings with that magic of yours?" Garrik gave her a look like she was crazy—well maybe she was.

Gabby laughed. "Don't be so cynical, Garrik. We can't grow wings."

"Well, at least you're making sense now," Garrik mumbled.

"But I know someone who can fly up there."

Calen appeared as confused as Garrik. "It's getting late, Gabby. We need to head back to the village before it gets dark."

"Neither of you get it," Gabby said, bouncing on her toes. "The dragon. Jaimon's dragon, Cholena. She can take us up there."

"No. No. No." Garrik continued shaking his head even after the words left his mouth. "I am most definitely not getting up on one of those things."

Gabby slapped him on the arm. "What happened to the brave elf we met in Mallek? The one who took on a group of renegade elves to save us and rowed at night to get us to safety?"

"The sea. The desert. Even the forest," Garrik said each sentence with more and more emphasis. "That's what I know. Water and Earth. Not the air. I'm not going, especially not up on one of those . . .those . . ." He folded his arms and planted his legs firmly, never finishing his sentence.

Gabby looked into his eyes for a moment and tried to figure Garrik out.

"Hey, get out of my head," Garrik hissed at her and backed up. "I thought your magic didn't work here."

Gabby's eyes went wide. "My wizard magic doesn't, but my family's *seeing* ability must still work." Gabby paused a moment to solidify the idea in her mind. Her father or brother hadn't shown any signs of wizard powers. In fact, in the history of their family she was the first in a long time. To have both the seeing and wizard abilities was rare.

"I'm still not going near one of those things."

Then Gabby got it and laughed.

"What's so funny?" Calen asked, perplexed at the entire conversation.

"Your cousin is afraid of lizards," Gabby said with an impish smile. "I *saw* it in him."

Calen snapped his head toward Garrick. "You mean you still . . ."

Garrik's face grew red. He opened his mouth and then shut it again.

Calen chuckled. "It's coming back to me. One day I was visiting Garrik's household, it must have been shortly before I left," Calen said. "He had a favorite pet lizard—a blue-tongued one. She had been acting strange, and one night Garrik fell asleep holding her in his hands, trying to comfort her. Sometime during the night the lizard burrowed down inside his pants. In the morning, Garrick found ten baby lizards crawling around in his night clothes." Calen couldn't continue without throwing his head back and laughing. "He jumped up and began running around screaming. We didn't know what was wrong at first. By the time he quieted down, lizards were lying all over the floor."

Gabby put her hands over her mouth and couldn't help laughing. Garrik's face turned even more red, matching the shade of his hair. "They didn't find them all. One had stayed there until I next went to the facilities."

Now Gabby and Calen were laughing so hard that Gabby thought she might never stop. But her ribs were hurting, and she had to. Soon Garrik joined in. Gabby hadn't laughed like that in a long time. It was a good release.

"But dragons?" she asked, trying not to start laughing again.

"They're just big lizards," Garrik said. "How would you like to find one of them in your pants?"

His ridiculous statement brought another round of laughter to the three of them. Finally, after everyone had settled down, Gabby tried to get serious.

"If we find Jaimon, we can find the dragon," Gabby said, directing the conversation back to where it needed to be. "I'm sure Cholena went to find him as soon as she dumped Rajamani."

"Last we saw of him, the dragon took him away," Garrik said.

"Yes," Gabby smiled, "but Rajamani was also there. He could tell us where Jaimon went."

"So, back to the village?" Calen sighed.

"Yes, I'm afraid so." Gabby shrugged her shoulders in apology.

"Well, the way is already cut, so it shouldn't take us as long," Calen said as he stepped out in front.

As Gabby turned to follow she thought she saw a bright orange-and-yellow light flash high up in the cliffs, but when she turned back and looked up, there wasn't anything there.

Are you up there, phoenix? The Dragon King needs your help— "If it isn't already too late," she whispered the last part out loud.

"What are you mumbling about back there, Gabby?" Garrik asked. "Hurry up before it gets dark."

"I just hope I'm not too late to save the Dragon King." Gabby picked up her pace and followed the two men. "We've been gone a long time. I don't know how long he will last."

They were silent for a few minutes, and Gabby snickered again, thinking about Garrik. He spun around and, sensing the point of her amusement, growled at her, turned around, and starting walking faster.

CHAPTER TWENTY-SIX

Alli stood behind a bush next to Nuri and Micha, a scholar wizard of some renown in Jor. She peered around the bush and watched the people filing into the castle's main entrance. The early winter darkness had provided appropriate cover for them, and no one saw them or paid any attention. Dressed in their darkest and finest clothes, nobles and other important city people streamed up the walkway to attend the state funeral for their king and queen.

Alli ground her teeth in frustration as she heard snippets of conversation blaming her for the killings. Nuri put a hand on her arm to keep her from jumping out and confronting the group. She was grateful for his calm presence—surprisingly calm, given the circumstances. Nuri had some strong mettle.

Miriel, are you ready? Alli asked her dragon. She would have liked to give her dragon more time to rest, but Miriel would be needed for Alli's plan to work.

I will be there when I'm needed, came the weak but positive reply.

The new king pointed his hand back toward the bushes, and the three of them retreated.

"Not all of them believe what they've been told, Alli," Nuri said.

Alli nodded, hoping he was right. Based on her recent siding with Delia, she wouldn't blame anyone for believing it of her. The hours since Delia's passing had brought more clarity to her mind, but the memories were still too overwhelming and painful to dwell on. So she stifled them. All that mattered right now was getting Nuri his kingdom back. And the funeral, aligned with the invaders' superstitions, had formed the background of her plan.

Nuri now led them around the side of the castle, then jumped behind a bush that still held large leaves, even in the wintertime. Alli and Micha followed suit and stood close to Nuri as he moved his fingers around the outline of a small door in the castle's foundation.

"We're going in there?" Alli asked. The door was hardly more than two feet tall.

Nuri shrugged. "Neither of us are very big."

Alli shrugged. "What about him?" she pointed her head behind her at Micha. He wasn't big, but his shoulders were broader than either Alli's or Nuri's.

Nuri smiled at the man. "He'll have to manage."

Micha frowned but stepped forward. He was at least twice Alli's age, and even though her reputation had preceded her, he didn't seem to hold much regard for her or her abilities. That's how it was sometimes with scholar wizards. Keeping their heads in the books all day long made them a little less social. But she was hoping he would be beneficial to her plan.

Bringing a small, thin, metal rod out of his cloak, Nuri ran it around the bottom of a lined crack in the foundation, and soon the door popped open. He held out a hand, directing Alli to enter first.

"You're the battlemaster here," Nuri said in response to her questioning look. "Lead the way."

Another memory she would have to come to grips with. She crouched and slithered through the small opening into a dark tunnel. Moving forward enough for Nuri to come up behind her, Alli brought out a small ball of light in front of them. The small crawlspace ended in fewer than ten feet, and she was able to stand. She wiped a spider web off her brow and flinched as something scurried off into a corner.

Turning back, she saw Micha begin to crawl through the opening. His shoulders were too broad, she thought. *He's not going to make it.*

Micha closed his eyes, and his shoulders collapsed inward. He squeezed through, turned around and replaced the door, then crawled back over to where they were and stood.

Alli was impressed. "How?"

He smiled and pointed to his head. "It's all in the mind."

Alli didn't know what to think of that. But before she could ask any more questions Nuri pointed forward, and they walked quietly for another ten steps before coming to a larger door. Opening the door carefully, they proceeded to climb up a dozen stairs before entering another thin corridor.

"It runs the length of the castle," Nuri said with a smile. "We'll never be seen in here."

"Perfect," Alli said.

Nuri led them to the right, and they walked thirty steps or so before stopping.

"Put the light out," he said, and Alli complied.

Total darkness fell on them. She heard a scraping sound against the wall, and then a few pinpricks of light appeared before them. Cracks in the wall. Alli leaned forward and looked through one. She saw the largest room in the castle. Up on a wide dais sat two coffins. Cherif, his main wizard, and a few other of his men stood next to them. Glancing around the room, she spied another dozen of Cherif's men placed strategically throughout the gathering.

"There's the counselor," Nuri whispered, and Alli turned to see where he was looking. Ezra had a hood on and hopefully wouldn't be recognized, but they had agreed on a color scheme for everyone in their party to use so as to recognize each other.

Once most everyone seemed to be in the room, Cherif stood. A smile grew over his face, and he bounced on his toes for a moment, looking over the crowd. Alli guessed the trader had never set his sights so high before.

The crowd quieted down, an apparent reaction to the strange power that Cherif was able to hold over people.

"People of Khazer," he began to speak, spreading his arms out to his side. He wore a dark burgundy coat over a white shirt and black pants. His dusty-dark skin reflected the plethora of candles in the room, and Alli could see tiny drops of sweat forming on his forehead. So he was nervous. Good. He was obviously way out of his element. "I am Cherif Kandori, a representative of the empress of the eastern kingdoms."

There were a few murmurs in the room at the mention of the eastern kingdoms. Long known for their power and aggression, the kingdoms periodically sent trading ships to the western continent. Rumors of eventual attack were always on the minds of those who lived on the western coast.

Now it was time for the next part of her plan. Alli waved a hand in the air, and at least half of the candle flames started dancing back and forth, as if a wind had blown through the room. The people began whispering and pointing. Cherif's people started to look around in worry.

Cherif faltered in his speech. He leaned sideways and spoke something to the wizard that stood by his side. The man scanned the room, and Alli swore that he looked right at their hiding spot. Now it was Micha's turn. Using spells of the mind, he turned the wizard's attention away from them. Soon the wizard was looking elsewhere.

Cherif tried to regain control. He stared hard out at the crowd, and Alli heard a faint voice in her head. *All will be fine.*

The voice was smooth and reassuring and she realized others were hearing it also. She almost faltered in keeping the lights moving. Micha grabbed her hand in his, and the voice soon went away. Alli noticed that Micha, standing between them, also held onto Nuri with his other hand.

"Cherif's spreading himself too thin," Micha said. "I can block him from us, but I can't do everyone."

Alli understood. She looked out and tried to find Ezra again. He, too, had a scholar wizard next to him. The crowd quieted down, and Cherif smiled. But some of his own men, especially his wizard, looked nervous still.

"My friends," Cherif began again. "Before your king met with such an untimely demise, we came to an agreement."

Alli saw Nuri take a step forward, but Micha held him back.

Whisperings grew louder in the middle of the room, and Counselor Wizard Ezra rose, removed his hood, and took a few steps forward.

"It's the counselor back from the dead," said a voice nearby—one of Nuri's own men that had been planted for this purpose.

"It's a spirit," said another one of their people.

The whisperings and murmurings grew louder, and the crowd turned to look at the counselor. He had bleached his graying hair lighter, and powdered his face to smooth out the wrinkles and make his face appear more ghostly, but younger.

Alli watched three of Cherif's men fall to their knees and began reciting something that sounded like a prayer. Cherif himself turned pale.

"It can't be," he mumbled.

"What can't be?" Ezra said loudly, amplifying his voice for all to hear. "I am Counselor Wizard Ezra Karaka, counselor to King Orian." He pointed a long and bony finger at Cherif. "What have you done here?"

Cherif took a step back, then turned to his men. "Get him. Bind him," he ordered.

Some of the men shook their heads, but a few, including his main wizard, moved forward. The wizard brought his hand up in an apparent move to cast a spell, but a loud roar outside the building shook the room.

Miriel!

Now it was time for her dragon to put on a show!

CHAPTER TWENTY-SEVEN

Still hiding behind the wall, Alli smiled. She hadn't been sure Miriel had the energy to come through, but her dragon hadn't let her down.

Miriel flew across the window, and both Alli and Miriel concentrated hard and changed her yellow scales to appear green. Through the glass, and in the dark, it would be hard to tell for sure, but they hoped it would be enough.

"My son!" Cherif shouted. "My son returns. All is now ready."

The people were in an uproar now.

"Silence!" Cherif yelled out over the crowd.

Alli felt the backlash in her mind. He had spoken to their minds also. Even Ezra stopped moving.

"I am your leader now," Cherif continued. "You will listen to me. Stop all this nonsense."

Miriel landed outside the largest window of the great room. On top of her back stood a man—someone they had found who resembled Raj enough to make it work through the windows. Through the small hole, she couldn't see exactly what was happening but by the tumult she guessed that events were going according to their plan. One of their other wizards brought up a bright light outside, and the crowd surged forward to see what was happening.

"Rajamani!" Cherif called out, and his men rallied around him.

All at once, Miriel flew toward the window. The crowd yelled and jumped back. At the moment of possible impact Alli swirled her arms and extinguished all the lights in the room. The Dragon pulled back, and the wizard's light outside also went out, bringing the entire gathering into darkness.

Then, inside the room, one of their other wizards, who was positioned by the window already and dressed liked Rajamani jumped through the air with a sudden gust of light. He jumped high overhead and landed on the dais. By now Cherif and the others had moved closer to the window. The wizard dressed like Raj raised his hands in the air, and Alli brought enough lights back on for the crowd to see the shadowed figure. This wizard had been picked for his ability to mimic voices.

The wizard pretending to be Cherif's son spoke with a loud echo, using power to both amplify his voice and mimic Raj's. It may not be perfect, but those attending the funeral had no idea how he really sounded.

"Father, the empress calls you," he began.

With a blinding light shining out toward him, Cherif couldn't really see the face of the person talking.

Cherif stepped forward and tried to shade the light from his eyes. "The empress wants me?" The man's voice shook with a fevered excitement.

"Of course, father," the wizard continued, his face shrouded his darkness. "She wants to reward you. That was our plan, right?"

Cherif's chest puffed out. "Yes, yes. We came in the name of the empress."

Alli could see Cherif's eyes grow bright.

"You poisoned the king and queen and the other nobles," the wizard continued speaking, "and now the empress wants to reward you."

Pandemonium erupted from the funeral attendees at this revelation. The crowd began to move as one toward the dais, shouting threats at Cherif and his men.

Cherif's eyes darted around the room, and he leaped forward to get control. As he got closer to his pretend-son he paused and cocked his head.

"You are not my son," he said and turned back to the crowd. "This man is an imposter."

But the crowd continued to surge forward with only thoughts of Cherif's betrayal on their minds. Alli heard Cherif's voice in her mind once again, signifying he was trying to manipulate the crowd again. She grunted with the effort of keeping his thoughts from affecting her.

"Now," Alli said to Micha.

With their combined power, Micha and Alli took Cherif's words in their minds and traveled back into Cherif's own mind.

His attitude of entitlement and the easy way he had poisoned so many people made Alli feel dirty as she delved through his mind. But there was something else there also. Fear. Not necessarily fear of the people around him—he saw himself as so far above these people that he couldn't see the danger in front of him. But the fear he felt was that he had displeased his empress.

We are not so easy to conquer, Cherif Kandori. Alli spoke to the man's mind now. *Your son has failed. The stolen dragon bond has been broken, and you will not rule this city.* She hoped what she surmised about Raj's dragon bond was true.

But? Cherif said back to her as he looked outside at the dragon there.

Alli laughed. The man had been a successful trader, but it took more to be a ruler. Cherif was cunning, but his conceit blinded him.

The wizard outside spelled a bright light, and Miriel roared in all her glory, her yellow scales reflecting off of the wizards light.

At the same time, Ezra moved up closer to the dais. The people, both those of Jor and those of Cherif's, still thought he had been killed, and all backed away from him.

He raised his arms in the air, and the caskets shook. Cherif's superstitious people fell to the ground and started mumbling to themselves.

"No!" Cherif shouted. "Your king is dead. I am your new king. You will listen to me!"

Alli laughed out loud at the desperation that filled Cherif's voice. His control upon the people was weakening with Alli's presence in his mind.

Nuri nodded at Alli and left her and Micha as he made his way farther down the hidden corridor. Now it was his turn.

"No," came another voice, younger and softer than Cherif's, but Ezra amplified it to fill the room.

Nuri stepped out of the hidden door behind the dais. Throwing off his dark cloak, he showed the tunic of royal blue he wore. His dark blond hair fell over his tanned face—the mixture of his father and mother. "*I am the king of Khazer.*"

"It's the prince," came a voice.

"Prince Nuri!" cried another. "He's alive!"

The crowd surged again toward the dais, kicking aside Cherif's men. His main wizard lifted his arms again and sent a bolt of fire into the crowd. People screamed, and while some moved forward, others now tried to find the exits. Alli took the moment to run down the hidden hallway herself and come out of the door behind Nuri. She jumped up on a chair and vaulted herself high into the air. With a somersault that brought her over the heads of the crowd, she landed on top of the wizard and took him hard to the ground. He tried to flick another spell at her, but she rolled to the side.

And unexpectedly, in her mind, she was in the arena in Turg once again, and she gazed out at her opponents. She remembered the suffering when her powers were denied her. She remembered the healing by doctor Abaddon each time, and she remembered Constantine giving her more and more power until she had beat everyone else and been given to Delia.

The wizard threw a punch toward Alli, and she, in her distraction, took a hit hard in the ribs. She heard something crack and collapsed to the floor. She rolled to the side in pain, barely avoiding another kick.

The arena opened up around her, and she knew she had to fight for her life. She needed to please her master. A flickering thought danced through her mind—who was her master now?

She leaped off the floor, grabbed a knife from her side, and advanced toward the wizard. She thrust it out in front of her, and he threw a bolt of fire at her. It hit her knife, but Alli hung on tight, and the flame reflected back at the wizard. Without a moment's hesitation she leaped into the air and kicked him hard in the chest. The man flew back ten feet, knocking over others as he did so. But Alli paid no attention to that. All she heard was the spectators around her. She had to please her master. And so she went in for the kill.

"Alli!" a voice called. One that shouldn't be in the arena, but one she recognized. "Battlemaster!" it called out again.

Battlemaster? The title sounded familiar.

"Dragon Rider," the voice came again, softer, and she stopped and looked around. The arena disappeared and the grand room in Jor came back into focus. She turned toward the sound of the voice.

"Nuri?" Alli whispered. She shook her head to come back to her senses.

The wizard stirred on the floor, but before he could do anything else, Counselor Wizard Ezra smashed him in the side of the head with his foot.

Nuri jumped off the dais and came running toward her, the remaining crowd parting around him. He skidded to a stop in front of her.

"Alli, are you injured?" Nuri said.

Alli blinked and glanced around her. Guards were dragging the wizard away, others, including Micha, held Cherif captive. The foreign wizard's head dropped low, his immense power obviously extinguished. Many of the people had left the room, and the few dozen that remained stood staring at her. Their eyes held a mixture of concern, fear, and awe.

She shook her head in response to Nuri's question.

"Hail Allison Stenos, Dragon Rider and Battlemaster!" called out Nuri.

Alli turned and looked at him. He winked at her, and her legs almost gave out. The action brought scenes of Roland to her mind. Her mind clouded with tears, and she wiped them away. What had she become? Who was she now?

"Hail the Dragon Rider!" said a small group off to her right.

"Hail the Battlemaster!" said another.

Nuri began speaking, giving her credit for the plan and recapture of the throne. The crowd began to give thanks and congratulations. But it all sounded far away to Alli. She was listening to someone else.

Welcome back, Rider.

Alli turned toward the window and saw Miriel still outside, now lying down and breathing hard. Alli didn't know if she was all the way back or not. But she had Miriel again firmly as a constant presence in her mind now. There were still vague memories of her past she would have to deal with, but this was the best she had felt in weeks.

Where to now? Miriel asked.

Alli thought about what she now knew from Cherif. The empress was coming to attack. She had to warn someone.

Elvyn. We fly to Elvyn. It was the closest place she could think of. She didn't know where Roland or Bakari were at the time. But she knew, above all, she could trust the elves.

CHAPTER TWENTY-EIGHT

The afternoon sped for Gabby, and soon the jungle began to darken. Gabby's stomach rumbled, and Calen passed out some jerky and bread. The three ate in silence as they continued their way back to the village.

As the sun set the jungle seemed to come alive with sounds and colors. Night-variety flowers opened along their path and glowed in the twilight. A sweet smell caught Gabby's attention, and she sighed. Peering around her, she could see small eyes up in the trees—animals intent on watching the travelers. The sounds of insects grew louder in her ears the darker it got.

Soon, aside from the glowing flowers, they could only see a few feet in front of them. Gabby wished she had access to her wizard powers to make a light for them to see better. Garrik stumbled once, and Gabby caught him from falling.

"Thanks," he mumbled. "Can't see a blasted thing out here."

A distant shriek stopped them in their tracks.

"What was that?" Gabby asked, but as soon as she did, she knew the answer.

Calen shrugged, but Gabby smiled and paused before saying anything.

"It's a phoenix, I think," Gabby said, excitement filling her voice. "They know we're here."

Deep inside of her, Gabby felt a sudden rush of power, and suddenly out in front of her a soft glow lit their way.

Calen stumbled into Garrik in surprise, then turned back to Gabby with questioning eyes.

"They want us to stay safe," Gabby said with a smile. She quickened her step. "Come on, let's hurry. The village can't be much farther."

She was right. Within a quarter of an hour, a woman and a man from the village spotted them, and a few minutes after that they all returned to the village.

"Where is the stranger?" Gabby asked.

The keeper came forward and pointed to a small fire. "Over there, wizard. He's gone through quite a shock being here. He's stayed by himself for the most part."

Gabby glanced over and noticed Raj wasn't secured at all.

"Why isn't he tied up?" she said. "He might escape."

The keeper smiled again, and he encompassed the village with his hands. "Why would he leave?"

Gabby rolled her eyes and remembered the power the island had over people. She noticed Garrik sitting down next to Calen and his family. He already appeared more relaxed. Glancing around at the small village, she smiled. It was a nice place.

No! she said to herself and steeled her thoughts. She had to stay alert. She strode over to the strange man. His hair was a bit darker than her own, and his skin darker than hers also, but more of a dusty brown, where hers was more olive. As she approached he stood up in front of her. He was tall and towered over her by at least six inches, but his demeanor seemed pleasant and non-threatening.

"Where is Jaimon, Rajamani?" Gabby asked without any other preamble.

"Jaimon?" The man furrowed his eyebrows. "And please call me Raj."

Gabby put her hands on her hips. She had walked a long way that day and was tired and in no mood for games.

"Jaimon, the man the dragon picked up out of the water," Gabby said. "Where did you put him?"

"Ah, the dragon rider," Raj said with more calm than Gabby would have expected from him, as he had just lost a dragon. "Cholena did seem happy to see him." Mention of the dragon seemed to drop his countenance to one of melancholy. "I have failed my father and the empress."

"Where is he, Raj?" Gabby asked once more. "I need to find him and his dragon."

Raj looked around him and sighed, his shoulders slumping. "It was grand to fly on her, but I see now that I was wrong. This is the place for me."

Gabby was getting more irritated. The man seemed to have been swayed by the island more quickly than she and Garrik had been. Speaking of Garrik, she glanced away and saw him lounging and laughing by one of the fires. She sighed deeply. Why did everything have to be so hard?

A soft voice came to her. *If it wasn't hard, it wouldn't be worth it in the end.* She didn't know if it was another entity that spoke to her or just her own voice.

"Raj!" Gabby snapped at him.

The easterner snapped out of his complacency. "The dragon dropped him off by a small cave about a quarter of the way around the island from where we picked him up."

"Is that where Cholena is now?" Gabby asked.

Raj appeared to be thinking for a moment, then shook his head. "I don't know. The bond is gone. I can't feel anything."

Well, at least she knew which direction to take. Jaimon's dragon shouldn't be too far away from him, she hoped.

"What are you doing here, Raj?" Gabby asked. "Not just here on this island, but away from your home?"

Raj sat down and took a deep breath. "It's really beautiful here," was all he said.

Gabby was about to pry again, but then he spoke more.

"From what I've heard, this is what the eastern kingdoms used to be like hundreds of years ago." He spoke slowly, his eyes looking out in the distance as if his mind was seeing what he was talking about. "Now it's overcrowded and dirty. We have used up most of our natural resources. Our empress is trying to make things better now, but in the twenty years she's been in power, only one of the ten great cities has returned to a state of beauty; a second one is in process. At least, that's what I've been told. My family has not been so fortunate to see it."

"And so she thought to attack us here and take our lands and make us slaves?" Gabby said, trying to understand.

Rajamani stood back up. "Oh no. No," he said with wide eyes. "She brings enlightenment to us. Brings us to a higher level of understanding."

Gabby snorted. "That's what all invaders in history say."

Raj fell back down on a log and put his head in his hands. "But being here, on this island," he mumbled before looking up. "Being here has shown me something different. I came to find the power that was here, but, but . . ."

His eyes teared up. Gabby didn't quite know whether to believe him or not.

"But?" Gabby prodded, anxious to get as much information from him before she left to find Jaimon. Once she left the village, she didn't know if she would ever come back.

"But . . . the stones . . . the power . . . the beauty," he stumbled on his words and shook his head from side to side. "I never knew. I never knew."

"What do you know of the stones?" Gabby jumped on him.

"The stones control all power in the east," Raj said. "The empress and her keepers control ours and keep them safe. But here, I can feel the power in the air. Here it is different."

"So why are you here before the empress?" Gabby asked. "Why were you siding with Delia?"

Raj looked down. "My father. He is a mighty tradesman. He knew that when the empress came she would need strong leaders here to maintain peace in the lands and to utilize their resources. He decided to come earlier. We infiltrated the royal house of Khazer. We found out about the previous death of their oldest son—something Delia hadn't known yet. We intercepted Delia's summons to the king of Khazer before he saw it, and I took Prince Ender's place."

Gabby paced back and forth, her mind racing to fill in all the details that were missing. "But why are you *here*?"

"My father felt a strong source of power here and ordered me to come find it. This power he would give to the empress when she arrived. It would guarantee him notice in this new land, and he would be rewarded. But my father got greedy and killed the king and queen of Khazer."

Gabby froze. She had met the king once when he had visited her father.

"Another dragon rider was there, but she escaped at the same time that I left," he finished his story. "I do not know what has happened since—only that that bond with the dragon has been broken."

There was only one other female dragon rider. "Alli was there?"

"Yes," he said. "She came to bring me back to Delia, but by then she'd found out I wasn't really Prince Ender. I think she escaped with Prince Nuri."

"And now?" Gabby asked him. "Now what will you do?"

"I want to stay here." Raj pointed around the village.

"I'm not sure that's possible," Gabby said.

She jumped as someone put a hand on her shoulder.

"Everyone is welcomed here," said the keeper. "I am getting old, and a new keeper is needed."

"What?" Gabby couldn't believe it. "He can't be a keeper! He is our enemy." Gabby felt her face redden as anger filled her heart. "He sided with Delia, his father killed a king, and he stole a dragon."

"All of which are irrelevant here on the island," the keeper said softly. "Magic is not territorial or worried about kingdom or continent. The stones of power and the phoenix must always be protected by those who care about the magic and want to stay here.”

At the moment Gabby really didn’t care if Raj stayed there or not. She was done with the delay’s.

Garrik!” Gabby turned toward her friend. “Are you coming with me?”

Garrik, who had been sitting back in a chair with his eyes closed, jumped to his feet, his eyes darting around the village. He glared over at her, and she glared back.

“I’m going after Jaimon,” Gabby said with determination. “Are you coming with me, or have you been spelled again?”

Garrik coughed and looked around. “Well, it’s not a bad place . . .”

“Calen,” Gabby called out, and Garrik’s cousin now jumped up. A few of the women placed hands over their mouths to keep from laughing. “Could you gather us supplies? I’m going around the side of the island.”

“Now?” Calen asked incredulously.

“Yes, now.”

“But you can’t see,” Calen said. “You’ll lose your way.”

“I’ll manage,” Gabby said. “I’ve wasted enough time.”

Garrik growled. “Do as she says, Calen. She’s one of those women who gets what she wants.”

Gabby smiled sweetly at Garrik. “Does that mean you’ve decided to come with me?”

“Yes, yes,” he mumbled. “Someone’s got to keep you out of trouble. You’d stick your hands in a hornet’s nest if you thought it the right thing to do.”

Gabby tried to keep herself from laughing. Garrik was probably right about that. At this point she would stick her head in the mouth of a dragon if she thought it would help her to save the Dragon King.

"Come on, we have Jaimon, a dragon, and a phoenix to find." Gabby crooked her finger at Garrik. "And then the Dragon King to save."

Garrik waited for Calen to give him a pack, and then he joined Gabby at the edge of the village. As they took a step back into the jungle, Raj called her back.

"Wizard," he said to Gabby, "if you see my father, tell him what happened. And if you see Alli, tell her I did enjoy sparring with her. Your land is much more powerful than we were led to believe."

Gabby nodded and, with Garrik in tow, stepped into the dark jungle.

CHAPTER TWENTY-NINE

Roland looked down from atop his dragon and took in the grounds of the Wizard Citadel below him. He used to think it the grandest place in the world, but now he had seen so much of the world he knew that Alaris was just one of many kingdoms on the Western Continent—and really not a particularly large or important one. Being completely landlocked without a quick way to get to other kingdoms—well, unless you had a dragon—Alaris was really at a disadvantage in trade as well as in bringing troops to help in Elvyn.

But what Alaris lacked in its ability to get around quickly, it made up for in wizard resources. The head wizard being Roland, of course.

Roland felt better than he had felt in a while. Knowing that Delia was no longer a problem and that the dragon bond would now revert back to the original dragon riders lifted his spirits. He wondered how Gabby and Jaimon's quest was going to bring a phoenix back to help Bakari. He shook his head in wonder at that. As much as he thought he knew about magic, the more he realized he didn't know. He ground his teeth, his peace turning to frustration.

Why can't I know everything about magic?

Are you ready for the price? the scepter spoke to his mind. It had been more silent lately.

Roland landed his golden dragon in the courtyard and slid off.

"Why the scowl, Your Highness?" Tam met him at the edge of the courtyard, with a short bow and a grin on his face.

"Nothing." Roland waved a hand in the air. "Nothing I can do about it right now, anyway. Gather the council," he ordered Tam. "We have a war to finish."

An hour later, Roland sat at the head of a table with ten council members present. He had just informed them of Delia's demise, a fact that a few of them had already known through the magical artifacts network they had created with wizards in each kingdom. Roland was impressed at how well this communication between countries was working.

Now, he turned to Hayden. "Tell me the status of each kingdom in its preparation for the war. We have only days left, a week at most."

Always one for protocol, Hayden stood to address the group. He adjusted his blue robes on his thin frame and cleared his throat before proceeding.

"Alaris seems to be rebuilding well under First Minister Patera," Hayden began his report. "Due to the country's recent war, I don't expect many troops from them."

Roland understood. "What about Corwan?"

Hayden smiled. "Good news there, Sir," he said. Roland noted the absence of any of Roland's other title's in the address. "A large group of survivors is said to have been found under the rubble of the governor's mansion there. They were stuck in a dungeon."

"Mericus?" Roland asked.

Hayden shrugged his shoulders. "I am sure we are all hoping he will be found," he said with a barely concealed smile.

Roland knew the man was hinting at the fact that Roland's reign as king of Alaris might be short.

"Continue," Roland said with a roll of his eyes. He held his scepter to the side and thumped it softly against the floor in a rhythm that calmed his nerves.

"Tillimot has sent troops around the Horn, but there is rumor of trouble with the desert elves at the port in Malek, and some of the troops may have been diverted there." Hayden looked down at some notes before continuing. "Quentis sent some troops up the west coast to help supplement those from Solshi. The rest, as well as most of the wizards from the sanctuary, are on their way to Elvyn."

Roland nodded. The king of Quentis pushed him, but he had done what was asked.

"Turg and Cyrene have been taken, Sir," Hayden said.

"But there is a question there on who rules," said another wizard on the council. He was one of the younger members, appointed by Roland himself.

"I rule there, Councilor Farrin," said Roland.

"Of course, Sire," Farrin said. "I meant no disrespect. But who represents you there? It's said that the Oracle's father, Nicholas, has resurfaced in Turg. King Abbas of Cyrene was taken in Solshi when his dragon failed him there."

"Inform General Guildmaster Ferdinand to hold both kingdoms with the military for now," Roland said. "I will meet with Nicholas Marinos and King Abbas when I have time. For now it is enough to know that they are part of my empire."

"Also news from Khazer, My Lord," said another wizard.

Hayden took up the explanation. "The king and queen and many of the nobles were poisoned. But Battlemaster Alli is there. Our wizard there is scheduled to check in again soon. It was rumored that a younger son of the king survived and was gathering support to take the city back from an eastern-kingdoms usurper."

Roland's heart stopped as he stood. *Alli!* Came his first thought, but out loud he voiced his concern. "They're not here yet, are they?"

Hayden shook his head.

"It does not appear so," Tam said. "This seems to be only a handful of people with one ship, but we aren't getting a lot of news out of Elvyn."

"They can't be here yet." Roland began to pace. "I'm not ready yet," he muttered under his breath. "We're not ready yet. I must go to Elvyn. We must all be there."

It figures those elves would be the problem, Roland thought to himself.

Unify them. The scepter spoke again to his mind. *All of them.*

Roland had heard that enough. The scepter would drive him mad with all the repetition.

He dismissed the meeting and went to his private suite. He had a servant draw up a nice hot bath and lowered himself into the tub. His body hurt in places that he didn't realize could hurt. The battle with Delia had been harder on him—both physically and magically—than he cared to admit. As steam rose around him he closed his eyes and let the water soak in.

Without any warning, he found himself in the magic stream.

Can't I even take a bath in peace?

He sighed and glanced down. At least he wasn't naked here. He wore black pants and a tight-fitting golden doublet over a white shirt. His favorite golden cloak seemed to blow in a breeze around him, though he didn't feel any wind on his face. He felt something on his head and reaching up to feel what it was

Ah, a golden crown for my golden kingdom, he thought with lazy pleasure.

He took a few steps and looked around. It was never without purpose that he was brought here.

Familiar pinpricks of light scattered around him. Some were brighter than others. He thought he could recognize those of the dragons. Two in Solshi still, one up in Khazer—that must be Alli. Maybe he should go there? He really wanted to talk to her.

No, as much as he wanted to see her again he couldn't get distracted from saving the continent— and most likely all they would do was argue. That seemed to be happening more and more lately, even before Delia had gotten a hold of her.

Toward Elvyn, he saw two bright lights moving together— brighter than most wizards except for the most powerful, but not as bright as the dragons.

The Cremelinos? Interesting. He wondered what that meant in terms of his unifying everyone. He could definitely use their power.

To the south were a few other bright lights. One must be the other dragon; one was much brighter and seemed to hurt his eyes. Could it be that Gabby had found the phoenix, after all? Speaking of Gabby, he searched her out and thought he had found her, but the light was different, more colorful. He shook his head and moved away. Thinking about Delia and her magic artifacts made him more cautious now with things he didn't understand.

Roland looked around for his own dragon; it should be close by. But he couldn't seem to find it through the magic stream.

Orelia, he called out. *Where are you?*

I'm always here with you, wizard.

But why can't I see you here? Roland couldn't quite figure out what his dragon really was. She was always cryptic with her answers. *Something else I don't understand,* he grumbled.

Before the dragon said anything back to him, Roland noticed another bright light up ahead and farther to the east than the Cremelinos. He watched it as it raced toward him, growing in brightness. He held his ground and prepared for what it might be.

The light exploded, and he blocked his eyes with his hands for a moment. When he took them away a lady stood in front of him. She was at least twice as old as he, maybe more. But she was a striking woman. Dusty brown skin, lighter than Bakari's. Her hair was jet black and sat in thick waves over her shoulders. Tiny jewels adorned her hair and matched a thick necklace that hung over her high-necked dress. The red-patterned dress flowed outward from its tight waist, cascading to the floor. The lady walked toward him with grace, and he took a step back from her penetrating gaze.

"Who are you?" Roland finally found his voice. He berated himself for jumping in so quick, as he knew it was a sign of weakness. But he couldn't help it.

She tilted her head to one side ever so slightly and smiled. Her teeth were perfectly aligned and white against her dark-red lips.

"I am Empress Aarunya Varma. I am coming to bring you enlightenment." Her voice had a musical quality similar to that of Breelyn, the Queen of Elvyn, and held a tone of sincerity.

Roland had a hard time finding his words in her presence; she radiated power that was almost too much for Roland to behold. Almost, but not quite. He had plenty of power of his own. Almost without thought he brought the scepter to his hand.

The empress let out a small gasp. "The Scepter of Unification." She couldn't keep her eyes off it. "Your people are more powerful than we had suspected."

Roland smiled. Now the conversation was turning the way he liked. "*I* am more powerful than you expected. I have unified the land and am prepared to turn you back from our shores."

The empress nodded, still looking at the scepter. Then she tore her attention away from it and gazed once again into his eyes. He felt himself swallowed up in them and felt her will trying to exert herself into his mind.

"Oh, no you don't," he growled and pushed her away.

"You will comply," she said evenly. "No one can resist the might of the new eastern empire. Your scepter is strong . . ." She paused as she looked at it again, her eyes coveting the power held there. She turned her attention back to him. "But you need more than unity to defeat us. We bring you enlightenment. Surrender now, great wizard, and save your lands, and you will be a great ruler among us."

The empress wiped her hand in the air, and another scene opened in front of Roland. He stood out on the balcony of a large building. The buildings and people beneath him seemed to go on forever. It was the most populated city he had ever seen in his life. Some of the buildings rose ten stories. Domes and spires sparkled from their tops in the sunshine. The people appeared clean and happy, and the air smelled of fresh fruits and spices.

"Behold Pathian, one of the ten cities of our empire," the empress spoke.

Roland's scepter sagged in his hand. *Ten* of these cities?

Another wave of her hand, and another city appeared. "Behold the city of Amidia."

This time he stood on a tall hill overlooking a beautiful land. A deep-turquoise sea stood off in front of him. He could see down a dozen feet in the water. White, sandy beaches ran the length of its shore. Buildings of all colors, sizes, and shapes ran from the beaches to the hill. Large lawns and ornamental trees dotted the landscape between many of the houses. Huge white-stone buildings stood off to one side, sparkling in the sunlight. Tall palms and other trees swayed in a breeze that Roland swore he could feel. He watched the people walking leisurely about their business. A blond-haired child ran with a dog at his heels, laughing with delight. A red-headed woman hugged a broad-shouldered man and a dark-skinned man, similar in size and color to Bakari, laughed as he sat and talked with another group of men.

Thinking of Bakari made Roland come back to his senses, and the scene disappeared before him. The cities were enormous and beautiful. She was enticing him! And, worse, he was succumbing.

"See, Roland Tyre, holder of the Scepter of Unification, I bring enlightenment to my people." Empress Aarunya spoke with intensity, power rolling off her tongue. "Your land could be our eleventh great city-kingdom, and you could be its leader."

"Me?" The words slipped out of Roland's mouth before he could think. But he had already unified the people. They were already his.

Roland, my friend, beware.

The voice was soft, barely a whisper, but he knew it as well as he knew his own.

Bak, Roland choked on his words and glanced around. *Where are you?*

The empress also seemed to glance around the magic stream, confusion filling her eyes. "Such power! Who is it?"

We need you, came Bakari's soft words. I *need you.*

Ha, Roland thought. All the power of the Dragon King, and he still needed Roland to save him. And that's what he was going to do. Save his people.

"I'm sorry, Empress." Roland gave a mock bow, ignoring her latest question. "I will have to decline your offer of enlightenment."

The empress's eyes darkened, the whites turning as black as her pupils. Her skin grew tougher, and her soft red lips paled and snarled at him.

"Then you will die!" She leapt at him without any warning.

The scepter was knocked from his hand as she fell on top of him. She placed her hand over his mouth and nose, and he couldn't breathe.

Roland struggled and thrashed beneath her, but she felt like a thousand pounds on top of him and he couldn't get up. He tried to breathe, but her hand was clamped too tightly.

The power to bind, Roland. Bakari appeared standing next to Roland. His face was pale and his eyes sunken. He looked about ready to fall over. *We need the power to bind.* With that he blinked out of existence.

Roland was beginning to feel lightheaded. But seeing his friend once again brought him renewed strength, and he pushed up against the empress.

Orelia, he called out in his mind. *Give me strength!*

All of a sudden, Roland was buried in water instead of the magic stream. He sucked in a mouthful of water and felt his head spin. Pushing up one last time, he shot a blast of golden fire out of his fingertips and pushed back whatever was holding him down. Sitting up out of the water, he gasped for air. He coughed and leaned over the side of the tub and spit up a stream of water. Looking to his side, he saw his servant lying on the floor.

He turned his head over to Roland. "I'm sorry, Sire," he spoke softly. "I couldn't help myself. She was inside my head. She made me do it. Please forgive me."

Roland nodded and coughed again. In his mind, he thanked Bakari and Orelia. Then he addressed the servant. "She is powerful. I do forgive you. But I need my clothes."

He had to get to Elvyn!

CHAPTER THIRTY

It was more difficult than Gabby had thought getting through the island jungle at night. It wasn't that she felt afraid. If anything, she felt more at peace and safe here than anywhere she had ever been. She hated to admit it, but they probably should have waited until morning to search for Jaimon.

She heard Garrik cursing in front of her as they tried to find the same path back to the coast that they had originally taken. After a few wrong turns, they found a small trail that appeared to lead in the correct direction.

"Sorry," Gabby said.

"What was that, *Princess*?" Garrik said.

"All right," Gabby sighed. "I deserve that. We should have waited until morning."

"You think?"

"But this place . . . it lulls us to complacency," Gabby said. "I had to keep moving and do something before I forgot why I'm here."

Garrik stopped. "You are remarkable, Gabrielle Von Wulf." His tone had changed.

Gabby didn't know what to say. "Thank you . . ."

Garrick started walking again. "Of course, you're a pain and bossy and too powerful for your own good," Garrik said.

"Doesn't sound so remarkable," Gabby teased.

Garrik threw back his head and laughed. "That's what I like about you. You speak your mind, you get things done, and you are fearless."

Gabby shrugged. "I care for my friends and believe in our cause."

Garrik was quiet for a few minutes as they found the bank that went down to the water's edge. On the small beach, they both stood silently for a moment, looking out over the water. The moon and stars gave enough light for them to see the outlines of their boat still lying on its side. The bank of fog that had made it so hard to get there still sat about thirty feet off the shore.

Looking up at the stars, Garrik sighed. "Sometimes . . . sometimes, I wish I had a cause so noble. My life has been torn between two worlds—I belong to both and neither. I've made mistakes; lots of them. I'm sure I'm a disappointment to my father. I'll never amount to much."

"Come on, Garrik," Gabby said with a smile while directing them toward the north side of the island. They walked side by side for a few minutes, the water lapping at their right and sending up a cool breeze. At the same time, Gabby could feel the unnatural warmth from the island on her left.

"You know," Gabby said, watching her feet carefully as they walked over bits of broken rock of differing sizes, "not many men would do what you have done for me and Jaimon. I think you are brave, and you are part of a great cause. What we do here is to bring the Dragon King and one of his riders back from the brink of death, then we will help Roland Tyre defeat the empress. Stick with us, Garrik, and you'll be a hero. Sung about by bards for years to come."

Garrick chuckled and turned and smiled at her. "As I said, Gabby, you are remarkable. Would that I could find someone like you to spend my life with. If only you were a decade older."

Gabby's face grew warm, and she knew she blushed brightly. She hoped the moonlight would not show how red she was. She looked up and met his eyes with a smile of her own.

They walked in silence for the next three or four hours, only occasionally conversing about some obstacle they needed to get around. They began to trudge in a daze, both tired from their long day. Soon the coast began to bend north, and Gabby became more alert.

"Look for a cave," Gabby said. "Raj said he dropped Jaimon off near a cave."

"You trust that man?" Garrik asked.

Gabby shrugged. "Not normally, but this island has a way of mellowing people out."

"That it does," Garrik said. "But I don't think we have to search very hard."

Gabby gave him a questioning look. "Why is that?"

"Look." Garrik pointed up ahead around another slight curve.

Gabby followed his finger. There was a bright light off in the distance ahead of them. Hope filled her heart, and she quickened her step. Garrik followed her now as they moved as fast as they could over the sandy beach. On their left, the bank began to grow higher up, until a steep, rocky cliff appeared on their left side.

"It's a fire," Gabby said to Garrik. "Jaimon! Jaimon!"

They were close enough to see a shadowed shape stand up in front of the fire. He lifted his eyes to shade the light from his vision.

"Gabby?" Jaimon called out. "Garrik?"

Gabby laughed and began to run. She slipped once on a rock, but Garrik was at her side to keep her from falling. Finally they reached the fire, and she ran into Jaimon's arms.

"Oh, Jaimon!" Tears fell from her eyes. "I'm so happy to see you."

"Me, too," Jaimon said. "I didn't know where to go. Cholena said to stay here." He pointed behind him to a small cave in the side of the cliff face. "My bond's back," he said with pure excitement. "My bond's back, Gabby!"

"I know! I know," Gabby said, pulling away from him and wiping her eyes.

Garrick stepped forward and gave Jaimon a hug, patting him on the back. "Good to see you again, son. Glad to see you're safe."

"My dragon saved me," Jaimon said. "Even without the bond, she couldn't bear to see me die."

"Oh, Jaimon." Gabby barely kept herself from crying again. "We tried to save you. We really did. I'm so sorry."

Jaimon smiled and shook his head. "I know you did. But I'm fine now. How did you find me?"

"Raj told us," Gabby said.

Jaimon's face went dark at the mention of the man. "Where is he?"

"In the village," Gabby said. "He's changed."

Jaimon huffed.

"I'll tell you later," Gabby said. "Right now we need to find your dragon."

"My dragon?" Jaimon asked. "Why?"

"I need her to take me to the top of the cliffs in the middle of the island," Gabby said. "That's where the phoenix is."

"She's gone off to hunt for the night," Jaimon said. "She went to the mainland. She'll be back in the morning."

Gabby was about to protest, when Garrick put a hand on her arm.

"Sometimes you have to rest, Gabby," he said gently. "You'll need your strength for later. I surmise talking a phoenix into coming with you will take all the energy you have."

Gabby was about to protest, but she knew Garrik was right.

"Let's rest for a bit." Garrik looked up into the stars. "At least as much as there is left of the night. Then when the dragon returns you can finish your task."

Rather than going back into the cave, they settled down next to the fire. Gabby took a bit of food out of her pack, sharing it with Garrik and a thankful Jaimon. After eating a small meal of dried meat and bread the three lay down by the fire, and soon Gabby fell asleep.

***

Deep in a dreamless sleep, Gabby woke up just moments before a hand clapped over her mouth. She struggled against it. Thrashing around, she noticed that two other men held Jaimon and Garrik with knives at their throats.

The sun was just below the horizon. A slight wind blew across Gabby's face. When she turned her head she saw a small ship against the shore. Thick fog rolled behind it.

"Who are you?" Gabby said, getting her mouth away from the man that held her. "I thought the island kept people away."

"Pirates," Garrik said in disgust. "They prey on those who travel between the island and the mainland on their way to the Horn. Apparently landing on the beach is possible—just like we did."

"But we don't have anything," Jaimon said. "We crashed here."

"We don't care about you, well, except to get rid of anyone who can talk about us," said a large man. His blond hair hung limply down the side of his face—one side of which had a scar running from his chin to his ear.

"We hear there are jewels here on this island," said a second man, the one holding Jaimon. His hair was shorter, but the same color as the first, though this man also wore a scraggly beard. Both were thin and appeared not to be very successful pirates.

The one holding Gabby spoke. "Shut up, you two."

Both of the other men shut their mouths.

Gabby tried to kick the man in the chins. She heard him grunt, and his hands weakened momentarily on her, but not enough for her to get away. Instead, he twisted her around and brought a knife up to her throat.

"Any of you try anything, and she's the first I'll kill," Gabby's captor said.

Gabby tried to see if she had regained use of her magic yet, but she hadn't. She could, however, feel the magic of the island. It pulled at her, but she didn't know what to do with it. She still felt the power of the stones this far away. *Unless there are more.*

The three were all shoved down next to the fire and their hands tied behind their backs. Garrick's captor threaded another rope between each of theirs in a way that it tied all of them together. The three of them sat facing the water, with Garrick and Jaimon's captors standing in front of them. Gabby's captor had gone back to the ship and was digging around trying to find something when Gabby noticed a dark shape up in the fog to the northwest. She elbowed Jaimon.

Jaimon tried not to smile, but it didn't work.

"What's wrong with you boy?" asked one of the men. "You think something's funny?"

"I sure do," Jaimon said.

The pirate walked over with his knife in his hand. "I should just kill you right now."

"I doubt that," Jaimon said, trying to hold back a laugh.

"Why you—" the man got out, just before Cholena roared.

They all turned and glanced up into the sky. Through the thick fog came a bright and beautiful green dragon; the early morning sun reflected a dark orange on the tips of its wings. And sitting on top of it was Gabby's brother, Kaspar. His face filled with a broad white smile, while his red cloak floated in the breeze around him. It was a majestic sight to behold.

"Cholena!" Jaimon yelled out.

"Kas!" Gabby cried out, tears springing to her eyes.

As Kaspar and the dragon approached, the other pirate came running out of the boat with a sword in his hand. Cholena flew about ten feet off the ground over the campsite, and Kaspar jumped off, landing in a crouch between the pirates.

The pirate with the sword brought the weapon up in both hands. As Kaspar walked toward him, he advanced at a quicker pace. He brought his sword up above his head and brought it down toward Kaspar, but Kaspar easily sidestepped, letting the man's sword hit the ground. Kaspar moved around and kicked the man in the behind, sending him sprawling on the ground, closer to the fire.

The two other men now approached, one with another sword, and the other with a long, curved knife.

The one with the knife dove in first, and Kaspar parried the weapon away with his sword. The pirate spun to the side, but in a surprise move, continued his spin and came back up behind Kaspar.

Now Kaspar had a pirate on one side and the other in front. By now, the first pirate had risen back up, wiped sand from his face, and moved forward on Kaspar's other side. The pirate in front came at Kaspar with the sword. He went low, trying to take out Kaspar's legs, but Kaspar jumped high in the air and, bending his knees, cleared the sword. He brought his own around and clipped the pirate on the shoulder, bringing a roar of pain.

The pirate with the knife took the moment to throw it from behind Kaspar.

"Kas!" Gabby called out.

Kaspar fell to the side just in time, and the knife flew past, now leaving its wielder defenseless. Kaspar rolled and brought his feet around to take the man down, but at that moment the first pirate entered the fray and brought his sword down toward Kaspar's middle. Bringing his own sword up at lightning speed, Kaspar blocked the hit, but the man held his sword there against Kaspar's.

Kaspar's eyes squinted with the weight bearing down on him, then his eyes widened. The man took it for fear and brought his sword up high above his head. He prepared to come down hard on Kaspar, but Cholena dove down from above, grabbed the sword by the blade, and lifted the man off the ground.

"Help!" the pirate screamed. The other two scrambled to get up.

Cholena flew over the ship and dropped the man on it. The weight of his fall caused him to crash through the deck and down inside the boat. With Kaspar on their tail, the other pirates ran to help. They jumped up into the ship. Instead of pursuing them, Kaspar stopped and hacked at the anchor rope, then pushed the boat with all his might. It creaked and moved.

Cholena came low and butted her head into the boat, loosening it from the sand and pushing it back into the water.

She blew out a heated wind that shoved them back behind the bank of fog.

With the boat gone, Kaspar turned back and ran over to the captives to untie them. As soon as Gabby was free she threw her arms around his neck.

"How did you know where I was?" Gabby asked.

"Roland Tyre," he said. "I was on my way, just about to sail over from the mainland, when Cholena came by. I convinced her to take me."

"Convinced her?" Jaimon asked with a frown. "You didn't hurt her, did you?"

Kasper pulled out a small carving of a dragon. "I have ways to communicate with them."

Jaimon continued frowning, and Gabby laughed. Garrik walked over and shook Kaspar's hand.

"Oh, Kas," Gabby said. "This is Garrik. The bravest elf there is."

Garrik blushed at the praise, though he tried to cover it up by turning his head with a cough.

"And I'm Kaspar Von Wulf," Kaspar said as Garrik turned back around. "Thank you for taking care of my sister. She has a way of getting into trouble."

"Don't I know it," Garrik said with a laugh.

Gabby joined in.

"Now what, little sister?" Kaspar said. "Seems you are in charge of this expedition." Turning to Jaimon, he nodded slightly. "No offense, Dragon Rider."

Jaimon smiled again. "None taken, my prince. I'm just glad to have the dragon bond back."

They all looked at Gabby.

"Jaimon, is your dragon strong enough to take us up to the cliffs?" Gabby asked. "We have a phoenix to find."

You don't find a phoenix, the echo of the guardian's voice came to her again. *It finds you.*

Well, it can find us easier if we knock on its door.

CHAPTER THIRTY-ONE

Cholena would need to make two trips to get the four up to the cliffs. Jaimon and Kaspar went first, while Gabby waited with Garrik. He had sat down on a rock and was staring at the ground. Gabby walked over to him and put a hand on his shoulder.

"You all right there, tough guy?" she asked.

Garrik took a moment before he looked back up at her. His red hair was a wild mess on top of his head, and his green eyes were tired. "Sometimes I wish I had never been in the harbor master's office that day," he said with a snort.

Gabby put her hands on her hips and gave him a mock glare.

Garrik laughed and stood up. "But you know what? This little adventure you've taken me on is quite a bit more exciting than my boring life of thievery, trickery, and underhanded deals."

Gabby felt wind at her back, and Garrik's face turned green.

"You're really going to have me fly on that thing, aren't you?" Garrik said, pointing behind her.

Gabby turned her neck and saw Cholena approaching them.

"You'll love it, Garrik," Gabby said. "Think of the stories you'll be able to tell the women!"

Garrik tipped his head back and laughed. "You are a wonder. All right, if we are going to do this, let's get it over with."

The dragon lay down, and Gabby mounted first, directing Garrick to get on behind her. Cholena stood up and began to flap her wings.

"Ohhh," a long groan escaped Garrik's lips.

"Hold on tight," Gabby called out.

Garrick grabbed her hard around the waist as they lifted into the air. The dragon soared over the water before reversing direction and rising higher up over the island.

"Look, Garrik," Gabby squealed in delight. "Isn't it beautiful?"

"I can't see anything," Garrik said.

Gabby, confused, turned her head. "Garrik!" she shouted back at him. "Open your eyes!"

A moment later she heard a gasp from behind her. She smiled at the wonder she heard in it.

With the height and speed of the dragon, it only took them a few minutes to reach the mountain in the center of the small island. Jaimon and Kaspar waved them over to a spot on top of the cliffs. Cholena dropped, and Gabby heard another groan from Garrik.

As soon as they landed, Garrick slid off behind her. He ran about ten feet away and leaned over and threw up.

Gabby climbed down and walked over to Kaspar and Jaimon, giving Garrik a bit of privacy.

"I guess he can't handle the heights," Jaimon said with a laugh.

"Don't tease him," Gabby said, but her eyes sparkled with shared mirth.

Jaimon nodded his head. "I remember my first time."

Garrik came back over to the group a few minutes later with eyes daring anyone to make fun of him. None did. Taking a few minutes to walk around, Gabby noticed tall pines growing on the cliff, and then the full mountain rising even higher behind them, the snow-capped top much closer now. A small creek ran down the mountain and traveled a dozen feet away from them and out over the cliff.

Gabby moved to the edge of the cliff, and the others followed, although Garrik stood back a bit farther.

Looking down, she could see half of the island. Tall palms stuck up, intermixed in places with other stout jungle foliage. A few colorful birds flew up from one tree and across the waterfall that fell below the group. Gabby's eyes were drawn down to the pool at the bottom of the falls. Even from this height she could see bright colors sparkling in the deep, clear water.

"Jaimon, can you ask your dragon if she knows how to reach a phoenix?" Gabby asked.

Jaimon nodded and grew silent for a minute. Then he turned back to Gabby.

"She says, you don't find a phoenix," Jaimon said. "They find you."

Gabby grunted. "That's the same thing the guardian said. But there has to be a way to get noticed. From what Raj said, I don't think we have a lot of time."

Cholena lay down on the ground, and the rocks shifted a bit with her weight.

"She needs to rest," Jaimon said to the group in general. "The dragons were taken out of their hibernation too soon."

Gabby paced along the edge of the cliff, trying to figure out what to do as the sun rose higher. "I need to think," she said to the others and moved over next to the stream. Finding a small, flat rock, she sat down next to the water. The others left her alone and made their own conversation. Gabby closed her eyes to think better.

She tried to draw on her power, but like before, the island seemed to constrain it. She had, however, felt the power of the stones, communicated briefly with Guardian Calanon, used her power of *seeing*, and Jaimon had his bond with his dragon returned. So magic did work on the island, but not in the way she was used to. It was just her basic wizard powers were constrained.

Dropping her hand to her side, she dragged her fingers in the cool water. Deep in the recesses of her mind she felt power. It was in the water. As her fingers numbed in the cold. The power grew within her. Soon the numbness spread up her arms, and then she felt it in her toes and legs.

Come, child. Come to me.

It was a soft female voice, full of power. Gabby took a deep breath and felt the numbness spreading farther over her body. It was cold at first, but now it felt as if a warm blanket covered her. The only thing that felt different was her head and face; they weren't as cold. She let herself lay down and let the unfeelingness wash over her. It hurt at first, but then felt warm and inviting.

A bright light appeared in front of her. Out of it stepped a beautiful woman with dusty-brown skin. Her eyes were deep-set and held Gabby's attention. The woman's black hair cascaded down her shoulders. Her red lips curved into a smile as she stepped forward.

"Another powerful wizard of the west." The woman laughed, almost as if taunting Gabby.

Suddenly Gabby found herself standing up in the magic stream. She carefully watched the unfamiliar woman approach.

The woman moved her hands out to the side and sleeves from her colorful dress fell down from her arms. "My child, you seek more power?"

Gabby didn't quite understand the question. Her mind wasn't thinking clearly.

"I seek a phoenix," Gabby said looking up at the woman, feeling like she could trust her for some reason. "Its power is needed to cure the Dragon King."

"You have a good heart," she said. "I can tell that. I'm sure a phoenix will come to you."

Gabby shook her head. "I'm not sure what else to do."

"I will help you and guide you," the woman said.

Gabby shivered but felt warm at the same time. What was happening to her? She felt her mind beginning to slip further away and she couldn't think clearly.

"Call for the phoenix, dear girl, call for them," the woman said, her voice growing more urgent. "Let's see their power."

Gabby tried to call out to them, but there was no answer. "I . . . I can't," Gabby said.

The woman in front of her frowned for a moment, and Gabby's heart went cold. She stumbled back in the dark grayness of the magic stream.

"You will, or you will die," the woman said, not appearing so beautiful or nice anymore. "Call them and give their power to me."

Gabby began to panic. She was having a hard time breathing. She tried to open her eyes but couldn't.

"I must have their power," the woman said. "It's my destiny. If you help me, I will reward you in my new colony of the west. I am Empress Aarunya Varma."

Empress? Warnings flashed through Gabby's mind now, but she didn't know what to do. Her mind was thick and her breathing growing more shallow. She couldn't feel her body at all anymore.

She tried to think. She had to learn as much as she could from the empress. Roland and Bakari would need to know. Thinking about Bakari brought her increased clarity. Her task was to save him.

Below the shivering, below the darkness and shortness of breath, Gabby took her mind deeper and farther away from the empress. She felt the trickle of water in the stream once again, and this time she followed it toward the stones of power. The empress in front of her began to recede and move farther away.

"No!" the woman screamed, her visage going darker. "Bring the power of the Phoenix to me!"

But Gabby moved along the water in her mind and down over the edge of the waterfall. She felt herself falling and falling, as if she would never land. Finally she felt immersed in the water again. Around her was darkness except for a few bright spots of power. *The stones of power.* She tried to grab onto them—to touch them. As she reached forward something broke in her mind—and her powers returned once again. All of them. Farther away in the grayness, she heard a loud howling of rage.

"No!" the empress bellowed. "Bring me the power, or you will die!"

Gabby struggled to breathe in the magic stream. She fell to the ground again, and her vision—what vision there was—grew dim. Her power left her again, and she felt so tired. If only she could rest a little before finding a phoenix. Even though her eyes were already closed, she felt as if she closed them again and began to sink into a blissful sleep.

Just before succumbing to it, she felt someone touch her, yanking her head up.

"Gabby!" called someone close to her. "Gabby, what happened?"

"Get her out!" said another voice. *Kaspar? What was her brother doing here in the magic stream?*

"Her body's like ice," said another man—*Garrik, maybe?*

She felt herself being carried now. She tried to open her eyes, but when she did the sunlight hurt, and she closed them again as darkness overtook her.

* * *

Gabby became aware of her thoughts sometime later when she heard soft voices around her. She shivered in the cold and without thinking reached for a blanket, but none was there.

"Gabby?" Kaspar said, his voice full of concern.

"I'm so cold," Gabby said, opening her eyes a bit. She blinked in the bright sunlight. "Where am I?"

"You're still up on the cliff, little sister," Kaspar said. "We moved you into the sun."

Gabby closed her eyes for a moment and then reopened them. Jaimon and Garrik now stood next to her brother. They tried to hide their worry, but Gabby could see it in their minds.

She looked down at her body. Her clothes were wet, and she couldn't stop shivering. Trying to take a deep breath, she coughed, and her chest burned.

"What happened?" Gabby asked.

"We found you submerged at the edge of the stream," said Garrik, walking closer. "You were lying on your back in the water."

Gabby shut her eyes and tried to remember what had happened. "I was thinking about what to do about the phoenix, and I dropped my hand into the stream. I jumped into the magic stream." Gabby turned sideways and coughed. "I'm so cold."

Jaimon leaned over and put his hand to her forehead. "She's burning up. I don't know whether she needs heat or cold. What do we do?"

Kaspar took her hands in his. "What happened in the magic stream, Gabby?"

Gabby thought a moment, then remembered. "The empress. She tried to kill me. She lured me under the water. She wanted the power of the phoenix, but I couldn't give it to her." Gabby groaned and shut her eyes again. "Kas, please help me."

Kas leaned over and softly kissed her forehead. "Just rest, Gabby. You'll be fine."

"Mmmm," was all Gabby could say. Sleep sounded nice.

She heard the others walk away.

"I don't know what to do," Kaspar said.

Gabby was worried at the desperation in his voice.

"She won't last the day if we don't get help," Garrik said. "Her body temperature is too low."

Gabby tried to open her eyes and protest, but she couldn't. Her eyelids were so heavy. She tried to breathe deeply but coughed once more. As she did so, she heard the three stop their conversation.

"Maybe Cholena can help," Jaimon whispered. "I'll ask her. She could start a fire to warm her."

"But her fever," Kaspar said. "I'm afraid about a fire. How can she be cold and hot at the same time?"

"Magic," Garrik said. "Magic caused this, and magic is the only way to cure it. I'm afraid not even a dragon can fix this. We need to find a phoenix."

"But you heard, Garrik," Jaimon said, his voice growing with concern. "You don't find a phoenix."

"Well," Garrik's voice rose as Gabby drifted to sleep, "my father is the guardian of the phoenix. I will find one now, or if Gabby dies, I will find it later and kill it for not helping."

CHAPTER THIRTY-TWO

Alli had left the city of Jor in the hands of Nuri and Counselor Wizard Ezra. Cherif had been taken to his ship and quarantined there with the rest of his crew. Other ships in the harbor held him in from escaping. All his men wanted to do was leave and never come back. They were a more superstitious lot than Cherif himself, and talk of ghosts, flashing lights, and things moving in the night spread through the rest of the crew.

Alli stood on the bow of a ship next to Scholar Wizard Micha. They had sailed all day and night for two days—much to the argument of the captain—to reach Lor'l. In the ship with them were five other wizards and two dozen soldiers. Alli didn't know what to expect from the elves. She didn't know when the ships from the east would arrive either.

Looking to her left, Alli scanned the horizon. The southern tip of a small island farther out in the sea was about as far as she could see. Beyond that, a loud black storm churned, growing stronger the longer the day went. The boat lurched a bit, and Alli grabbed the rail and peered ahead again. She shielded her eyes from the setting sun and gasped at the number of ships that sat in the harbor east of Lor'l.

"That's not normal," Micha said, brushing his blond hair out of his forehead—hair that reminded Alli of Roland.

She quickly shut that line of thinking down. Over the last two days she had remembered more of her past, but with those memories came shame at not being strong enough to withstand her masters. And she berated herself, too, for thinking that way. She shouldn't think of them as her masters anymore. They were Constantine and Delia. But she still felt shame and didn't know how she could ever face Roland again. He had tried so hard to reach her.

She turned her thoughts to the task at hand. "The elves have not been known to join in the fights of the other kingdoms. That's a lot of ships, and based on the flags, they are from Quentis, Tillimot, and Elvyn."

Micha pointed in one direction as they came closer. Alli followed his finger and opened her eyes wide in surprise. One of the ships was on fire.

"There appears to be fighting," Alli said, then turned to the captain. "Bring us in carefully, Captain. There may be trouble."

The captain grunted. He hadn't liked his ship being commandeered by Alli—a foreigner with no authority in Khazer. She had pointed out to him that she was a dragon rider and did what she did by the authority of the Dragon King. She winced now a bit at the lie. She had tried to kill the Dragon King herself at the Coliseum and wasn't even sure where he was at now.

Alli looked up, hoping to see her dragon Miriel. She had stayed behind to rest more. But she had promised to join Alli later.

As they sailed into the northern part of the harbor, another, smaller ship intercepted them. Alli was surprised to see an Elf on the bow. She thought they normally didn't leave their forests.

The Elf saluted the captain. "State your business," he said tersely.

Alli smiled in recognition. She moved in line of sight. "The business is mine, Gloron."

The Elf frowned for a moment, his usual soft features turning dark. Then his slanted eyes opened wider. "Dragon Rider!" His frown turned to a smile, and he stood up straighter. "Forgive me. I had not been informed of your coming." He looked the boat up and down and turned serious. "But on whose business are you here?"

Alli let out a sigh. They had heard of her siding with Delia, no doubt. She knew she would have a hard time explaining that for years to come. Even now, she still felt a small compulsion to obey the woman, and finish her errand for her. But Delia was dead, and time would increase Alli's freedom of thought.

Before anyone could say anything else, Alli leaped onto the rail of the ship and jumped the ten feet across to the other one. Five elves behind Gloron had their bows out and arrows trained on Alli herself. She jumped down in front of Gloron, who took a step back.

"I'm here on my own, Gloron," Alli said. "Tell Lan I would speak with him."

Gloron cleared his throat. "I will inform King Lanwaithian of your arrival. He is busy at the moment." The Elf's eyes flicked toward the burning ship.

"What is going on there?" Alli asked.

"The desert elves have rebelled," Gloron said. "The warlord instructed them to send troops here in preparation for the fight, but they have attacked instead. A few from Tillimot have also sided with them."

"Need some help?" Alli asked.

Gloron smiled. "It would be good to have a dragon rider with us."

"Where are the other dragon riders?" Alli asked.

Gloron frowned and shook his head. "You do not know?"

A feeling of dread hit Alli's heart. Had she done something that she couldn't remember doing? She shook her head.

"The Dragon King and Rider Liam lie at death's door; Healer Kharlia has been tending them, but . . ." he paused for a moment before continuing. "Rider Jaimon and Wizard Gabrielle have gone south to find a phoenix to cure them, but they have been gone a long time and, I'm afraid, may have come to harm."

The news sobered Alli, and she felt guilty again. If she hadn't been so weak, she might have been able to stop harm from coming to Bakari. She couldn't face the thought of him dying. She owed him everything for making her a dragon rider.

She steeled her shameful thoughts and turned her attention back to the fight in the harbor. This was something she could do something about.

"Captain!" she ordered the man, jumping back to their ship. "Take the ship over there." She pointed toward the fighting. "We have more important foes to fight than ourselves."

The captain sullenly turned the ship, and Alli felt an increase of wind on her face. A heavy storm would be upon them that night or, by the latest, the next morning. As the ship pulled away from Gloron's something he had said tickled the back of her mind.

"Gloron," she shouted, gaining his attention, "who is this warlord you spoke of?"

Gloron's eyes twinkled. "You don't know about that, either?"

Alli shook her head. Apparently there was a lot she didn't know about.

"The Warlord of Elvyn is Roland Tyre."

Alli grabbed the railing for support. Once her composure returned she cupped her hand and yelled back with the wind. "Is he here?"

Gloron shook his head, his long hair flying around him in the increasing wind. Concern etched his face, and his slanted eyebrows furrowed. "No. We don't know where he is."

Alli let out a deep breath she hadn't realized she had been holding. At least she wouldn't have to face him yet. She turned now and instructed the soldiers and wizards of their needed help in securing Elvyn for the king. Some of the wizards stood ready, while Micha and a few others took a few steps away from the others.

"We are not prepared to fight like this," Micha said. "We are not soldiers."

"We are all soldiers, Micha!" Alli took two steps closer to the pacifists. "If the eastern empire does come, we will all be fighting for our lives."

Alli was impressed that he didn't back away, but he did bow his head slightly to her and nodded. "We will do what we can."

Alli turned and moved to the bow of the ship. They were approaching the fight. Before they were close, a volley of arrows came through the air toward them. Alli put her hands up in the air, and a flash of fire burned them all before they hit the ship or the men.

Alli and another battle wizard threw out their hands, and lightning raced into a nearby ship of men, blasting a hole in its side. A loud boom sounded in the air, and a cannon ball blasted the side of the Khazer ship, knocking many to the ground. Alli ground her teeth and looked in the direction it had come. Men with flaming red hair stood on deck of another ship and let loose another volley of arrows. Alli was about to knock them out of the air, but before she could let loose her spell the ship hit a wave, and her aim went off.

A few soldiers cried out as the arrows struck.

"Ram their ship, Captain!" Alli yelled out.

"That could damage us as well," the captain said. "I'll not harm us intentionally."

"Do what I say, Captain," Alli said, her voice hard and firm.

The captain's face turned red, and he turned the ship's wheel hard, making Alli slide across the deck and hit her head on one of the masts poles.

She rolled over and glared at the captain. Her first thought was that as soon as this was over, she would kill him. That's what her master would want.

The sudden and horrible thought floored her, and she barely moved out of the way of another volley of arrows. She shook her head angrily to clear it. She was still a monster! Would she never be rid of what they had done to her?

Alli stood back up and jumped up on the railing of the ship. "Full speed, Captain," she yelled out.

The men on the other ship stopped what they were doing, and their mouths fell open. They knew that the ship from Khazer was coming in too hard. Alli grabbed a pole with her hand and held on tightly as their ship's hull smashed into the other ship. Men went flying overboard on both sides. Others drew their swords and charged forward as Alli jumped onto the other ship's deck. With a flash, her own sword was in front of her, and she advanced through the men without a thought. Slicing into a man's arm here, kicking another man in the gut there. She sent a spell of fire into another group that came for her. She jumped up on a crate, spun around, and with a broad swing of her leg took down four of them.

A soldier brought a sword around toward her arm, and Alli swerved to the side just in time, receiving only a small nick. In automatic reprisal, her sword moved to hit the man, but he was quicker than the others and blocked it. They circled each other for a moment, and the man dove in, thrusting toward her middle. She brought up her sword tight inside her and blocked his with the upper part of her blade. The force sent shivers down her arm.

Suddenly she was back in the arena fighting off opponents for her master. The crowd cheered around her, and she pushed forward. The man parried her thrust, and Alli swept a leg around, catching him in the thigh and knocking him down. Another man came from behind her. She dropped to the ground, and when the man fell over her she stabbed up into him and he fell lifeless on the ground.

The scent of blood filled her nostrils, and the sound of battle faded into the distance. It was only she against them all. That's what she did. She fought for her life every day, and when she did well her master would give her powers back to her.

Her powers! She had them. With the sword in one hand she pointed her other hand, fingers out, at another soldier, and fire spewed forth, taking his life away without another moment's thought. She jumped up on a ledge and flipped into the air. On her way back down she blasted five others with one hand while cutting down another with her sword.

"Dragon Rider!" came a call to her. She ignored it for a moment.

"Alli!" someone else said. She took a breath, and the sounds of battle came rushing back to her. She noticed soldiers from Khazer standing in front of her with hands out in front of them.

"Stop," said a voice to her right, and she turned and saw Micha marching toward her. His face was full of rage. "You're going to kill our own men!"

Alli stood for a moment and turned in circles. Every last desert elf on the opposing ship lay on the deck, many of them dead, a few still alive and squirming in their own blood. What had she done?

Her right arm dropped to her side, her sword clanking on the wooden deck. She closed her eyes and in anguish let loose a shuddering sob.

High up in the air came an answering bellow. She opened her eyes and beheld Miriel, in all her beautiful yellow, diving down for her. Fire burst from her jaws, and soldiers in neighboring ships, both friend and foe, scrambled out of the way.

Alli leaped up on the railing and jumped into the air. Miriel came swooping down for her. Alli landed with a jolt on her back. With another roar from Miriel, the two flew back up into the air.

The air stilled for only a brief moment, then another echoing roar came from the shore. Alli looked, and flying from the west over the treetops came Roland Tyre and his golden dragon. The young man's blond hair flew back around his face. He wore a red vest and black trousers, with his bright golden cloak blowing in the wind around him. He held on to his dragon with one hand, and in the other sat a long, bright, golden scepter.

Within moments, his golden dragon circled Miriel and Alli. He stared hard at her.

"They were attacking Lor'l," said Alli. There was so much more she wanted to say.

Roland continued to circle her, his blue eyes never letting go of hers. She felt adoration, joy, shame, and embarrassment all at once.

"You didn't need to kill them all," Roland said as his dragon shot golden fire in the air. "They are my people, too."

"Not everyone is yours, Roland Tyre," Alli said without thinking.

Both dragons continued to circle each other in silence. The fighting below had halted.

"But are you?" Roland finally shouted, his face contorted in anguish.

"Am I what?" Alli said. She wasn't following him. They needed to get back to the fighting.

"Are you mine, Allison Stenos?" Roland asked. His scepter crackled, and lighting flew out around him. "Or do you still belong to another?"

Alli almost fell from her dragon with the force of his words. Her heart broke, and she swallowed hard. What exactly was he asking? Did he want to know if she still sided with Delia's ideals, or was he literally asking if she was his, in a more personal way?

She opened her mouth three times to speak but couldn't find the right words. Memories flooded her mind. Memories of almost losing him before, of his arrogant smile, his teasings when they first met, his swagger and selfish desire to be the most powerful wizard in the world. But under it all, she knew that she and Roland Tyre had always had some kind of special connection.

Roland continued to fly around her, never wavering in his gaze, but the longer she waited to answer the more grave his face became.

As he moved closer and closer to her, she watched his firm jaw, his deep, intelligent eyes, his longing face, and then . . .

then he winked at her and smiled. And her world made sense once again.

"I could never belong to another, Roland Tyre," Alli said with a force that surprised her—and all around heard.

Lighting flashed out in the sea and thunder boomed. Alli turned and saw a blackness she had never seen before. Roland turned and brought his dragon back toward Lor'l. Alli followed.

Someone has to look after that boy!

CHAPTER THIRTY-THREE

Once again, Gabby didn't know how long she had been out. She could feel her body burning up, and her breath wheezed. She didn't have the energy to open her eyes or to even hear what was going on around her.

Bakari, I'm sorry, she whispered in her head. She was sure they were close to her final thoughts. *I have failed.*

But we have found you, came a soft voice, a voice full of compassion, kindness, and strength.

Gabby's heart lifted, but she still couldn't open her eyes. Her mind, however, did open, and she found herself farther up the mountain from where she and the others had come. She stood on a small ledge high on the mountain side. Five trees stood in a circle around her. There was a noise above her, and she peered up through the branches. Someone was up there, climbing higher.

"Garrik!" she said, startled to see him there. He couldn't hear her, though, and continued climbing.

The trees must have been three hundred feet tall, and he was almost at the top. Her perspective changed, and she was up above him, looking down into his weary face. He stopped and looked around.

"Where are you, you blasted phoenix?" Garrik shouted into the air. "She is dying!"

Gabby's heart swelled with gratitude to him.

"As the son of a guardian, I command you to come forth!" Garrik shouted. "We have protected this land of yours for hundreds of years. I now demand a reckoning. Heal Gabby!" His voice dropped lower. "Heal her, please."

His pleading brought a sob to her lips and tears to her eyes. The tops of the trees stirred in the breeze, but no answer came.

Garrik grabbed another branch and pulled himself farther up in the tree. Gabby didn't understand how, but she could see him clearly. His muscles bulged, his arms shook, and his face glistened with sweat. Gabby thought of what it must cost him to be this high up.

No, Garrik, she said, but her voice was lost in the vision. *You don't have to do this.*

Branch by branch, he continued to climb. The wind picked up and his body swayed back and forth with the tall trees.

Phoenix, if you are truly here, why don't you stop him? Gabby tried to access her powers. To her surprise, they came bursting forth now. Not only her wizard powers, but the power of her family's *seeing* and the powers of the stones. She felt them all. They churned and burned through her.

No, Gabrielle, you must not pull so much power here, came the soft voice. Gabby realized it was a phoenix. *Your body is weak. It can't handle it.*

Gabby looked around but couldn't see the bird. *But he'll die if I don't help him,* Gabby said. *He'll never have the strength to climb back down. Or he'll panic and fall.*

Before an answer came, Garrik cried out again.

"Heal her, please!" His voice rose, then dropped to a quiet whisper. "As a son of the guardian, I ask this one favor." His earlier anger seemed to have left him.

A life for a life.

Gabby gasped. Garrik looked around, eyes wild. It was the voice of Garrik's ancient father, Calanon, the guardian of the phoenix.

A life for a life, came the same words, although this time from the voice of the phoenix in Gabby's head.

Garrik's face relaxed, and he peered around once again.

"No, Garrik, no!" Gabby screamed as loud as she could. She could almost reach out and touch him, he was so close. But he couldn't hear or see her.

A bright light blazed in the top of the tree, and a brilliant, red bird with orange and yellow tips shone forth. It was about three feet tall, with a wingspan of four or five feet. It flapped its bright wings, and wisps of fire rose out of them. But the fire did not burn the branches of the tree.

A life for a life, the phoenix said again.

Calanon's voice came to her again through the magic stream. *The life of a phoenix comes from the ashes of death; so does its ability to heal. The power of spirit, the power to bind, is strong in all mythical creatures, but the power to bind a life is the most precious.*

I can't let him do it! Gabby cried out, sobs racking her body as she pulled more power into her. She looked down and saw her own body glowing in the magic stream.

The phoenix turned and glared at her, eyes boring into her own. *You must stop, wizard. Your body will burn up.*

Then save him, she wailed.

It is up to him. He has the right to ask the bargain.

Gabby choked back the tears and let the power recede.

"I will do it," Garrik said softly, and for a moment he looked in her direction and smiled, but she didn't think he could see her.

"Oh, Garrik," was all Gabby could say.

He glanced around, as if hearing her for the first time. "Tell them about me, Gabrielle. Tell them to write a song about me."

Gabby squeezed her eyes shut for a moment before opening them back up. She stifled a whimper from her lips.

A life for a life, he whispered in the air.

And let go.

Gabby could only stare as his body fell in silence through the five trees. Halfway down a bright red and orange light erupted, and the phoenix flew across her path. Gabby shielded her eyes for a moment, and when she looked again, Garrick was nowhere to be found.

* * *

Gabby coughed and opened her eyes. The first thing she saw was the bright feathers of the phoenix high in a tree above her. Jaimon and Kaspar were at her side.

"Her fever's broken," Kaspar said as he touched her head.

"Help me up," Gabby asked, her voice hardly more than a croak.

Kaspar helped her sit up while Jaimon brought a waterskin to her lips. She drank hungrily, feeling her strength return with every swallow. Power flared inside her again, but this time it didn't burn her, only healed.

A lone red father dropped to her side. *Take this to the Dragon King.*

Jaimon and Kaspar looked up, but then turned back to Gabby.

"Is this from a phoenix?" Jaimon asked with excitement in his eyes. "Where is it? Where is Garrik?"

Gabby shook her head, and tears filled her eyes. She leaned over onto Kaspar's shoulder and sobbed. "Garrik's gone."

After a short time, she wiped her eyes.

"Where's Garrik?" Jaimon asked. "What happened?"

"He gave his life for mine," Gabby said with a throb of pain in her head. She still couldn't believe he had done it.

Jaimon and Kaspar's eyes went wide.

"And the phoenix?"

Gabby held the feather in her hand. "They will help us. We must bring this to Bakari," she said. Inside she wondered what the price would be.

A life for a life, came the echoes of the earlier words.

She stood up and stretched. Her energy had returned, and her powers were back, stronger than before.

"What now, little sister?" Kaspar asked.

"How's Cholena, Jaimon?" Gabby asked.

He paused a moment, then smiled. "Much better. The island has given her renewed strength."

"We need to get to Elvyn right away," Gabby said.

Minutes later, the three mounted Cholena and headed north as fast as they could.

CHAPTER THIRTY-FOUR

Roland Tyre stood next to Alli Stenos and observed Bakari and Liam lying in the small healer's hut. Kharlia stood opposite them. No one spoke.

The appearance of the dragons had stopped the uprising of desert elves and Tillimot traitors. Upon landing, Roland had led Alli here.

Roland now glanced sideways at Alli. They had not spoken since landing. He wasn't sure what to say at this point.

Kharlia shifted and looked at Roland and Alli. "I don't know what else to do." Her voice broke, and she hung her head. "It's been difficult keeping them alive this long. We've done all we could."

Roland glanced down at what he would consider to be his best friend. Bakari's brown skin was pasty and pale, his legs and arms thinner, and his braided hair—although Kharlia must have freshly braided it—void of shine and luster.

Oh, Bak, why, why, why? He had been angry at his friend. Bakari's inability to stop Delia from taking the bond and forcing Alli to do her bidding had been more than Roland could stomach. But what Bakari had done for him during the empress's attack, and having Alli at his side again, erased anger from Roland. Bakari couldn't die!

"I could try again," Roland said. "I have more power now. More than anyone."

Kharlia shook her head, her dark Mahlian hair falling softly on her shoulders. "No, Roland, using magic on him will just speed his death."

Roland growled. "There must be something I can do. What good is being all-powerful if I can't heal him?"

They stood in silence for a few moments longer. Roland took a deep breath and wondered what he was supposed to do now. He knew he put up a tough exterior, but he had to admit to himself for once, maybe he was in over his head. Thoughts turned to Alli and he began to turn in her direction, but before he did, Roland felt Alli's fingers against his. He turned quicker, anticipation fueling him. She gave him a small smile and grasped his hand tighter.

His heart burst with thankfulness that she had come back to him. He knew they had a lot to think about. But just having her here brought him renewed strength.

"Welcome back, Alli," Kharlia said.

Alli nodded. "I still can't remember everything, and I know I have a lot to atone for, but it's nice to be among friends again." She glanced back down at Bakari and Liam and her voice caught. "I just wish there was something we could do."

"Gabby may yet return," Kharlia said.

Roland nodded at Kharlia's optimism and wished he could share in it. He didn't resent her for holding out hope. It was all she had. Maybe Gabby would return.

Outside the hut, the wind picked up, and rain fell hard on the roof once again. Lightning and thunder rolled overhead as the three resumed their silent vigil.

* * *

Roland woke from a restless sleep and walked out on a high deck of one of the nicest Elvyn guest chambers. The air was damp, but the storm had moved on, with only a handful of clouds hanging low over the Lor'l trees.

"Warlord," an Elvyn messenger called up to him from a level down and a tree over from where he stood. "Ships are approaching."

Roland sighed. It would be today.

Unify them. The scepter's command came once more. It hadn't said much to him lately, and Roland wondered about that.

Nodding to the messenger, he went inside and put on his golden cloak, strapping a sword on one side and carrying the scepter in his other hand. He crossed to the deck for a moment and took a deep breath. Power from the scepter sizzled through him, and he stood straighter with the new jolt of energy.

He followed the messenger down the tree and across bridges and levels, to the ground. He was led to a spot that was on high ground, overlooking the bay. Both his and Alli's dragons sat not far in front of him. Alli stood next to hers, her hand to Miriel's snout and a smile on her face. She turned around as if sensing him, and her smile broadened. As did Roland's. They had spoken alone briefly the night before. They had both been too exhausted after the day's ordeals to say much, but it was enough to know that she was there to help him. He hoped it would turn into something more, but for now he felt comfort and strength in her presence.

"Sire." King Lanwaithian walked up beside him.

Roland bobbed his head at the king. "Lan, it's good to have a dragon rider back with us."

"And this particular one lifts your heart," Lan said.

Roland felt his face grow warm, and the king chuckled.

Roland cleared his throat. "I wish them all here for this, but I'm not sure how that will be accomplished. Unity is the only way we can beat back the ships."

The night before he had pulled out the dragon artifact from the Citadel he had brought with him, the small figurine that Bakari had given him to call the help of the dragons if ever needed. In Bakari's current condition, Roland didn't know if the dragons would respond or not, but it was all he could do about them at the moment.

The king nodded in agreement and pointed into the lifting fog. "The first ships look to be only a few hours away, Warlord."

Men and women began to gather on the shoreline. Many of the troops had been gathering from the other kingdoms for the last few days. The crowd stretched for at least a mile. He had tens of thousands of men and women—hundreds of them wizards—and at least sixty ships at his disposal. But would it be enough? They did hold the advantage of being on land, but the number of ships he had seen was astounding.

Alli came up next to him now, and Breelyn, the queen, a powerful mage in her own right, joined the king. The four of them stood on the small sandy knoll and looked out over the troops.

Men and women from many lands stood looking up at him. Blond, black, brown, and a few redheads with white, dark, and olive complexions. They were young and old, nobles and peasants. They had all come at his call to protect their land, and he swelled inside with love and pride for his people.

Roland held the Scepter of Unification in the air, and the crowd applauded. He heard the praise for him and Roland let it continue for a moment, relishing in the power he held and the people he loved. He had done what the scepter had asked him to do, and now the people were unified behind him.

But would it be enough? The thought plagued Roland as often as the scepter's chant of unification echoed in his mind. He raised his hands, and lightning flew from the scepter and filled the sky with wonderful colors.

Suddenly hoof beats sounded behind him, and he turned around. Two Cremelino horses trotted up next to him, their coats wet with perspiration. A double roar filled the sky, and two more dragons—Ryker, the red, and Abylar, the blue— soared over the trees. Hanging down from them were the transportation contraptions Delia had built to move her troops around. As the dragons lowered them to the ground, hundreds of additional troops from Solshi, Turg, and Cyrene poured out of them, many of them wizards.

We heard your call, High Wizard. The voice of Ryker, the red dragon, spoke boldly, yet with a hint of sad desperation.

More help is coming, came Abylar's voice, though with much more of a melancholy tone.

Roland understood the subdued nature of the dragons. Both of their riders, Bakari and Liam were still lying unconscious in the healer's hut.

Roland smiled at the additional strength the dragons brought and felt things clicking into place. Now all the southern kingdoms were represented in the gathering, as well as powerful counselor wizards of the heart, scholarly wizards of the mind, and battle wizards of the earth—Alli being at the forefront of those.

The two dragons and Cremelinos joined Alli and Roland's dragons, and Roland felt the power of unification swell inside him. The dragons and the Cremelinos were the last piece.

He let out a deep breath. He had kept a frantic pace, but he had done what no one else had. He had unified them all. Now his power would be complete. Now he could save his people!

The crowd quieted down. Roland glanced out at the sea for a long moment before turning back to his people.

"Today is only one day in your life, but a day that marks fate for all of us. Today we stand together, unified as one people. We put aside our differences of kingdoms, race, religion, and whether we have magical powers or not. Today we stand unified against the aggressors of the eastern kingdom."

Some in the crowd turned and stared at the approaching ships, but Roland continued. He had been promised all power for unifying the people, and today he would use that power to defeat the enemy.

"How we live our lives in the future will depend on what we do this day, this hour, this moment. Nothing is more important than the now. Rise up, my people of the unified golden empire, and let's push back the aggressors and tell them who we really are. As High Wizard of the Citadel, King of

Alaris, Monarch of Tillimot, Regent of North and South Solshi, Conqueror of Turg and Cyrene, Protector of Quentis, Warlord of Elvyn, Ally of Khazer, and . . .” Roland paused for a moment. The last title was a weak one at best, but he could hope for any additional strength it would give him. What was he to Mahli, Bakari’s homeland? He had left them alone in this fight, but there were those here from Bakari’s homeland, nonetheless, in support of their Dragon King who still lay at death’s door.

“. . . and Friend of Mahli,” he decided would work. “I, Roland Tyre, the holder of the Scepter of Unification and rider of the golden dragon, do now call on all humans, elves, wizards, and magical creatures from all kingdoms and all ages to rise up today. Let us fight! Let us call upon all the powers at our disposal to show the empress of the east that we will not be her next conquest, her next city, her next slave.”

Excited voices cheered.

“Today we fight as a unified people!” Roland shouted as loud as he could. “Today we fight for freedom!” He raised the scepter once again, and powerful bursts of light flew out from its orbed tip and up over the heads of the people. They hollered with excitement and began chanting Roland’s name once again.

Off in the distance, over the sound of the crowd, a loud boom sounded. Something flew up high in the sky from one of the ships. It exploded in the sky as a beautiful firework.

Lan leaned over to him. “Too bad something so beautiful signals the beginning of something so ugly.”

Roland nodded in agreement, then turned to Alli. “Battlemaster, ready the troops.”

CHAPTER THIRTY-FIVE

Three hours later, the first volley of cannon balls from the warships hit the Elvyn ships. Suddenly the battle was real. A battle so huge that none in the present generation had ever seen or thought it possible.

The fog in the Blue Sea sat about a mile off shore, and Roland marveled at the number of ships that continued to sail out of it. The sea was black with them. His heart sank as he realized he was actually leading the defense of a war without any prior knowledge. He was not a fighter—oh, he had trained with weapons and could hold his own, but he was born to rule, not fight.

The ships were huge, with three to four large sails each. Their sides were tall, and the hulls were equipped with tree-sized spears coming out from the front. He marveled at the size of the crew each ship must hold.

He ground his teeth and hopped up on his golden dragon. With Alli close behind, and the other two dragons following, he made a sweep down the shore between the ships and the coast. The soldiers cheered and dug in their feet for the start of the battle.

Roland turned his dragon around and headed out over the water. Not knowing the enemy's full strength, he was hesitant to get too close.

It was lucky for him that he held back. He barely missed the net of magic that shot out from one of the ships and grabbed ahold of his dragon's foot. With a roar Orelia flew up higher and out of the net.

Alli flew by him and signaled that she was going down the line a bit. As he watched her fly away, his heart soared at having her with him.

A whoosh of air signaled a blast of cannon fire that barely missed his back. Orelia dove and spit a line of fire directly at the attacking ship. The wizard on it fell back to the deck, and fire from his fingers found the ropes on the masts. Sailors scrambled to keep the fire from the sails.

Flying over the next ship, Roland pointed his scepter down at it, and a bright explosion enveloped the hull. Soldiers and sailors dove off the side to escape the destruction.

That was more like it!

An explosion rocked Roland, and he grabbed on tightly to keep from falling. Looking in the direction of the noise, he saw an Elvyn ship engaging two other eastern ships. Before he could do anything about it, Abylar soared overhead and dove down. His giant mouth opened up, and a stream of fire spewed forth, disintegrating the opposing ship in one breath.

Roland began to feel a bit of hope. With four dragons they might have a chance. Looking down the line, he saw Alli and her dragon blasting a wall of fire between the enemy line and the shore. Bolts of lightning blasted up and down from Alli to the ships.

Roland realized that each ship must have at least one wizard. And there were so many ships. They didn't stop. A few of them had made it through the dragons and were now approaching the shore. A shout went up, and a volley of flaming arrows came from the shore and landed on three ships. Screams and yells ensued as men and women leapt from the burning ship.

Dark-haired southerners fought alongside heads of blond and red, and Roland felt a lump in his throat at the sight. His chest burst with pride for his people.

A larger ship came through the fog, and Roland could see five men standing at the bow. Each held his hands high in the air, and above them a creature materialized. Roland's heart sank at the sight.

It was three times the size of his dragon and at least twice the size of the other dragons. It had a long, spiked tail that snaked through the air; its head was horned and rimmed with long spears. The face was grotesque, similar to a dragon, but with all the worst characteristics magnified. The eyes were too large, the mouth even larger. It had shorter legs and was more like a flying snake.

Roland took his dragon closer and while holding the scepter in his hand sent a blast of fire into the creature. However, at the last possible moment the flying snake turned translucent, and Roland's fire flew right through without doing any damage. Roland cringed at first, but then smiled. Maybe this creature was only for show and couldn't really harm them.

The creature slithered with incredible speed through the air and past Roland. He took his dragon up higher, turned around and followed the creature toward the shore. The creature lowered its head and dove down toward one of the ships from

Tillimot. With a crash and crunch, the creature tore the ship apart.

So much for it being just for show.

Roland began to race toward it when he saw movement out of the corner of his eye. He turned and saw another creature, and another. His heart fell. A few opposing ships had reached the shore, and men were disembarking. The hand-to-hand combat for the ownership of the western continent had begun.

"No!" Roland yelled out. This wasn't the way it was supposed to be. *You promised me,* he told the scepter.

You were promised glory. The scepter vibrated in his hand and in his mind.

Then give me glory. Give me victory. Roland raced his dragon toward the enemy wizards and their ships, their hands still in the air. He flew low and, with the scepter stretched out, called upon its power. A blast of liquid fire raced out of the glass orb on the end and consumed the five men where they stood. The snake-like creature they had been conjuring disappeared in thin air.

Roland turned in a circle and counted at least five more of the creatures wreaking havoc on his ships. The men on the shore were holding their own, and Alli and the other dragons seemed to be destroying ships one after another.

He raced for another ship of magickers and pointed his scepter. The ship split in two. Racing toward the other creatures, he used the scepter to destroy each of the eastern wizards who were forming the creatures.

The morning fog began to lift, and Roland could see farther than before. Warships stretched for miles and miles. Roland spied the biggest ship he had ever seen in his life. Five tall masts rose above a massive vessel. It was colored red, with a red and gold flag flying atop its tallest mast. Even from as far away as he was he could see a woman standing on the bow.

The empress!

Four dragons and a puny army is all you have, Roland Tyre? The throaty voice came to his head.

Roland tried to shake it away. "Get away from me!" he said out loud and with a quick burst of mental energy pushed the empress back. He saw her stumble on the deck and grab the rails.

Where is the mighty Dragon King I have heard of? Did Wizard Gabrielle fail in her quest? The questions bombarded Roland. Roland pushed at each one in succession. But the words sank inside him.

Could they win this battle without the Dragon King? He had been told to unify everyone. Well, he had four dragons, but only one true dragon rider. He had thought he could do it himself; now he wasn't so sure. Doubt began to expand in his mind.

Wizard, came the voice of his dragon, *beware of her trickery. Be strong!*

Roland sat up straighter. The power of the empress was mental. He smiled at the realization. She sent her troops to fight the physical battle, but it was all in the mind with the empress.

Then that's how he would beat her.

The sounds of battle filled his ears. Orelia took a broad circle, and Roland took in the scene. For miles up and down the coast from Elvyn, hundreds of warships attacked his people. But between dragon, wizard, and human, whether on ground or ship, they were holding their own.

Taking a route closer to the fighting, he brought his scepter out in front of him once again. He needed to believe his own words of motivation. Today was the only day that mattered. Today, this moment, would determine the fate of the continent. Roland let Orelia guide him, and he closed his eyes. With three deep breaths to steady himself he breathed it all back in and with it all the energy and power at his disposal. The power of his dragon, his scepter, his years of training, the power that came with this people and their unification. Power blazed through his heart and mind.

In the corner of his mind, he heard the words of the Elvyn Ambassador Rassdurthian warning him of too much power. But he ignored it and brought more and more. He wasn't afraid of the power. "I am magic!" he yelled as he opened his eyes. The brilliance surrounding him even startled himself. He was glowing.

Roland pointed his scepter toward the sea and drew a line of demarcation between the shore and the eastern warships. The water broiled; the waves turned gold. The point of contact sliced through sea and ship alike. Enemies screamed and fell from their ships as hundreds of ships cracked in half.

Cheers went up from the shore, and hands were raised in triumph. Alli and the other dragons came from both sides, attacking all those Roland had missed. He spied a few skirmishes on shore and raced to stop them, but by the time he had arrived, his people had stopped the advance. Roland smiled and let the power subside. He put a hand to his head to steady himself.

Smoke filled the air, and none of them could see farther out than a few hundred feet. Roland relaxed. *That wasn't so bad!* He waved toward Alli, and she smiled back and pumped her fist in the air.

A roaring sound filled his ears. About to land his dragon on the shore, he rose back up and watched the smoke clear away. Before it all disappeared, he saw faint outlines farther out in the water.

And his stomach fell.

"Roland!" Alli yelled and pointed.

Roland could see. "It can't be." For all the ships they had destroyed there were at least three times that many still sailing toward them. But each one was two to three times the size of the previous ones.

Roland flew next to Alli. "That was just their vanguard. Those they were willing to lose."

Alli nodded and said nothing. Her mouth hung open. Her eyes were wide.

"How do we win, Alli?" Roland asked.

Alli turned to him with fire in her eyes. "This is your doing, Roland."

Roland's eyes went wide.

"If you weren't so bent on gathering so much power and glory for yourself, you could have helped Bakari, and the dragon riders could be here with the might of the Dragon

King. That is our duty, to protect the land and keep the peace." Alli's words flew out quickly. "You thought to take it on yourself. That's not how it works."

"I'm . . . I'm . . ." Roland didn't quite know what to say. Was Alli right? "No," he yelled back. "You're wrong, Alli," Roland argued. He could do it. "Bakari made his choice and fell to Delia's trickery, and I am left to clean up the mess."

"It's not all about you, Roland! That's only what you want to see, and it skews everything you do see!"

Her words hurt Roland more than he cared to admit. Not for who said them—one of the things that attracted Roland to Alli in the first place was her fierceness and desire to defend those that couldn't defend themselves. It was the meaning behind the words. Had he truly lost sight of the things of more importance in his quest for power?

Roland glanced back at the shore, lined with people—his people. The people he had sworn to protect. Words caught in his throat, and he shook his head back and forth. "You don't understand," he said. "I do it for my people. I did everything for them. The scepter told me to unify them."

"The scepter has used you for your own vanity!" Alli yelled over the sound the battle, but her expression softened. "Now look."

Roland did look, and he truly didn't know what to do. The additional ships were coming within range of the shore now.

Before Roland knew what was happening, his battlemaster started her own war. She dove down upon each ship, and between the power of her dragon and her own wizard powers she took on an entire army. The way she moved with her dragon as one was beautiful and mesmerizing. Colors of power flew around her as she blasted one ship after another.

Why can't we be like that? He spoke to his dragon. He realized they had never moved together like Alli and Miriel did.

Unify them! The scepter pounded again.

Roland roared. What more was there to unify? At this rate they would all be unified in death—all his people. It tore him up inside.

Unify the powers!

Roland hadn't heard that before. Something coming from the south caught his eye, and he drew up higher out of the battle for a moment.

"Roland!" he heard Alli scream out. "Get back here and fight!"

But something drew him away from the battle. Something bright and beautiful was coming toward them. Something powerful! Something that could help him win the war.

CHAPTER THIRTY-SIX

"Gabby!" Roland yelled out far too soon for the young wizard to hear him. He felt almost giddy with excitement. Had she really found a phoenix?

Roland raced toward the oncoming dragon. As he flew down the coast, he watched his people fighting. They couldn't see the endless ships from their perspective, but they fought. A few wizards raised their hands to him and waved. As he approached the dragon, he could see three people on its back: Gabby, Jaimon, and Kaspar.

Roland sighed. Why did he always feel nervous around the prince of Quentis? A small contingent of men and women from Quentis raised cheers up to their prince and kinsmen. Kaspar waved toward them as Roland flew up beside them.

"Protector," Kaspar said with a small bow of his head.

"Kaspar," Roland nodded back, then turned to Gabby and Jaimon.

Jaimon couldn't seem to keep the smile from his face. "High Wizard, the bond is back."

Roland nodded. "I know. The rest of the dragons are here."

The two dragons rode side by side, but Cholena seemed to ignore Orelia.

"And Alli?" Gabby asked.

"She has returned," Roland said, though he knew he didn't sound happy.

"What did you do this time?" Kaspar asked.

Anger flared up inside of Roland, and he bit back a retort. His and Alli's relationship had nothing to do with Kaspar Von Wulf.

Roland felt a power around them that he couldn't see. "Did you find the phoenix?"

Gabby's face fell. "Yes, we did."

"And, where is it?" Roland continued to look around.

"Let's land and talk," Gabby said.

There was something that wasn't being said. Roland didn't have time for this, but he agreed anyway.

"They're so many," Kaspar said, pointing out to sea. "How can we hold them off?" He looked at Roland. "Why are you not out there fighting?"

Roland did let his anger rise this time. "Because I'm here with you! Do you have a phoenix or not? It may be our only chance. We need more power."

Cannons from the newly arrived warships blasted their balls through the air. Roland surged lower for the moment and took his dragon down over one. With a roar from Orelia, the ship caught fire, and with a blast from Roland's scepter, three others were pounded with lightning. Roland circled back around and looked out in the bay for Alli. She sat on Miriel, with both Abylar and Ryker flanking her. They were keeping most of the ships at bay. The ones that did get through were currently being taken care of by his troops. But the warships continued coming. At some point his people would tire.

Roland bit back a moan.

Soon both Orelia and Cholena landed, and Roland directed Gabby, Jaimon, and Kaspar up and away from the fighting. King Lanwaithian joined them and offered his greetings. The three travelers appeared exhausted, and food was promised them soon.

"I need to see the Dragon King first," Gabby said and started running toward the hut.

Roland gritted his teeth. "We need to win this war. I need the power of the phoenix."

Gabby glanced at him with sad eyes but then turned away. She shook her head at him. "The power is for the Dragon King."

Roland grabbed her arm and spun her around. Before he could say anything, Kaspar had a knife pulled and pushed Roland away. With his hand on his scepter, Roland glared at Kaspar.

"Don't touch my sister," Kaspar said as he stood between the two.

"He's not going to make it," came a small voice from farther down the path. It was followed by a sob. "He's almost dead. Both of them."

"Kharlia!" Gabby ran toward the healer and gave her a hug.

Roland and Kaspar stole one last glare at each other before they and Jaimon joined the two women. All five walked back inside the small hut. They stood crowded around the invalids.

"Did you find it?" Kharlia asked with hope in her eyes.

"It's a long story," Gabby said as she pulled out a long, red feather. A splash of orange decorated the tip.

"Where is the phoenix?" Roland asked. "Is all you have a feather?"

"The phoenix's power is in the magic stream, Roland," Gabby said. "I've been there. I've seen what it takes to reach them."

Kharlia softly touched Gabby's arm. "Are you all right?"

Gabby nodded. "I think so, but I can't go there again."

A wailing scream was heard out on the beach, and Jaimon clutched his head. "Cholena!" He bolted to the door.

"Jaimon!" Gabby called.

"Someone's trying to hurt the dragons," Jaimon said with a turn of his head. "I need to help."

Roland stuck his head out the door and yelled after the racing young rider. "What about Alli?"

"Miriel's hurt, too," Jaimon called back.

Roland took a step outside, but someone grabbed his shoulder. Roland snapped around, thinking it was Kaspar. A loud retort disappeared from his lips when he beheld Kharlia watching him.

"Bak needs you, Roland," Kharlia whispered, tears falling from her eyes.

Roland turned and peered down the path toward the shore once again. "They all need me," he sighed.

But he came back into the hut with the others.

Bakari's chest barely moved. It seemed like seconds between each rise. His skin was still pale and his lips almost white. Liam didn't look any better. His face was pure white, and his thin body was barely more than bones.

Roland knelt next to them, holding onto his scepter. He looked up at Gabby and she reached down and gave him the feather. He took it in his other hand.

A feather! Is that what this all came down to? All his glory, the war, his friend? Down to a single feather? Roland brought the feathered hand to Bakari's forehead and laid it there with his palm on top. He closed his eyes and, with all the strength that he had, pushed the war raging outside out of his mind. A vision of Alli standing up on her dragon and throwing bolts of fire down on the enemy brought a small smile to his lips—but then he pushed that away also.

The magic stream came to him easily now. The amount of power he held was a raging torrent there. He stood in the grayness and looked around. Hundreds of pinpricks of light stood around him. All the wizards from both sides of the fray. A few here and there blinked out, and Roland steeled himself. He had preached to his people of the importance of a day, a moment. Well, now it was time for him to prove it to himself.

Taking a deep breath, he pulled in the power of the scepter.

Unify them! Came the familiar taunting. And he reached out his mind and powers.

He grabbed a wizard from each of the kingdoms under his control and from each of the three disciplines of magic and pulled some of their power into him. And the power flowed into him, first a stream, then a mighty river.

He reached out to the magical creatures. First, the two Cremelinos.

High Wizard! They acknowledged his presence.

Then he reached out to the dragons: first his own, then Ryker, Cholena, Abylar, and last of all Miriel.

What are you doing, Roland? Alli's voice came to him, whether directly in the magic stream or through the dragon bond, Roland didn't know.

I need to unify them all, Alli. I . . . I . . . I need to save Bakari. There he had admitted what he feared all along. He couldn't do it himself. He needed the strength of the Dragon King.

No! she said. *I will not let anyone steal this bond again. It's mine. Get out here and fight.*

I am doing what I can, Alli. Please, Roland begged. She could be so stubborn!

But Alli cut him off.

Roland growled and dove deeper into the magic stream. But as he did so he felt the presence of the other dragons around him. They were in trouble and fought against other wizards trying to control them.

All of a sudden, a bright light flared in front of him.

A phoenix! he thought.

But instead, it was the empress again. She stood dressed in red. With her dark hair pulled back, her face more angular than before. Darkness circled her eyes, and her lips twitched in anger.

"Get out of my way, Roland Tyre," the empress said.

"This is our land," Roland retorted.

The empress brought a hand out in front of her and pushed it at Roland. He actually fell backwards—something he didn't think was possible in the magic stream.

"You'll never win," the empress sneered.

Roland knew he couldn't win the war physically; it had to be won with magic. "I am the most powerful wizard in the land," Roland said. And he heard a thunderous boom off in the distance of the magic stream.

With both him and the empress there, the magic stream was becoming unstable. There was too much power in once place. Lights blinked and flew around him in crazy patterns. He saw those he knew. Tam, still back at the Citadel, Tabitha safe in Turg, Danijela, the High Wizard of the wizard conclave of Arc, Mezar, the Emperor of Gildan, and Darius, the king of the Realm and Liam's father.

Save my son, came Darius's voice, and he shared his power of the heart with Roland.

Be careful, Roland, came Danijela's voice, and she gave him some of her power of the earth.

Protect us all. The mighty wizard, Mezar, lent Roland his powers of the mind.

As they did this, the ground underneath the empress and Roland shook again.

"If I can't destroy you in person, wizard, I will destroy you here, forever." The empress stomped her foot on the ground, and Roland felt a shift in the magic stream. The normal grayness churned a multitude of colors.

Roland couldn't let this happen. His body jumped a bit in the hut when someone touched his arm. He felt something slide into his palm, between his hand and the scepter. He glanced back up at the empress in the magic stream and suddenly saw into her mind.

An artifact. Roland felt a small dragon artifact in his hand. Kaspar had shared it with him.

Save us, Protector, came Kaspar's fading voice.

He didn't hesitate before pushing into the empress's mind.

"No!" she screamed.

Suddenly her mind was open to Roland, and he saw into her so-called mighty empire. But it was not the beautiful cities she had shown him. Now he saw them for what they truly were. Dirty, poor, starving people. Ten cities in all; ten conquered lands. His heart went out to them, and he vowed that his land, the western continent, his golden empire, would not be the next land for her to trample on.

Leave! Roland commanded, and the empress swayed on her feet in the magic stream. She shifted in and out for a moment before solidifying once again. Her once-beautiful face now became contorted and filled with rage. The smooth skin went dry and wrinkled, the dark glossy hair went dull and gray, and Roland saw her for who she really was. It had all been an illusion. Once her mind was opened to him he saw all that was real.

Roland threw the weight of his power at her again, and she screamed and winked out of the magic stream. Roland leaned over, hands on his knees, and tried to take a deep breath. Had he beat her? He reached out for Alli's bright sparkle of light and grabbed hold; he was there with her on her dragon. Whether in body or spirit, he couldn't tell.

Alli almost jumped out of her seat when Roland whispered in her ear. "How goes the battle?"

"Roland?" Alli yelled, turning her head around. "What are you doing here?"

"I defeated the empress in the magic stream," Roland said.

"Nothing has changed here," Alli said.

Roland looked out and his heart sank once again. She was right. The war raged on below them. His people were doing well, but slowly, bit by bit, they were being pushed back by the onslaught of ships.

Alli pointed to the biggest ship, and once again Roland spied the empress standing there in her physical form.

"We can't let them beat us, Alli!" Roland cried out. "I've seen her empire. I can't let my people live like that. I owe them more."

"I thought you were all powerful, Roland," Alli said with a harsh tone. "I thought you had a plan to save us all."

"That's not fair," Roland cried out. "I've done all I can. There is nothing else I can do."

A loud crash drove Roland to turn around. Three large ships had crashed into the docks of Elvyn, and hundreds of enemy soldiers were taking the beach.

Alli turned her head again, and her eyes softened. "I'm sorry Roland," she said with a change of tone. "I really, really am."

Roland put his hand up and caressed her check from behind. Alli moved her head closer to his hand, and Roland felt the tears roll down her face. A bolt of lightning shot by them, and Alli moved away from his palm and turned her dragon toward the offender.

"If we can't win, Roland, I will die taking as many with me as I can," Alli said. "Go. Do whatever you can do. Let's not let all this fighting be in vain. There must be something you can do."

A life for a life.

The soft whisper burned through Roland's mind. He reached his hand out to touch Alli once more, but all of a sudden he found himself back in the magic stream.

He shaded his eyes from the brilliant red and orange light in front of him. Rising up out of the light was the most beautiful bird he had ever seen. His voice caught in his throat as he realized what it was.

A phoenix. The most powerful creature alive.

He found himself holding his scepter once again.

Unify, it spoke again. *Unify the magic and truly be the most powerful wizard in the world, Roland Tyre.*

And now he knew what that meant. He had unified the people and gathered all their power; he had linked with the Cremelinos and had his own dragon, but until the other dragons shared their power with him he couldn't defeat the empress. But they would not obey him—they needed their king, Bakari. And the phoenix was the key to saving Bakari.

Standing in the magic stream, but feeling his hand still on Bakari's head in the small hut, he reached out for the power of the phoenix but hit a block.

A life for a life, came the voice of the Phoenix once again.

What? Roland didn't understand. *Stop the riddles and tell me what you want from me.*

You wanted all power, came the voice of the scepter now. *This is the price.*

The price? What price? You never talked about a price.

You said you would do anything to be the greatest wizard. You wanted glory, and we gave it to you. Each kingdom has bowed to you, and they chant your name in praise. You hold inside you the power of earth, mind, heart, and a portion of spirit. If you truly want it all. If you truly want to be the greatest, you must sacrifice the most. You must sacrifice all to be all powerful.

A life for a life, the phoenix spoke again.

And Roland finally understood.

The weight of it all brought him to his knees. His mind opened again, and he saw the barrage of ships in the Blue Sea. More and more of them were making landfall. The dragons were tiring, and his people were beginning to die.

Tears came to Roland's eyes and his head sank lower. He couldn't let them all die. They needed the Dragon King.

As if in response to his thoughts, he found himself in the small hut once again. His hand still rested on Bakari's forehead. But the Dragon King's skin grew cold, and his breathing barely existed. Roland looked over at Liam and groaned. He couldn't save both of them could he?

He turned his face upward and caught Gabby's kind eyes. Tears streamed down her face. She understood. Somehow she understood the sacrifice that was needed. A life for a life.

"Roland?" Kharlia asked, her voice forlorn and desperate. "Is there nothing you can do?"

He dropped his head and studied his friend. A man who never wanted glory or power for himself, but had taken the role of the Dragon King to heart.

Realization blossomed red and orange in Roland's mind. Now he knew what made a man great. It wasn't the amount of his power, but the strength of his heart. Here lay the lowly scholar wizard who had scolded him about wanting too much magic, but whose power could save them all. The Dragon King's power was pure and untainted and his ability to unite the dragons could save them from being destroyed.

And Roland truly realized he was not the most powerful wizard alive.

He felt shaken to his core. Hollowed out. Yet he knew, with every fiber of his being, what he had to do.

Unify them!

He looked up at Gabby once again and nodded. With a sob, she covered her mouth.

Well, whatever he was, whatever power he had or didn't have, Roland still knew he was different from others. Tears smarted his eyes. But he turned to Kharlia.

And smiled.

CHAPTER THIRTY-SEVEN

Bakari couldn't distinguish how long he had lain in this state. Time had slowed for him days or weeks before—he didn't really know. The last thing he truly remembered was being in Hillside with Jaimon, Liam, and Gabby. He had met his Uncle Auni there and had received a present. He remembered opening the matching glove to what Liam had gathered in the cave. Before anyone could say anything about it, Liam, Jaimon, and then he had started having excruciating pains.

He had been poisoned.

In the time since then, Bakari had had glimpses of events from time to time. He knew Kharlia watched over him. And he longed to reach out and touch her hand or give her a gentle word. But his body continued to decline any such command.

The magic stream had called to him from time to time, and he had slipped in and out of it. The bright spot was that he had felt the dragon bond return. It had been a glorious and wonderful moment. He knew Abylar fought the onset of a great horde of ships alongside the other dragons, but he didn't truly understand what it all meant.

Then moments before, he'd felt a touch on his head, and power had flared through him. It was a power like none other. A cool hand had touched him, and he knew Roland was there. His body was too worn to hear or understand what was happening in the room around him, but he knew that a decision hung in the balance.

Roland's magic flared in his head, and he felt the poison in his body respond negatively. "Aaargh!" he screamed out in his head and tried to twist away from it. The poison fed off the power and drove deeper into this body. He knew he couldn't last much longer.

Roland! He yelled out in his mind. Then he was transported away. He stood now on a hill of sand overlooking the usually serene seashore of Lor'l. Today, however, thousands of ships crowded the harbor, and a heavy battle raged around him. Bakari had never seen so many people or ships.

Roland came running down a path from the forest and out onto the beach. He jumped on his golden dragon and flew high up in the sky. Higher and higher he went until he was hardly more than a speck. Then a desperate and pitiful roar came from above. The paired voice of man and dragon together tore the fabric of the sky. Thousands of men and women turned to look up, the frenzied battle pausing for a moment.

And then the speck grew bigger and bigger as Roland and his dragon dropped from the heavens. It was glorious and dreadful at the same time. Roland's blond hair flew around his handsome face, which was bathed in the golden glow of his scepter. His golden cloak rode behind him in the increasing wind. He closed his blue eyes, and when they opened again his face was as serene and tranquil as a spring morning.

Bakari had never felt so much power in his life. A bright red bird popped up between him and Roland, and Roland's power grew even more. At the same time, Bakari's pain began to retreat, and he felt his own strength beginning to return.

A life for a life, the bird said—a phoenix—Bakari now realized.

A lump formed in Bakari's throat. He reached a hand in desperation toward Roland as his friend continued to plummet toward the largest ship of the fleet—the one with the grand lady standing at the bow. "No, Roland," a mere whisper left his dry lips.

Roland turned his head, and although the distance would say otherwise, Bakari could see him clearly. Roland regarded Bakari for a moment, and nodded to him in respect.

"Bak, it's up to you now," Roland whispered. "Save these people. Please, save my people."

With the golden Scepter of Unification held out in his hand, Roland and his dragon plunged into the largest ship of the fleet and directly into the empress herself. As Roland landed, he struck the ship with the scepter and roared with all his might. An explosion rocked the air, and a golden blast of fire raced over the ship destroying it and everyone on it in mere moments. From the depths of the ship a red and orange ball of fire roared up into the sky farther than Bakari could see. It hung above them all for a moment and then plunged back down to the water, hitting the spot where Roland had gone with such force that its splash covered hundreds of ships.

With the force of the blast, Alli and the other dragons fell from the sky, barely gaining control before landing on the beach in front of him. Bakari searched for Roland and his dragon, but nothing was left of him or the empress's ship.

After a moment of silence, the phoenix flew up from the fires of the ship Roland had destroyed. Bright red feathers outstretched, tinted with edges of orange and gold, the bird flew directly toward him.

Bakari lifted an arm into the sky, and the phoenix landed on it. Bakari felt a power that dwarfed all others. Along with the dragons and the Cremlinos, it was the power of spirit: the power to bind. And with that power, Bakari felt the poison leave his body. His strength roared to life.

The phoenix disappeared back into the magic stream, but Bakari now found himself standing on the shoreline, but in full physical form. He stretched his hands out and called upon the power that was his and his alone. "Dragons, to me!"

Jaimon and Alli on their yellow and green dragons flew to him from one side, while Abylar and Ryker came from the other. Bakari mounted his blue dragon and relished once again the bond that he held with him, amplified more so due to the healing power of the phoenix he still held inside him. He took the dragons up in the sky and ordered them into a line along the shore. Looking down, he saw the Cremelinos—and for a moment wondered if Liam was also healed.

Still feeling the power of the phoenix coursing through his veins, Bakari pulled all he could into himself. He was at a breaking point, but he pulled on more. He felt more alive than he had ever felt in his entire life. Blue fire crackled around him and his dragon.

Through his bond with the dragons, and as the Dragon King, he connected himself to all the magic down below him. He connected himself to each wizard, elf, and magical creature and they all gave to him willingly. He glanced from his left to his right and nodded at Alli and Jaimon. With hardly more than a blink of an eye, through their dragon bond, he shared the power he had with each of them—also willingly. Alli's eyes opened wide, and she flexed her fingers, powerful yellow light escaping out between her knuckles. Jaimon appeared for a moment like he might be sick, but then he sat up straighter, and a broad smile spread across his face. Crackles of green lightning raced around him, and he yelled out in glee.

The three dragon riders and four dragons held their line at the shore and, upon Bakari's command, the riders shot forth their hands toward the opposing warships. A hurricane of wind formed in front of them and began pushing the water back, the ships with it. Lighting crackled from the sky, diving down into each of the thousands of ships. Thunder boomed around them, and the sky darkened as a huge dark cloud formed between the shore and the ships.

With his last strength, Bakari screamed out loud and pushed his hands out in front of him. The ships were instantly driven back miles upon miles on the sea, many of them overturning and sinking. Those that weren't destroyed continued to be blown by the wind and rising storm until nothing could be seen of the enemy in the distance. Without a leader, they limped back east.

Bakari dropped his hands, his strength depleted. His braids flew around his head in the air as the wind subsided. He signaled the others to return to land with him. As they landed on the sand, the crowds around them cheered and hollered in a celebration of victory.

"Hail the Dragon King!"

"Hail the Dragon Riders!"

Bakari smiled, glad they had been able to defeat the enemy. But his face dropped as he remembered the price that had been paid to do so.

Alli came up beside him and gave him a questioning look. He shook his head, not trusting himself to speak of Roland at the moment. The price of this war had been too great. Tears welled up in Alli's eyes and she fell to the earth and sobbed with heartbreak and emotion. Eventually she looked up to the sky and with tears still streaming down her face and shook her head. "Stupid man. How am I supposed to live without you."

Bakari turned away from Alli and toward another sound. Running down a path from the trees came Kharlia, Gabby, and Kaspar. Kharlia pushed the others aside, almost knocking them over, and fell into Bakari's arms.

"You disappeared from the hut," she wept. "I didn't know . . . we didn't know what happened to you. I thought . . . I thought . . . " She couldn't finish the words.

Bakari held her close, and tears streamed from his own eyes. Gabby and Kaspar hugged him, and soon they were joined by Lanwaithian and Breelyn. After congratulations were said, the king ushered them back under the trees and ordered a feast.

"What about Liam?" Bakari asked before stepping away.

"What about me?" came a voice from a few yards away.

Bakari turned and saw two Elvyn healers carrying Liam on a litter.

"When you were healed," Liam said to Bakari, "your power as the Dragon King along with the re-established bond with my dragon began to heal me too."

"I had magic for a few moments, Liam!" shouted Jaimon. "It was incredible."

"I'm sorry I missed the fight," Liam said as he looked around behind the other dragon riders.

The healers brought the litter down, and Liam stepped off. A loud roar was heard behind them, and the great red dragon took a step closer.

"Ryker!" Liam called out and ran to his dragon.

Bakari smiled. He understood the feeling. He wished he could leave with Abylar right now and just fly off with him by themselves. He glanced at Kharlia standing next to him. *Well, with Kharlia and Abylar.*

"My foot, Bakari!" Liam turned and yelled. "My foot is better than ever!"

Bakari laughed in delight as he realized his eyesight had returned also. The power of the dragons was once again working with the dragon riders.

The group set back off again to the feast being prepared.

As they sat down later to eat, and at Bakari's urging, Gabby filled them all in on that had happened since Bakari and Liam had been poisoned. Alli sat mostly to the side, only joining in the conversation when asked to clarify something.

Bakari couldn't believe all that Roland had accomplished in such a short time. He glanced at Alli and caught her eye. He nodded to her to join him outside.

Walking out the door, they stood on a wooden platform that looked down on Lor'l. From where they stood they could see the shoreline. Men and women of all lands and races were helping in the clean-up effort. Many had been killed.

"Well, he got what he wanted, didn't he?" Alli said with a soft, sad voice.

Bakari nodded his head. "For a moment there he was the most powerful wizard in the land."

"And stories and songs will be told of his sacrifice." Alli blinked as she stared out at the ocean. "All he wanted was power and adoration."

"And he did it all in his usual extravagant style," Bakari said softly.

"Oh, Bak." Alli turned and grabbed Bakari into a warm hug. "I've never seen such a display of magic in my life. He lived large and died even larger . . . but what am I going to do without him?"

"What are *we* all going to do without him, Alli?" Bakari added. He really couldn't believe that Roland was gone.

They pulled away from their embrace at the sound of a voice on the ground below them.

"You're both giving up on me so soon?"

"Roland!" Alli screamed and leapt over the deck, almost knocking Roland over as she dropped thirty feet to the ground.

Bakari jumped down too and joined his friends in an embrace. The others from the feast ran outside after hearing Alli's scream and looked down over the edge of the railings. A few shouts and hollers drifted down to Bakari, Alli, and Roland down below.

While the others took a lift down from the tree, Bakari took a step back from Roland. Alli continued to hold onto him tightly around the waist. Roland's face was dirty, and his golden cape hung in scorched tatters around his shoulder. Part of his shirt and pants were missing, and he seemed about ready to fall over.

"How?" Alli asked, her arm around his waist.

The others joined them and they all waited for Roland's explanation.

"Roland," Bakari didn't really know what to say. "What you did . . . I don't know how to even thank you. You gave up everything for me."

Roland shrugged. His bravado seemed gone for the moment. "I did it for the people. For everyone, Bak."

King Lanwaithian bowed his head low, and others followed suite.

"So what do you think about me now, Alli?" Roland smiled, but Bakari noticed the smile was forced and didn't reach his eyes.

Alli moved closer to Roland as others came in to hug him. "You are either the most stupid man I have ever met, or the most brilliant and brave one I will ever know," she said. "I haven't decided yet."

Roland sagged against her, obviously tired from the ordeal. "I'll take the latter, if I have a choice."

"Oh, Roland!" Alli said and then hugged him again.

Gabby stepped forward with a concerned look on her face and spoke to Roland. "But, how did you come back? I know the price, Roland." Gabby's eyes clouded up again. "It's a life for a life."

Roland considered for a moment, then he winked. "Well, it seems my charms work on a phoenix as well."

Bakari laughed, and Alli rolled her eyes.

"As with all mythical creatures, they talk in riddles and hold secrets within secrets," Roland began to explain.

Bakari chuckled. He knew of what Roland spoke.

"There are many lives we can give up," Roland said. "I gave up my physical life for Bak—um, the Dragon King," he corrected himself, "but I struck an additional bargain—you know how I can be."

The gathered crowd laughed.

"I gave away my old life for a new one," Roland said.

Bakari felt as confused as the others appeared. He noticed that Roland's eyes glistened and his smile appeared shaky.

Alli spoke first. "And, Roland, what life did you give away?"

Roland's smile faded away now. He held his trembling lips tight for a moment, and tears filled his eyes.

Bakari's heart skipped a beat.

"Roland?" Alli asked again, confusion covering her face. "What did you do this time?"

"I . . ." Roland paused, trying to compose himself. He took a few deep breaths. "The Scepter of Unification is gone and all my wizard powers with it. All of them."

"Roland!" Alli cried out, reached up, and grabbed him by the shoulders. "You did that for us?"

Bakari groaned and wiped tears from his own eyes. He knew how much magic meant to Roland.

"I did this for us, Alli." Roland smiled through his tears. "I did it for all of us. For all my people. I didn't think you could survive without me around."

Alli socked him softly in the shoulder, leaned up on her tiptoes, and kissed him on the cheek.

Bakari took a step closer and shook his head at his friend. "You always were one for the dramatics. What will you do now?"

Roland bowed to Bakari, his tattered golden cloak blowing up behind him. "Dragon King, I'm afraid I may have made a little mess of things. It may take a while to untangle my golden empire and make sure the kingdoms are stable in their own right."

King Lanwaithian Soliel of Elvyn laughed and raised his hand in the air for everyone to quiet down. "Roland Tyre, for your ultimate sacrifice today and your willingness to lead the kingdoms against the might of the east, I name you Elvyn-friend forever more. Wherever your travels take you, you will always have a place to contemplate, rest, and heal in the magical kingdom of Elvyn."

The crowd gathered around Roland, and even Jaimon, Liam, and Kaspar seemed to join in the revelry of the situation. Bakari heard the roar of the dragons behind him and looked back at each of his dragon riders and grinned.

Over the crowd, Bakari caught Roland's eye and mouthed, "Thank you."

Roland nodded his head, smiled, and winked back.

EPILOGUE

Roland sat in his personal office in Cassian, the capital of Alaris. He leaned over his desk and finished writing a missive to Andre De Luz, the king of Solshi. Some of Roland's titles had been ceremonial to get the support of each kingdom, but King of Alaris and Regent of Solshi were not. He was still their leader.

He turned and stared out the window for a few moments. Without the use of his dragon, he had to rely on messengers to deliver his letters around the continent—well, an occasional favor from a dragon rider would get things there quicker, but he couldn't always rely on them. They had the peace to uphold.

Thoughts of the dragon riders made him think of his own dragon once again. It was still a confusing thing to think about, but at the end he thought he finally figured it out. Orelia had never been real. She had been born of Roland's magic and the scepter. All the dragon's power was really Roland's own power. When they had dived together into the warship of the empress, they had both given their lives for Bakari and his people.

Walking to the window, Roland peered out over the city. He spied the gray ribbon of the Corwan River just to the east. The sky was cloudy and the air growing colder. A few flakes of snow began to fall outside, gathering on the edges of the castle wall and the rooftops out in the city.

Opening the window, Roland took a deep breath and felt the cool air fill his lungs. Holding his hand outside, he waited only a moment or two before a beautiful bird landed on his outstretched arm. Roland smiled and pulled it back inside. It was a little bigger than a falcon. Its feathers were a dark red, and its head darted around the room in a quick clip.

I wish they could see you for what you really are, Roland said as he ran his fingers over the smooth feathers.

I am too much power for the people to see, the disguised phoenix said back to Roland's mind.

But you will stay?

For now, said the bird in Roland's mind. *Someone has to watch over you. You are still a dangerous man Roland. Not many people can cheat a Phoenix.*

I didn't cheat. I just used your own riddled words against you.

That as it may be, I am staying around to look after things.

"Roland," Alli called out from the hallway. "Are you ready for dinner?"

Roland's face lit up. With the Citadel having to choose a new High Wizard, Alli had resigned her post as battlemaster, and now, aside from her duties as a dragon rider, never wavered far from Roland's side. Which was all fine with him.

"Coming," he called out and headed toward the door.

Exiting the room, Roland reached to hold Alli's hand.

"Does that bird have to come with us?" Alli wrinkled up her nose at the disguised phoenix sitting on Roland's shoulder.

"I like her," Roland sighed. He didn't want to leave it, but he was really trying not to make Alli mad at him anymore and so, while Alli waited in the hallway, he turned and went back into the room and put the bird on a perch that had been created for her by the window.

Coming back to the door again, Roland turned around and faced the room. With a quick look out into the hallway to make sure Alli wasn't watching, he snapped his fingers and the window shut on its own accord, while the candles snuffed themselves out.

A life for a life, Roland Tyre, the phoenix admonished him. *You bargained away all the magical powers you held, remember.*

Roland laughed. The phoenix obviously didn't know who it was dealing with. *You can't take something I can't give* away, Roland smiled as he closed the door.

"What are you so happy about, Roland?" Alli gave him a sly smile. "What did you do this time?"

"Me?" Roland asked as he escorted her down the broad hallway of the castle.

Roland just shrugged without admitting anything. He had realized soon after the battle that his basic nature of magic was still embedded deep inside of him. It was as much a part of his nature as his hands or feet. He may have given up what the scepter had given him and much of what he had gained in his time as a wizard. You could give up something you have, but you couldn't give away who you were. Because . . .

I am magic!

***

Thus ends The Dragon Artifacts. If you haven't read how Roland, Alli, and Bakari first met, make sure you read The Alaris Chronicles, starting with The Dragon Orb.

Other Series By Mike Shelton
The Alaris Chronicles

Read about how Bakari, Roland, and Alli first met and how the Dragon Riders came to be!

A magical barrier. Civil war. Power-hungry Wizards.

The fate of a kingdom rests on the shoulders of three young wizards who couldn't be more different.

As the magical barrier protecting the kingdom of Alaris from dangerous outsiders begins to fail, and a fomenting rebellion threatens to divide the country in a civil war, the three wizards are thrust into the middle of a power struggle.

When the barrier comes down, the truth comes out. Was everything they were taught about their kingdom based on a lie?

Will they all choose to fight on the same side, or end up enemies in the battle over who should rule Alaris?

Sign up on Mike's website at www.MichaelSheltonBooks.com and get a copy of the prequel novella e-book to The Alaris Chronicles, Prophecy of the Dragon.

Protect the youngest heir of the Dragon King. That is the mission given to Imari in this prequel novella to The Alaris Chronicles.

The Cremelino Prophecy

A Prophecy. A Powerful Sword. A reluctant wizard.

Darius San Williams, son of one of King Edward's councilors, cares little for his father's politics and vows to leave the city of Anikari to protect and bring glory to the Realm.

When a new-found and ancient magic emerges within him, he and his friends Christine and Kelln are faced with decisions that could shatter or fulfill the prophecy and the lives of all those they know.

Wizards and magic have long been looked down upon in the Realm, but Darius learns that no matter where he goes, prophecy and destiny are waiting to find him.

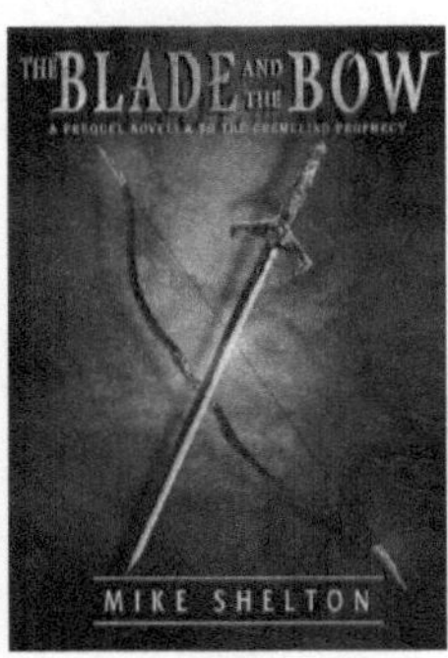

Sign up on Mike's website at www.MichaelSheltonBooks.com and get a copy of the prequel novella e-book to The Cremelino Prophecy, The Blade and The Bow.

Follow Darius and Kelln in one of their more fantastic adventures prior to The Path Of Destiny.

The TruthSeer Archives

On an island far out in the Eastern Sea join a new adventure of magic through the stones of power.

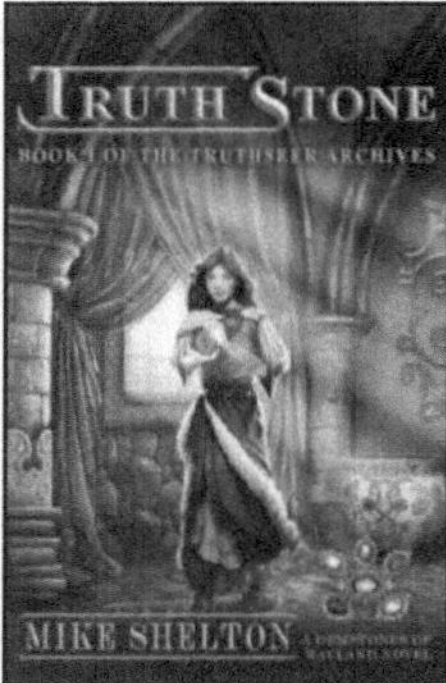

Everyone lies.
What if you could tell when they did?
What if this knowledge caused you immense physical pain?

Given a rare TruthStone, Shaeleen suffers immense agony with every lie she hears or tells. While struggling to control her new power and curb the pain she learns a powerful truth that could thrust an entire continent into civil war.

The stones of power protect the five kingdoms of Wayland - and have done so for two hundred years. Now those stones are failing and a dark power threatens to take control. With the help of her brother, and a young thief, Shaeleen sets out on a dangerous journey to gather and restore the power of all the stones.

The lies could kill her, but the truth could destroy a kingdom.

Will she succeed before the endless lies destroy her?

About the Author

Mike was born in California and has lived in multiple states from the west coast to the east coast. He cannot remember a time when he wasn't reading a book. At school, home, on vacation, at work at lunch time, and yes even a few pages in the car (at times when he just couldn't put that great book down). Though he has read all sorts of genres he has always been drawn to fantasy. It is his way of escaping to a simpler time filled with magic, wonders and heroics of young men and women.

Other than reading, Mike has always enjoyed the outdoors. From the beaches in Southern California to the warm waters of North Carolina. From the waterfalls in the Northwest to the Rocky Mountains in Utah. Mike has appreciated the beauty that God provides for us. He also enjoys hiking, discovering nature, playing a little basketball or volleyball, and most recently disc golf. He has a lovely wife who has always supported him, and three beautiful children who have been the center of his life.

Mike began writing stories in elementary school and moved on to larger novels in his early adult years. He has worked in corporate finance for most of his career. That, along with spending time with his wonderful family and obligations at church has made it difficult to find the time to truly dedicate to writing. In the last few years as his children have become older he has returned to doing what he truly enjoys – writing!

mikesheltonbooks@gmail.com
www.MichaelSheltonBooks.com
https://www.facebook.com/groups/MikeSheltonAuthor/
http://www.Twitter.com/msheltonbooks
http://www.Instagram.com/mikesheltonbooks

www.ingramcontent.com/pod-product-compliance
Lightning Source LLC
Chambersburg PA
CBHW051608100726
47898CB00001B/273